Marsanne looked at Sir Philip. His face appeared cold and sculptured under the bitter sweep of the wind; yet she now knew he could be extraordinarily winning. She had never admired coldly handsome men. And now Marsanne faced a frightening thought: Could she be one hundred percent certain of him? And if she could now trust him, could she trust herself and the physical attraction for him that was growing stronger? She decided, in any event, that she could not honestly avoid admiring this strong man who seemed in control of almost any situation. And how could she not at least be attracted to such a man?

MARSANNE

Virginia Coffman

A FAWCETT CREST BOOK

Fawcett Books, Greenwich, Connecticut

MARSANNE

THIS BOOK CONTAINS THE COMPLETE TEXT OF THE
ORIGINAL HARDCOVER EDITION.

A Fawcett Crest Book reprinted by arrangement with Arbor House

Copyright © 1976 by Virginia Coffman

ISBN: 0–449–23373–1

Printed in the United States of America

10 9 8 7 6 5 4 3 2 1

For Donnie and Johnny
from old Ning,
with all my love

Chapter One

"*Mark my words, mademoiselle, you will regret the* journey," Marsanne's landlady advised with gloomy satisfaction.

The recipient of this unsolicited advice, a slender attractive brunette, continued to fold and pack a fashionable new pelisse without looking up; so Madame Rivarol gathered more ammunition to combat the departure of a lodger who had always paid her rent on time.

"You'd not catch me traveling all the way from Paris to a sinful place like that England. And in a public coach, with only an addlepated maid for protection. Didn't the English put a cannonball through my nephew at Trafalgar? Them with their highwaymen and footpads and smugglers and what-all, they'll cut any throat for a sou."

Marsanne looked up and explained lightly, "My Cousin Sylvie hasn't found footpads or cutthroats in England. In her last letter to Mama she speaks of England as that dazzling place where the Prince-Regent is the chief ornament of society. She calls it a silver web of intrigue and romance. It sounds splendid to me, all a-sparkle with jewels and lovely gauze gowns, and—" She smiled.

"Not the place for a young lady, if I may say so," Madame Rivarol began again on a new tack. "Those fine relations of yours! Like as not, they're after your new inheritance. I note they didn't ask you to come visiting them before you got the estates."

Marsanne began to find her landlady a trifle monotonous. It was getting late and she had a singularly important visit to make before boarding the coach for Calais that evening. "I haven't got the estates yet. The king's court has only just ruled that they are mine." She knew all sorts of misinterpretations would be put upon her next remark, but she added, in all fairness, "I can thank Cousin Sylvie's financial aid to the king when he was exiled in England. Her influence weighted the scales in my favor when the ownership of grandpapa's estates came before the courts here in France."

"Ugh!" exclaimed Madame Rivarol, doubtless picturing all sorts of peccadilloes between the fat tired old king and ebullient Cousin Sylvie. Like many of the working class of France, Madame Rivarol was still an ardent supporter of the deposed Emperor Napoleon.

Marsanne said hastily, "Last year, when the Allies brought the king to France, we were lucky to be related to Cousin Sylvie."

Madame muttered, "Last year was a dreadful one for France. I'll not deny it."

For Marsanne, one good thing had come out of the last year. She had discovered a gift for languages and during the Occupation had acted as interpreter between the English invaders and the Paris citizens. At this time she also discovered the perfidious English to be charming, well-mannered, and far more attractive than the savage Cossacks or the arrogant Prussians. The contact gave her a desire to see that stubborn island of Britain, and Cousin Sylvie had obliged with an invitation.

Having finished with her portmanteau, Marsanne glanced at the small, corded trunk that had belonged to a wealthy ancestor. Would the gowns so carefully laid in that trunk be grand enough for Cousin Sylvie's routs, soirées and balls?

And will I be grand enough for them? . . . She wondered if that insecurity showed in her face or manner . . . Madame Rivarol, however, threw up her hands, and conceded: "Well then, I say nothing of the matter. Go where you will, mademoiselle. Your property shall be kept safe in my cellars."

Marsanne finished tying the big mulberry satin ribbons on the bandbox she had inherited from her late grandmother with whom she had lived until the old lady's death a year ago. Madame Rivarol cleared her throat.

"But I trust you will not rely too heavily upon that wretched maid of yours as a chaperone. A more man-crazy chatterbox I have never—"

Warned by Marsanne's mischievous smile and the creak of floorboards in the open doorway, Madame Rivarol swung around to catch a full view of Clotilde Lefebre, who was employed as Marsanne's maid and companion. The sight was enough to make anyone stare: young Clotilde was all golden curls, huge eyes, and over-generous lips, framed by a feathered pink bonnet. Her curvaceous form, barely concealed by pink round gown and dainty pelisse, emphasized her fondness for bonbons.

She curtseyed to Marsanne, beamed and giggled, ignoring the landlady. "Mamselle! They have promised to wait for me, each of them. Even Captain Luneville with the King's Guards, who is so popular with the new ladies at court." She clapped her small hands in their knitted gloves. "Do you think I shall have such luck in England?"

Marsanne glanced at the landlady, saw that she looked positively swollen with disgust, and told Clotilde dryly, "I have no doubt of it. But you won't find out if you don't finish packing. I want to go and see Mama before we take the coach tonight."

Trying to look suitably penitent after having been almost two hours late, Clotilde rushed into the room, removing her bonnet. "You packed everything yourself, and I meant to help you. I deserve a monstrous scold. But, indeed! Etienne—he is the Bonapartist—would not let me go until I promised on my honor to be true to him."

"Name of God!" the landlady cried, rolling her eyes heavenward. "She has no political discretion either. A Royalist captain and a Bonapartist at the same time!"

"Oh, not at the same time, Madame!" Clotilde protested innocently. She added, encouraged by Marsanne's laugh, "At all events, I persuaded Etienne that I don't barter my honor so easily."

Goodnaturedly, Marsanne observed, "What a rattle you are! Find something warm to wear. We are going to my mother immediately. She is waiting for us, and her time is a deal more valuable than ours."

Taking this as a hint, both women departed, Mademoiselle Rivarol downstairs to her ground floor lodgings and Clotilde into the adjoining bedchamber where she slept in the trundle bed but made up for this indignity by occupying three-quarters of the big armoire with her wardrobe of frills and furbelows.

Marsanne came in, tying the ribbons of her street bonnet.

"I see the streets are full of soldiers. Do you think there will be any difficulties?"

Aroused from dreams of male conquest, Clotilde turned. With the self-assurance of a born beauty, she informed Marsanne, "So many are my friends . . ." Her eyes widened as she saw the cluster of little flowers with curled stems in Marsanne's hand. "Oh, no! You will not carry those violets where all the world may see them!"

"They are Mama's favorite flowers. Surely, everyone

who carries violets in Paris is not trying to restore the Emperor!"

"But they are. It is the Bonapartist sign, mamselle. They wear violets and whisper passwords to total strangers on the streets. Something about 'violets coming in the spring.' That means the Emperor Napoleon will escape from that nasty island."

"I know what it means." All the same, Marsanne covered her hand with her cloak. She waited while Clotilde put on her second-best pelisse and bonnet, stopping to enjoy the dainty picture she made in the looking-glass that hung on the armoire door.

Marsanne watched the girl, impatient to be on her way but amused and a little envious of her companion's self-confidence. Marsanne had been taught to be sensible and totally lacking in personal vanity, but she knew instinctively that if she tried she could break at least a few hearts. Her chief problem was the reserve which had been bred in her through her twenty years.

Clotilde made a soft, moist-lipped moue at her own reflection. Then she trotted after Marsanne. "Do you walk fast across the city because of your mama's fear, mamselle?"

They were going down the narrow, ancient staircase to the street two stories below and Marsanne stopped so suddenly Clotilde trod upon her heels.

"Afraid? Mama is never afraid of anything. As for me, I promise not to show anyone these poor little violets."

"No, mamselle. It isn't that. Your mother is afraid for you. I saw it in her eyes when we were all at Mass the day before yesterday. I am persuaded that is why you are being sent to your cousins in England."

"I am going to England to attend the wedding of Cousin Sylvie's daughter."

"It's more than that," Clotilde insisted.

This time she really caught Marsanne unawares. "You are imagining things."

"Begging your pardon, she's afraid now. Day before yesterday, she kept watching everyone in the cathedral."

Marsanne chose to ignore the remark. Everyone knew that the only thing Clotilde wasn't afraid of was the "danger" she faced at the hands of her admirers.

Marsanne pushed open the window and looked at the street. Soldiers wearing the white cockade of the new King Louis the Eighteenth were still busy arresting suspected Bonapartists among those Paris citizens going past them to the various shops in this ancient street. There had been a riot in the night, as there had been frequently that winter of 1814–15, with passions rising for the exiled Emperor on Elba.

Clotilde said easily, "If you are wary of the soldiers, you needn't be. Just give them a pretty smile. And—" She caught a glimpse of the flowers in Marsanne's hand. "Really, mamselle, take care. I saw a man stuck with a bayonet not half an hour ago, just because he said something about violets."

"Very silly. If he is a Bonapartist, he shouldn't call attention to it like that. He sounds stupid enough to be one of Louis the Eighteenth's agents."

Clotilde was so shocked she almost forgot the deference due her young mistress. "Hush. Please do take care."

Marsanne stepped out onto the noisy, crowded street and started off with Clotilde's reprimand trailing after her.

Seeing two Royalist soldiers at the end of the block she carefully tucked the fragrant violets under her cloak. She would not have admitted it to Clotilde but she was relieved when the soldiers let her pass without comment.

The girls reached the Pont Neuf without trouble, but the bridge itself was alive with angry citizens throwing rocks, clods of mud and cobblestones at the king's troops who grew more impatient until a volley of shots was fired skyward as a warning. Marsanne looked up. The sky had been piercingly blue all day, but at this late afternoon hour it was streaked with pink and orange in a fiery sunset.

Hearing the rifle fire, Clotilde clutched Marsanne in a panic.

Marsanne pulled the girl out to the edge of the unruly crowd. "We'll cross over the Pont au Change. Nothing seems to be happening there." She pointed ahead along the quai past a fishmonger's shop, a café, and an ancient alley with roofs nearly meeting across the narrow shadowed cobbles between. Feeling Clotilde's hand tremble against her arm, she turned to calm the girl. At that second a buzzing noise passed above her head.

Marsanne raised her hand in a panicky flutter, felt the crown of her bonnet and at the same time saw Clotilde's horrified face. The girl stammered, "It—it—your b-bonnet—"

True enough, Marsanne's finger went straight through a surprisingly neat hole in the layers of dark blue cloth and stiffening that made up the crown of her bonnet.

Her first reaction was astonishment. "What was it?"

The fishmonger came bustling out of his shop waving his bare muscular arms. "Mademoiselle! The shot. It came from that alley. Take care . . . clumsy recruits. They shoot anywhere . . . anyone."

In blind panic Clotilde started on a run along the quai toward the next bridge. Marsanne swung around, saw nothing in the silent alley, nor any careless soldier on the Pont Neuf behind her. They had already moved in a body after their Bonapartist prey on the Ile de la Cité beyond the bridge.

Removing her bonnet to examine the neat hole, Marsanne, realized the fishminger was right. The "buzzing" *had* been a bullet.

"You are quite well, mademoiselle?" the fishmonger asked, then glared pugnaciously toward the alley. "I shall confront the Royalist butcher who can't aim straight."

Replacing her bonnet and retying the ribbons with unsteady fingers she followed the fishmonger to the opening of the alley. . . Only a drunken old vagabond sleeping close to a barrel of rotting fish. . .

"You!" The fishmonger kicked the vagabond in the rump. "You saw soldiers here a few minutes ago? . . . Shooting off their long rifles at the mob on the bridge?"

Nothing could be gotten out of the drunk whose eyes scarcely opened for these intruders. But at the far end Marsanne noticed a half-dozen soldiers jog-trotting past to reinforce their beleaguered brothers on the approaches to the Pont Neuf.

The fishmonger pointed to them. "I say this, mademoiselle. Those Royalists cannot shoot straight. Mind, the Emperor Napoleon's Old Guards were real soldiers. They would not send bullets through the bonnets of innocent young ladies."

Shaken by the episode, she muttered her thanks to the fishmonger and hurried off to join her companion cowering at the entrance to the Pont au Change.

Chapter Two

"*Are we safe, mamselle? Why did they shoot at you?*"

"I am safe, thanks to their bad marksmanship. One of the soldiers apparently thought he could get a better shot at the rioters from that alley, and I happened to be in the way. At all events, the soldiers have left, for which I confess my gratitude."

Still uneasy, they stepped onto the bridge. As always, it was crowded with hucksters, beggars, and carnival performers. The two girls threaded their way between an aged seller of broomstraws, and a woman peddling a drink of cocoa and licorice on a wooden tray suspended from her shoulders. The point of the tray struck Clotilde in the ribs and she squealed indignantly. The woman leaned over in pretended apology, muttering, "The violets will return in the spring."

Marsanne stifled a smile. She found this dream of the poor and the working class of Paris sad. Their hero, the Emperor Napoleon, was bound fast to the island of Elba, and would stay there as long as King Louis the Eighteenth led the entire army of France.

It troubled her that others, including her own dear mother, dreamed of his return. . . Her mother, who had organized and become the skilled administrator of the public hospitals in Paris under the Empire, was now to be superseded by an emigré nobleman who had never set foot in Paris until three months before. Marsanne understood quite well why her mother's favorite flowers were violets. It frightened Marsanne to think of the older woman's daring, but Marsanne knew from twenty years' experience that her mother like Marsanne's Royalist grandmother before her was a born survivor. Had not both women come through the bloody Revolution with their heads intact?

The huge gloomy Hôtel-Dieu, the largest public hospital in Paris, cast its shadow not only over the far side of the Ile de la Cité at this time but over one channel of the Seine and the Left Bank as well. It was separated from Notre Dame cathedral by a jungle of wretched slum shacks. Marsanne and her maid always hurried through this area.

Inside the great hospital Clotilde hung back, carefully avoiding the patients awaiting treatment. Marsanne made her way among the crowded beds and private cubicles, not certain from one day to the next where she would find her mother. Several patients looked up as she passed, touching her cloak, greeting her, asking her: "Will you send Sister Veronique to me? I have not been given my dinner soup yet" . . . "Mademoiselle Vaudraye, would you ask your sainted mother if she will give me a drop of laudanum? This damned leg may have been cut off, but I feel it yet. I swear it."

Marsanne did her best to remember all their messages and complaints; for her mother never forgot such things. Her mother knew every occupant of every bed. And the Emperor had complimented her dedication by taking her advice about improvements at Les Invalides and other military hospitals.

Would all this end now? The new administrator had already announced that under the king's protection certain economies would be practiced—beginning, of course, with the amount of meat permitted in the soup that was the main meal of each patient's day.

"Poor Mama!" Marsanne thought. "She has survived so much. To have all her great work hacked away now . . . It isn't fair." But she remembered something her mother had said long ago to one of Marsanne's complaints: "The world is not fair or unfair. It simply is. Then we make it what we wish it to be."

A tubercular young female reached out gaunt fingers, caught them in Marsanne's cloak.

"Tell Sister . . . make my confession . . . Tell dear Sister . . . fetch a priest."

Marsanne covered the hot, dry hand with her own. "I'll tell her, mademoiselle. May I bring you something? Water? A little wine?"

"Priest."

Marsanne released herself gently and went on to the staircase. All the pity she felt did not blind her to the truth about herself: she had no vocation for her mother's work. If she were permitted to make a living of her own, she would buy a little café on a street corner and cook meals exceedingly well.

A young jolly-faced nun approached and Marsanne curtsied, asking, "Is Sister Veronique abovestairs?"

"Very much so. And putting us all to drill like one of the Emperor's own grenadiers. All the things we must remember when she is gone. A bad day for us when we see the last of Sister Veronique, my child. She is our conscience. Our very backbone."

It always warmed Marsanne to hear such praise, but it again brought the bite of conscience. Why was she going off to faraway England now when her mother might need her most? Marsanne felt she should remain here in Paris. Sister Veronique, after all, was always there when Marsanne needed her. Busy as she was, the nun always made time for her daughter yet seemed to have enough time left over to mother all of these lost souls in the public hospitals.

Marsanne gave quick instructions to the nun about the three patients who had stopped her and hurried on to meet her mother who was generally presumed to be her "Aunt Veronique."

Sister Veronique had just dismissed her acolytes, two nuns, a priest and a lay surgeon and came rapidly toward Marsanne, her strong spare form seeming to push against her heavy robes and the blood stained pinafore that covered her bodice and skirts. She held out her hands to Marsanne. Clotilde pattered along behind and the three women moved into a little cubicle with a long, narrow window overlooking the Seine. Here the nun and her daughter could meet more privately than in the general wards, with only Clotilde standing in the curtained doorway, first on one foot, then the other, trying not to yawn. This relationship shocked her a little, for whoever heard of a nursing Sister of Charity—a nun—with a daughter? That Revolution they all talked of must have been a very wild time!

Marsanne hugged Sister Veronique as if they had parted months ago instead of two days before. Mindful of the patients nearby, she protested in a passionate whisper, "Mama! I don't want to go away now when you might need me."

Sister Veronique, who had momentarily yielded to an emotion of deep tenderness, regained her composure, held her daughter at arm's length and said lightly, "What's this? You don't wish to go? And you want to disappoint your old gray-haired mother as well?"

That made Marsanne laugh. No one would ever believe

that, beneath the coif which framed Sister Veronique's strong unlined face, she might have gray hair. "Mama, what if they try to arrest you because you served under the Emperor Napoleon?"

Sister Veronique said in her matter-of-fact way, "It would not help me in the least to have you stand up for me. My darling child, the new regime would think you were a greater hindrance to me than my Bonapartist sympathies. A nursing nun with a grown daughter! Sacrilege. And worse. Your English cousins are right. I must remain as I always have been to those outside our family . . . your devoted aunt. Much more practical in the world's eyes, I assure you."

For most of her twenty years Marsanne had understood that no young lady acknowledged a Sister of Charity as her mother. But living with her grandmother, the Vicomtesse de Vaudraye, Marsanne was reared to understand always that she was the product of a great love which had occurred long ago during the stirring days of the Revolution. She knew nothing of her father except that he had died before she was born. That and one surprising admission from her mother, made on a bright April day when Marsanne was seven years old: "I hate April. The world died for me that month. It was when I lost your father."

Marsanne never knew the circumstances of that loss, nor was she told any more about the artist, Gile Marsan, who was her father. At the age of seven she found the subject too embarrassing to pursue, for it was the only time she ever heard that harsh passionate emotion in her stoic mother's voice.

Marsanne took the little nosegay of violets out from under her cloak. "It's crushed. I wanted it to be nice for you."

She would never forget her mother's smile as she raised the violet cluster and breathed the fragrance. Sister Veronique said after a moment, "I'll take it to old Amboise. He is dying and he talks of nothing but the Emperor. This may make his going a little easier to bear. And now, my girl, are you packed and ready for that exciting journey tonight?"

Suddenly, it seemed to Marsanne that all her fears and objections poured over her to smother her enthusiasm, her previous high hopes of the journey ahead. "I feel it, Mama. I don't want to leave you alone at a time like this."

"What nonsense! One would think I had never weathered a storm. I don't doubt King Louis will call me back, once he discovers what a fool my successor at the hospital proves to be. But I'll not be satisfied until you are on your way to Calais. And better yet, I shall be delighted to find you have reached Cousin Sylvie's estate in England. You must write to me frequently. Our cousin will find someone to frank your letters. But I must know you are safe."

Marsanne had been caught by a peculiar and thoroughly unexpected note in her mother's voice, the note of urgency . . . and fear. She recalled that curious observation made an hour before by Clotilde.

"Mama, what are you afraid of? It isn't politics, surely."

Sister Veronique laughed away such a notion. "If you and I survived the Occupation by wild Cossacks and those thoroughly detestable Prussians, we needn't concern ourselves with politics." All the same she glanced over her shoulder, through the curtains behind Clotilde.

"But there is something," Marsanne prompted her.

"When you had nothing, I was not afraid for you. But now . . . I am waiting only for the royal signature on the deeds, and then the Vaudraye estates will be yours."

Marsanne felt breathless, apprehensive. These facts were all known to her. Why should they trouble her mother now? "Surely, there is no other heir. Cousin Sylvie's influence . . ."

"My dear child, Sylvie put the very food in the mouth of King Louis when he was exiled in England. The king could do no other than restore our property to the last direct descendant of the Vaudrayes. I confess it might be difficult if I claimed Papa's estate with my political affiliations, but you—granddaughter of the Royalist Vicomte de Vaudraye—are the natural heiress. There remains nothing now but for Maitre Louis Reynaud, the lawyer I hired, to deliver the royal deeds. He asks payment in kind, two of the fields on the High Road to Rouen. But that shouldn't trouble you." She hesitated, considered the traffic on the river and looked back at Marsanne who felt that this was not all of the story.

"Are you afraid someone will marry me for my fortune, Mama? They won't, you know. I am not gullible."

Sister Veronique patted her hand. "I know you aren't. But I want you on guard at all times."

"But why? Will the king change his mind?"

"No. Unless something should happen to you before you yourself have heirs."

Startled, Marsanne asked, "Who else is there to inherit the estates? Cousin Sylvie is now the widow of an Englishman. It's hardly likely that she would qualify."

"You forget this Joseph Binet who bought the property when it was confiscated during the Revolution."

"But Binet died last year, didn't he? And with no direct heir?"

Veronique shrugged. She lowered her voice. "I have an agent. That is, a friend who is working for the restoration of the Emperor."

"Mama, how dangerous in these times!"

"Yes, yes. I daresay. But the point is, this sailor—this agent—visited Normandy on political business, and learned of the threats made by Joseph Binet as he lay dying. The neighbors all insist that Binet swore his little nephew would inherit the property."

"I didn't know he had a nephew."

"Ten years old, living with his mother and a stepfather in the West Indies. The family, including the boy Pierre, visited Binet several years ago and the child gained his affection, so old Binet swore to everyone that if the government took the property from the Binets at his death, they would do so over the body of the Vaudraye heir."

Marsanne burst out laughing at the melodrama of the threat. "Really, Mama, we are not in some renaissance castle. Will my soup be poisoned? Or—"

Clotilde gasped, "Or be shot by mistake for a Bonapartist!"

Marsanne said pettishly, "Don't talk rubbish. That was a stupid accident. They were aiming over my head at the crowd behind me on the Pont Neuf."

"What!" There was no mistaking the authority in Veronique's voice. "What is all this? Were you shot at today? Marsanne, tell me!"

Marsanne sighed, gave Clotilde a warning frown and explained that a bullet, obviously fired in error from the alley near the Pont Neuf had passed through her bonnet.

"We saw the soldiers passing the alley only a minute or two afterward."

"Did you see any of them in the alley itself?"

"No, but—"

"I don't like it, Marsanne. I want you out of the city until my sailor friend locates this Pierre Binet's stepfather, a man named Gris."

"What is the man like? How would we know him if we saw him?"

"Thirty to forty years old, my friend tells me. He gained only sparse information from the people of the Normandy countryside nearby. No one can give us a closer description. A dull, prosaic-looking fellow from all accounts. But if you were dead, this man could claim the estate for his stepson—with a payment here and a bribe there, they could get it for a song."

Marsanne grinned. She did not want to believe any of this and yet could not quite overcome a growing queasiness.

Veronique looked over her head at the wide-eyed

Clotilde. "I trust you to look out for my girl. This child heir, Pierre Binet, is innocent and doubtless deserving. But that ambitious fellow, his stepfather, who sailed from the island of Martinique two months ago, landed at Calais. He was supposedly going to visit the grave of old Joseph Binet. My . . . informant tells me the man visited the grave, and asked questions about the heiress to the Vaudraye lands. He seemed most interested in your description and where you live. The Normandy peasants could say nothing. They have never seen you. But my informant and I both regard the man as dangerous."

Clotilde's horrified whisper did not help matters. "Will this stepfather of the little boy try to carry out Monsieur Binet's vow?"

Veronique put her hands on her daughter's shoulders and said solemnly, "I too scoffed at all this business at first, but the shooting accident today worries me greatly. Do you *know* that soldiers were in the alley?"

"I moved to speak with Clotilde just as a—soldier fired."

Veronique shook her gently. "And you saw no one else? You are certain?"

"No one but the fishmonger. And he was in the doorway when the shot came. He had nothing in his hands."

Clotilde coughed. "Mamselle, what of the drunken vagabond curled up in the alley?"

"Don't be ridiculous. He was—" Marsanne stopped. She did not actually know anything about the vagabond. She had scarcely noticed him. But had there been anything strange, anything suspicious there?

"Now that I think of it, even a drunkard might have been disturbed by a shot fired over his head, and then by the soldiers when they left the alley. The soldiers themselves would have roused him even before they fired."

"Did this fellow get to his feet? Could he have been hiding a gun of some kind?"

Marsanne nodded.

No one said anything for a minute. Then, as her mother started to speak, Marsanne recovered and added teasingly, "I shall watch everyone, turn my head frequently to avoid bullets, and—and become suspicious of handsome young men who court me for my riches."

"Marsanne, I am serious. Would you know this vagabond if you saw him again?"

Marsanne kissed her cheek. "I know you are serious, Mama. I don't even know how old he was. He looked unshaven. The alley was heavily shadowed. At all events, I will take care."

"I wish you need not travel by the public coach. If you could have traveled in your own carriage, with your own coachman and postilions to protect you!"

"Heavens! I'm not rich yet. Besides, you would take all the adventure out of the journey."

"I wish I might," Sister Veronique sighed, then reached into the deep pocket of her pinafore whose many stains had long since been thoroughly laundered into the material. She drew out a silver chain to which were affixed not the crucifix Marsanne expected but a pair of silver miniatures closed together by a hinge and clasp. She slipped the chain over Marsanne's head, her fingers barely caressing the wiry dark curls of hair that emerged from her bonnet in spite of her efforts to keep them respectably smooth.

Marsanne looked down at the miniatures, opening them in a gingerly way; she had often seen her mother studying one of them when she supposed no one noticed. The portrait that had so mesmerized Sister Veronique was not her own no-nonsense face with its unexpectedly passionate mouth and its clear direct gaze. The other portrait was of Marsanne's father, a man just under thirty, his dark, somber gaze relieved by the warmth and tenderness of his smile.

Marsanne said softly, "I shall never love anyone as you loved Father. How handsome he was!"

Sister Veronique looked at the portrait for a few seconds, then deliberately broke the spell it cast upon her. "He loved you very much, before you were born. He wanted you. We spoke of you at the end, that last hour. Since we could not marry, I named you for him, Marsanne." She smiled, shrugged. "But when you praise his looks, that is very like conceit, my girl; for you are the image of him."

Flushed by the unexpectedness of that, Marsanne promised fervently, "I'll keep these forever and ever."

Her mother permitted herself to be hugged so hard she found herself breathless. "Well, well, I believe you. And I promise you something. You will find a man as wonderful as your father was. And every bit as handsome."

Marsanne had been on the verge of weeping for her mother and father but this made her laugh instead.

"Mama, I have never doubted your word in my life, but this is one promise you cannot possibly keep. All the same, I love you for it."

Sister Veronique suddenly admonished her daughter: "No more nonsense. You've your packing to finish and your supper to take. Be certain to take a fiacre from the hospital to your lodgings, and later to the coachyard. Take care. And trust no one until you reach Cousin Sylvie."

This farewell had been the most wrenching in Marsanne's life. They walked together to the staircase where Monsieur Dureau, the surgeon, met them.

"Sister Veronique, there is a piratical fellow who claims you sent for him. A sailor, I believe. He is at the river door."

"Thank you. You may send him to me in five minutes. He is here to remove the gilt N's and replace them with L's."

Since they could now be seen by many strangers in the wards, all endearments were excised from their farewell. Marsanne curtsied to her mother, gave her one long last look, and they separated.

Clutching the silver miniatures, Marsanne started out in

the direction of the nearest Left Bank bridge. From this vantage point she saw her mother's visitor. She had no doubt that this was the Bonapartist agent who had brought Sister Veronique the news about Binet's dying threat and the arrival of the boy's stepfather who might very possibly carry out that threat.

The sailor was waiting by the river door. Marsanne made out only the red headband, the striped shirt and wide-legged trousers. His face was turned away and he was leaning over a stone embankment so that she got only a vague notion of his size.

Marsanne reflected nervously that it was just like her reckless mother to be involved with Bonapartist spies. Ironic that Veronique was so concerned over her daughter's safety when associations with such fellows might bring Sister Veronique herself to the executioner. Marsanne shivered.

The sailor remained at his place. Once he waved to someone on a barge passing in the river below. Perhaps he was simply as her mother had described him, and no more.

They walked back up onto the Cité to hire a fiacre. It was now dusk. Three hours before tonight's coach would leave Paris. . . Marsanne found herself looking around suspiciously as she and Clotilde rode in splendid privacy back to their lodgings.

Chapter Three

The streets were no longer scenes of agitation, though clots of citizens had collected here and there to discuss politics. Snatches of conversation reached the girls in the hired fiacre:

"The Emperor would never have allowed it. This new king cuts our pay by two-thirds. How are we to live? He's none of us. He don't understand the poor. Not like our Emperor."

It was sentimental talk but Marsanne was forced to agree with them in part as she watched the lamplighter at the new gas lamps, another of the Emperor's legacies.

Unfortunately the new king had alienated much of the populace within six months of his return. Among the more atrocious of his errors were his efforts to turn back the clock, wiping out all social and political advances made since 1789. It was a situation building to an explosion.

A man passed Marsanne as she and Clotilde alighted from the carriage—his two little eyes peering at her like dull beads . . . But now Marsanne shrugged off her own absurd imaginings and started up the stairs with Clotilde following.

Madame Rivarol looked out of her own parlor, calling up to Marsanne, "Mademoiselle, a gentleman called. He was curious to see you."

Marsanne felt her skin prickle with fear. "What was he like? How old?"

"Older than you. Maybe not so old as my husband."

"What did he look like?"

"Tolerable. One might call him good-looking. I like them ripe. Like my husband."

"Whatever did he want?"

"He wished to know when you would leave your lodgings. He wishes to rent them when you are gone."

Marsanne asked abruptly, "You told him?"

"Of course. Tomorrow, I said. Your property will be moved to my cellars tomorrow for safekeeping. I must have my rooms rented, so I said he may come back the day after."

"Do you remember anything about the man? His eyes. His height. Fat or thin? Anything?"

Madame Rivarol raised her head indignantly. "I am not a fool. A tall man, to my way of thinging. Not fat, no. Not like my husband who is comfortably fat. The eyes I do not recall. Not too dark, I think. The gentleman wore a great-coat and a high cravat. I did not look into the eyes. Why these questions?"

Since Madame Rivarol could give no more information, Marsanne ignored the question and hurried up to her lodgings where she ordered Clotilde to bolt the door. "We must appear as if we were to remain here all night. When we leave, it will be by that long window at the back of the ground floor . . . and it *will* be tonight."

Marsanne gathered up all the luggage she could carry, signaling Clotilde to do the same.

Clotilde obeyed, grumbling all the way down the stairs

with the bandboxes, while Marsanne made two trips, the second time dragging a small, corded trunk down and then managing with a little effort to push it out over the sill of the long window. She raised her skirts to her knees, settled a moment on the sill, swung out into a dark cul de sac between several buildings in the block, and turned to help Clotilde. . . .

Full darkness shrouded the city when the girls arrived at the innyard where the coaches made up for Normandy, Brittany and Calais—departure point for Dover and the British ports. They arrived scarcely five minutes before the coach was to depart.

Climbing up into the coach Clotilde mumbled unhappily over the absence of any helping male hand, and she squeaked and squealed so much when she and Marsanne found themselves seated and facing the boot of the carriage that a courtly old gentleman facing front insisted on exchanging his place with hers.

Out in the yard an agitated young man suddenly joined the coachman and the agent with the way-bill, and announced news unpleasant enough to arouse the attention of the passengers.

"Messieurs," the gallant old gentleman called to them, "what seems to be the delay?"

"A riot on our route, monsieur. Royalist troops forced to arrest a score of citizens protesting the newest pension cut."

The passengers exchanged glances. No one could be certain how contagious such riots might be during these uncertain days. The excitable dark youth leaped up the steps into the coach and with a grin intended to be both winsome and apologetic squeezed in beside Marsanne. The coach door slammed shut and before anyone was ready, the horses leaped forward jerking passengers backward and forward violently. A chorus of screams and curses followed. This broke the ice among the strangers and by the time the coach had rumbled out into the city's streets, the new young man had introduced himself as René Nicoletti, the jolly fat man was Jacques, a butcher, and a frigid-looking woman announced haughtily, "Madame Hauteville. I hope we are well protected. One does not know from one hour to the next when the Corsican Ogre will rise up from Elba and murder us all."

"Bah!" said the butcher, hiding a belch with some difficulty. "They've got him right and tight. He'll never rise up again. More's the pity."

"Pity, indeed! I will not share a conveyance with one of the Usurper's creatures."

Marsanne watched René Nicoletti's lively green eyes studying herself and Clotilde. Perhaps it was natural that a man his age should be more concerned with females than politics. He looked harmless enough—especially to Clotilde who had noted his interest and was smiling coquettishly as she toyed with her little pink gloves.

Nicoletti returned Clotilde's smile but also seemed to understand the relationship between the pretty blonde and her more soberly dressed mistress. For a few minutes this realization seemed suspicious to Marsanne. Wouldn't a normal, ordinary traveler express more interest in the pretty blonde?

"Mademoiselle," he asked Marsanne, "do you go far?"

"Somewhat."

"Ah, yes. Amiens, perhaps?"

"No, monsieur."

"Farther, of course. A fine young lady like yourself, and very properly accompanied." His grin was directed at Clotilde who leaned forward and eagerly added, "Much farther, monsieur," then caught Marsanne's frown and subsided in a pique.

"Calais. You are bound for Calais." He said this as if he had achieved a notable victory in their little game. With a flash of teeth he went on triumphantly, "Then across La Manche—the Channel—to England, yes? And by glorious chance, I go there as well."

Clotilde clapped her hands. "What a delightful chance. Monsieur!" After a glance from Marsanne she blushed prettily at her own indiscretion.

"Delightful, indeed, mademoiselle."

With some curiosity the other passengers watched this happy little flirtation. Rebuffed by Marsanne's indifference, the young man pursued his advantage with Clotilde. Before the coach reached the nearest customs barrier, the two were leaning toward each other, exchanging amenities. Marsanne could only pray to heaven that the girl would not confide their entire story to this good-looking stranger.

Two customs officials opened the coach door. Their new white Bourbon cockades looked strange and foreign to Marsanne. Only Madame Hauteville gleamed with obvious satisfaction at the sight of the two Royalist officials. The junior officer was supercilious and very taken with his authority. The senior possessed the polished manners of another day.

"Messieurs . . . Mesdames . . . your papers, if you please." He smiled charmingly at Marsanne, examined her papers with a casual air and replaced them. "Mademoiselle. A pleasant and safe journey . . . may you return soon."

"Thank you, monsieur. You are too kind."

"Not at all, mademoiselle. I knew your grandmother, the Vicomtesse. A gracious lady. And I am also deeply indebted to . . ." He hesitated. Obviously, he knew of her birth, but everyone in the coach was listening, and he added tactfully, "to Sister Veronique. She nursed me back to life once, after the Malet Treason in 1812."

Feeling infinitely cheered, Marsanne settled back against the worn leather cushions. It seemed to her that the junior officer showed an inordinate interest in René Nicoletti's papers. He gave the young man a sharp look while Nicoletti stared back—all innocence. What was going on between them? Marsanne wondered. Did they suspect

Nicoletti of something? Bonapartist tendencies, probably. His name suggested Corsican ancestry.

The two officials saluted and stepped back to make room for a new passenger, a tall man in a black tricorne hat with white hair clubbed at the nape of his neck in the old-fashioned way. Although his black travel cloak enveloped him to his boot-tops, it did not hide the exceptional pallor of his flesh. It was evident to the other passengers that he was a gentleman, and by his manner a man of some authority. The senior officer studied his papers very briefly and returned them with a bow. To his junior the officer repeated aloud in broken English, "Sir Philip Justin. English. Passing through this kingdom from the Swiss Cantons."

"Not remaining in France," the younger officer snapped in French. "No permission to remain here."

"I cannot imagine anyone remaining in this benighted country by choice. I sail from Calais on the first tide," said the Englishman in his own language, throwing the reply over his shoulder as if to a lackey.

Marsanne, whose gift for languages, especially English, had been so useful to her mother and to the hospital during the Occupation, wondered at this elegant man who spoke no French. There had been many Englishmen like him during those months—men who took pride in speaking nothing but their native tongue, but this man's appearance implied a series of contrasts . . . not the least of which was why such an obviously wellborn man traveled by the public coach. She decided to watch him.

Ten minutes later she wondered if she need concern herself. In the semidark of the coach the Englishman took the corner seat opposite her, pulled his cloak tightly around him—long legs, and a trim, fencer's figure, she guessed—and turning his face to the cushion he apparently went off to sleep under the stares of his fellow passengers.

By the time the coach had rumbled out across the

countryside the older passengers were also making an effort to sleep, which left only the murmur of conversation punctuated by an occasional giggle—from Clotilde and René Nicoletti. Marsanne paid scant attention to anything but her hope for a pleasant visit in England, a visit she had greatly anticipated until that mysterious bullet punctured her bonnet.

She first met her mother's Cousin Sylvie in the winter of 1802 during the brief peace between Great Britain and France. At that time Marsanne was seven years old and had found the flamboyant Sylvie de Vaudraye a fascinating companion: Sylvie spent money freely, ate superb food, and gave balls which Marsanne could watch from behind the velvet portières in one of her grandmother's salons. Sister Veronique had been much too busy to attend soirées, but Marsanne's grandmother, the Vicomtesse, was present at every entertainment, and led off half the balls. Those were good times.

Later, after Alex de Vaudraye, Sylvie's husband, died, she married seventy-six-year-old Sir Peverell Lesgate who died while leaping a hurdle to impress his French bride. Sylvie now boasted that she owned half of Sussex County and had traveled to Paris during the Allied Occupation to visit her "poor" French relatives. Much too lively and goodnatured to give offense, however, Sylvie used considerable influence to get her cousin Veronique's Vaudraye estates restored to Marsanne. Veronique herself was clearly unacceptable to the Royalists. Marsanne now looked forward to seeing Lady Sylvie Lesgate again and meeting her daughter, Amy.

Perhaps the betrothal and marriage celebrations of young Amy would restore the gaiety of former times for Marsanne . . .

The carriage lamps cast occasional flickers of reddish light into the coach's interior and Marsanne saw that even the indefatigable Clotilde and René Nicoletti had settled into their seats and were sleeping soundly. Marsanne shifted her position and closed her eyes. Suddenly she sensed movement in the coach and raised her eyelids a fraction. The Englishman's eyes were wide open and watching her. She frantically hoped he could not see her looking at him.

She would not have believed it possible, but half an hour later, and despite herself she was asleep. Nor did she wake up until the coach rattled and bumped over the cobblestones of a country innyard, and came to a rocking stop.

"Ah, breakfast, and about time!" the butcher cried in his jovial booming voice. "A cold chicken and a bottle for me."

With a flourish René Nicoletti offered an arm to each of the young ladies as they descended from the coach. "Mesdemoiselles, you will need a strong arm to defend you from the ruffians in these country taverns."

There seemed to be no alternative . . . Clotilde was already moving jauntily beside him, her muslin skirts briskly sweeping the ground, so Marsanne allowed herself to be piloted as well.

At the public room door Nicoletti turned back toward the coach which stood alone now. The hostler was leading out a fresh team of horses. Marsanne, noting Nicoletti's interest, asked curiously, "You are fond of horses, monsieur?"

"The hostler does not handle them well. You see the skittish mare? Mind you, trouble there." Marsanne thought this a reasonable observation, but suspected his attention had not been entirely occupied with the coach's new team.

Marsanne glanced beyond the lively team to the coach itself. She saw the tall Englishman who stood beside the open coach door, calmly studying the busy innyard scene, where chickens and ducks were running about in great panic, upset from the noisy arrival of the coach and passengers.

Nicoletti said, "I do not believe that gentleman is English."

"What!" It was not the comment Marsanne had expected. "Why not? Are you yourself an expert in the English tongue, monsieur?"

He denied hastily, "Indeed, not. I should regard such skill as very near to treason. After all, they have been our ruthless enemy since before we were born. But—"

"Yet you are visiting England."

She had caught him unawares. For a second or two he was almost flustered. "Quite true, mademoiselle. But I am going on my father's business. He is a merchant in Corsica. Olives and olive oil, you understand. I only mention that gentleman because he takes an extraordinary interest in you." Seeing Clotilde's wide-eyed gaze he added, "In you both."

A shrewd young man, this René Nicoletti, Marsanne decided.

Clotilde batted her long, pale lashes, acknowledging the compliment and adding vacantly, "The English gentleman's eyes are blue."

"Even blue-eyed gentlemen may be cutthroats," Marsanne reminded her tartly, rather pleased to hear Monsieur Nicoletti's laugh at her sour joke.

"Oh, but when he looked at me this morning—such a keen gaze! I swear, I did not know which way to turn." She raised her dimpled chin. "I found his appearance quite . . . unexceptionable. For an Englishman."

"If he is one."

Marsanne seized upon that. "Monsieur Nicoletti, what do you mean? What are you trying to say?"

"He speaks French like a native."

She pretended not to be startled by that. "Perhaps he prefers not to speak with his fellow passengers. When did you hear him speaking French?"

"During the night. The coach stopped to test a bridge after the winter rains. That gentleman got out and discussed the roadway with the coachman."

"Dear me! How very observant you are! One must take care not to deceive you in any way, Monsieur Nicoletti."

"Another thing. His pallor. Has he been—where?—to acquire such a pallor?"

"Perhaps the poor gentleman was ill? He did say he came from the Swiss Cantons where they go to recover from the lung sickness," Clotilde put in charitably.

Marsanne agreed without actually believing what she said. "I suppose that might explain his hair." She glanced at Nicoletti with amusement. "Unless you would suggest that his hair is dyed."

"No. I saw the roots. It is genuine, I think. All the same, our Sir Philip Justin, as he calls himself, is not as old as he looks. He is scarcely above thirty-five, or I'm a Dutchman! The question is—why? What is he doing here . . . what is he?"

Clotilde's eyes grew round. "At the Charity School the girls talked of legends. Vampires, strange creatures of the night. Do you think . . . ?"

Marsanne and Nicoletti laughed. "I leave you to refute that," she told him. "You are responsible for this tale having been started."

Nicoletti was in no way abashed. "I'd give a thousand francs to know who this man really is. Or should I ask—what is his purpose here?"

Chapter Four

They breakfasted in a private parlor beyond the taproom, and Marsanne thought over her conversation with René Nicoletti. Aware that she was influenced by Nicoletti's comments, she decided to gain what information she could from the coachman. But she did not want the Englishman to catch her spying. She had a notion that the handsome stranger could be very cold and very cutting if he discovered her watching him. When the tailor and the butcher had gone off to purchase bottles of the local apple brandy for the journey, she suggested, "Clotilde, do you think you might hold Sir Philip here at the inn for a few minutes if he appears about to leave?"

"Ah! So the fellow does arouse your suspicions. And while mademoiselle holds him in conversation, we might get a glimpse of his luggage and learn something." René Nicoletti seemed ready to follow her outside, which was not her intention . . . she had thought she might discover what she could about the young olive merchant from Corsica as well.

She sighed. "What a pity! I am very much afraid Clotilde might not know precisely the right things to say to him, to draw him out. Whereas you, monsieur, would know . . . but perhaps you are no longer curious."

Marsanne got up abruptly and left her co-conspirators. She passed the Englishman without looking his way but got the distinct sensation that he turned his head and was watching her. Clotilde was right about the man's good looks. To Marsanne this made him fit even more closely the portrait her landlady had drawn of the mysterious fellow who asked questions about renting Marsanne's lodgings.

She went out through the taproom to the innyard, wondering that Clotilde and René had been so much more observant than she was about the Englishman. Whatever the cause of the man's white hair, the rest of him was unquestionably in its prime. According to his passport papers, he had been living in the Swiss Cantons. As Clotilde had suggested, for his health? . . . That would explain his sallow complexion, but after René Nicoletti's suggestions, she doubted it. Somehow, even in her brief encounters with the Englishman, she suspected there was a dangerous, steely strength about this "invalid from the Swiss Cantons." She felt that he was quite capable of contriving her removal from the path of the boy, Pierre Binet.

When she caught the coachman, he had just left the public room and was smoothing his long moustaches, the relics of his years as a grenadier in the Emperor's army. Marsanne began by congratulating him upon his Imperial service and he thawed at once. It was a little difficult to maneuver him toward the subject of the Englishman at this moment. The young hostler had gotten the help of a local peasant who finished harnessing the team, but the skittish mare was still giving them trouble, much to the coachman's disgust.

"It was not so in the army, mamselle. In those days they knew how to care for the poor beasts. There was a time—we were chasing the English out of Naples—"

"Monsieur," she cut in, seizing her chance, "was it in Italy you learned to speak English?"

His hand fell away from the sleek strands of his moustache. "I, mamselle? I do not speak English."

"But in the middle of the night you talked with the Englishman, didn't you? There was a bridge, part of the high road washed out. He came around to speak with you?"

The coachman scowled at her. "But I say to you, I do not speak English. And this monsieur, he speaks as well in French as these ears have heard."

"What did the gentleman speak of when you talked?"

The coachman shrugged. "Of the bright weather which came too hard upon the rains. This caused the difficulty with the roads. He mentioned other roads in the area. Said he had seen them recently, and we might take one of those roads, but it was not in my orders."

"And he talked of nothing else?" She wondered if the Englishman had actually expected the coach to wander off into some byway recommended by him.

"Only to ask in what regiment I had served. He said he had lived in Genève—Geneva, he called it—for many years. For the lungs."

"His lungs are affected?"

The coachman looked at her with impatience. "If he is there for his lungs, then that is evident, is it not?"

"He does not appear to be an invalid."

"Appearances can deceive, mamselle."

That was perfectly true. So René Nicoletti had been right. He was obviously a young man who did not miss much.

She decided to return to the inn and determine if she could what passed between the Englishman and Mademoiselle Hauteville. She moved cautiously past the four-horse team, still considering what she had heard. A sudden noise, like a shot fired, or a sharply broken stick, set the skittish mare to kicking.

After that, everything happened at once. Marsanne found herself thrust violently out of the way and went crashing to the ground. The muddy runnels between broken cobblestones did not cushion her fall and by the time the coachman and René Nicoletti lifted her to her feet she could not be sure where anyone had been a few minutes before.

The fretting team calmed down under the hands of the Englishman who certainly had not shown "invalid" tendencies in controlling them. But had he caused the trouble near the Pont au Change? Nicoletti had pushed her out of the way this time, yet he too might have fired the shot or otherwise arranged to play the hero.

Most probably both men were innocent and Marsanne's suspicions unfounded. Shaken as she was, she much preferred this answer.

Using his heroic rescue as an invitation to greater intimacy, Nicoletti put an arm around Marsanne's waist and led her back toward the posting-house. Marsanne was limping slightly, and she thought the Englishman had reached out to help her as she passed him.

In the private parlor Clotilde and Mademoiselle Hauteville fussed over Marsanne, brushing her cloak which was torn and mud-stained and rubbing the dirt off the left side of her face. There were bloody scratches underneath the dirt. Marsanne winced but let herself be made presentable. It was kind of Nicoletti to help attend to her, she mused, when Clotilde seemed so much more his type.

All the same she was annoyed by his presumption: Marsanne had always been sure she would react strongly to the sensuous attractions of a desirable male. However, when René Nicoletti had held her around the waist in an intimate way, remarking softly, "What a tiny waist, mademoiselle!" she had resented his lack of subtlety in trying to take advantage of the situation.

She was much relieved when the coachman called his little flock to attention and they all poured out to reclaim their places and resume their trip. She went out between an anxious Clotilde and a possessive René Nicoletti, started to take her seat facing the boot of the coach and found "Sir Philip Justin" calmly settled in her seat. His long legs were crossed at the ankles, and the point of his tricorne hat had been tilted down over his forehead toward his nose, almost, but not quite, to hide his eyes.

"Now, see here," Nicoletti began before Marsanne could stop him, but the Englishman merely pointed to the seat across from him—an obviously preferable seat at that. Then he closed his eyes in a bored fashion and appeared to go to sleep.

Marsanne did not for a moment believe he was actually asleep, but his surrender of the excellent corner seat in the coach had been generous; he must have paid extra to obtain it. Without expecting any reaction from him, she murmured her thanks. This time she could have sworn his lips curved into a smile, but he made no reply and did not open his eyes.

The coach started off with its usual backward-forward jolt. Clotilde caught her breath, pressed her handkerchief against her mouth, explaining to the concerned Nicoletti, "My stomach, monsieur. When we rock like that my stomach behaves very . . . oddly."

"My dear mademoiselle," Nicoletti observed quickly, "what will you do on La Manche, the rough channel? You must go instantly to your berth and remain there until we reach Dover. That will do the trick. You need not feel concern for your mistress. She will excuse you. And I—well, I will keep you both company. By turns."

This advice did not strike Marsanne as particularly

notable, but to her surprise the sleeping Englishman opened his eyes and fixed his gaze upon Nicoletti and Clotilde who were leaning toward each other as they talked.

Marsanne was puzzled to find anything of interest in that little exchange about seasickness and could not imagine why it had attracted the Englishman. She said nothing, however, and merely determined to watch him for the rest of the journey while she nursed the bruises from her fall at the innyard.

There was a long delay later that day when the coach was forced to abandon the Amiens high road because of the recent winter rains. The passengers crowded into an isolated manor house and Marsanne got a chance to ask Clotilde privately, "How long did the Englishman wait this morning before he left the private parlor to stop the coach horses? I asked you and Monsieur Nicoletti to detain him, remember."

Clotilde was vague. The event had passed and, to her mind, was settled. "But it was Monsieur René who went first. Monsieur René noticed you were standing too near the horse. He told me so. And then, after he left, the Englishman followed him. He did not even give Mademoiselle Hauteville a by-your-leave. The English are very impolite when they choose to be."

"Well, it's no matter." Or if it was, the facts apparently solved nothing.

By the time the passengers had been herded back into the coach they found their number increased by four lively men bound for a gaming house in Calais. Over the stern protests of Mademoiselle Hauteville and the Royalist tailor the gamblers tossed coins to see which of the men took seats in the coach and which two inherited the cold and windy coach-roof.

This time the Englishman wedged himself between Marsanne and Clotilde with the butcher occupying the far corner, leaving Nicoletti to share the opposite seat with Madame Hauteville, the tailor and two of the cheerful drunks who persisted in the illusion that five could find comfort in a space meant for three. René Nicoletti was in a foul mood and glowered at Sir Philip Justin, who innocently stretched his legs out and went to sleep.

After they had been racketing along well over five hours, with most of the passengers in alcoholic slumber, Marsanne became more and more convinced that, though the Englishman's tricorne hat was pulled over his face, he was not asleep. What was his cat-and-mouse game? And was it directed against her or someone else?

She would have what she thought was her answer to that as they entered Calais late in the morning and the coach stopped for the showing of passport papers. Everyone fussed nervously except the Englishman, whose papers were produced with a bored air, and Marsanne, who carefully held her own and Clotilde's papers for ten minutes before they were needed. No one questioned her papers or Justin's, though they seemed to find more papers among Justin's Through Passage permits, and the officer give him a long thoughtful look as he returned the papers.

Next Nicoletti handed over his papers. To the astonishment of Clotilde and Marsanne the official showed the papers to his fellow officer, then raised his rifle.

"René Nicoletti? Out!"

The young man stared, not moving. "Why? What is the delay, messieurs?"

"Out!" The rifle with its long, gleaming bayonet terrified the two women as it felt its way into the coach's interior.

"What—" Nicoletti licked his lips. "What is the charge, messieurs?"

"You admit you are René Luigi Nicoletti, born Ajaccio, Corsica, currently resident of Paris?"

"Yes, but—"

"You are to be searched."

"René Luigi Nicoletti, you have been denounced as a Bonapartist agent, working in the cause of the Usurper,

Napoleon Bonaparte. You will come with us. As for the rest . . . messieurs, mesdames, you may be on your way. Captain Justin, we will expect your testimony as soon as you have delivered these ladies."

The supposed Englishman yawned, touched his mouth gently, agreed. "As you say, officer."

The coach rolled off along the cobbled streets of the port town. Marsanne was no longer confused. She knew now that the man who called himself Sir Philip Justin had made the accusation. What a scoundrel to have betrayed another man so brazenly!

Chapter Five

What an evil man! We must be very careful of him,"
Clotilde whispered as Sir Philip leaned out to ask the
coachman if he would drive by the Dover Quai, the inn
nearest the point where the cross-channel English boats
docked.

Marsanne was busy wondering how the Englishman
knew she and Clotilde were bound for the Dover Quai
Inn. Perhaps a reasonable assumption. It was the logical
resting place for anyone sailing to or from the port of
Dover in England. The Englishman pulled his head back
in and raised the window.

"I assume you have some explanation for betraying
that unfortunate Bonapartist," Marsanne challenged him.

His gaze shifted blandly from Clotilde's shocked expression to Marsanne.

"Yes, Miss Vaudraye. All in good time."

Clotilde's presence apparently inhibited his explanation.

Marsanne tried to imagine what excuses he could give in betraying a man who might be executed for a crime of which her own mother was guilty.

"How do you know we are staying at the Dover Quai Inn?"

Again came the faintest glance in Clotilde's direction. He shrugged. Marsanne said sharply, "What if we turn you over to the Royalist authorities? For all we know, you may be the Bonapartist."

One of his eyebrows raised and she knew he was laughing at her. "If I am a Bonapartist, you won't betray me."

"You are much too sure of yourself on that score."

"Not at all. I am sure only that you won't wish to betray the—" He hesitated. "—let us say, the Bonapartist who sent me. And incidentally, it was I who suggested the Dover Quai Inn to this Bonapartist."

Dumbfounded, Marsanne could think of nothing to ask without telling Clotilde more than such an incurable chatterbox should know. "Good God!"

Clotilde's big eyes widened. "Really, mamselle, your sainted mama would be shocked to hear you use language like that."

"Very true," the Englishman observed gravely.

Marsanne gave him a look but could do no more without betraying him as well as her mother. She found herself in a state of utter confusion by the time they reached the quai and saw the angry gray Channel beyond. Clotilde looked out, her fingers slipping down the window in panic.

"It looks so big. You did not tell me it went so far. I can't even see England."

With an effort Marsanne controlled the nervousness that had grown with Sir Philip's partial confession. Could she believe him? After all, Pierre Binet's stepfather was sure to know about Marsanne's mother and half of Paris was aware of Veronique's politics. Marsanne turned her attention to the immediate problems of reassuring Clotilde, whose chatter had leaped from the terror of the vast expanse of water—her first sight of such a natural phenomenon—to the subject of the late lamented René Nicoletti.

As the coach pulled up before the two-story, half-timbered Norman inn facing the busy harbor, Clotilde whispered, "I am persuaded this horrid man lied about Monsieur René. Can't you make him tell the truth?"

Marsanne looked quickly at Sir Philip who had heard every word. As the postilion opened the door, the Englishman helped Clotilde out before her mistress, and while the girl was occupied with picking out their luggage and trying to test her bruised leg, he explained to Marsanne, "My note to the customs merely said I had heard this Corsican make anti-Royalist statements boasting that the 'Little Corsican' would return."

In spite of her anxiety to play fair with the young Corsican, Nicoletti, Marsanne reminded Justin, "But when he is interviewed, he will be freed to follow us again."

"Not unless he has Royalist connections and can prove it. Meanwhile, we will be across the Channel on the tide. If he does follow you to England he may expose his employer."

"You can't mean that! You have no proof."

He said lightly, "I know his sort. One learns to smell them out in prison."

He left her with that revelation about his own past as he helped her out of the coach, told her he would collect her and Clotilde for the sailing, and having recovered his cape from Clotilde, strode off along the quai, easily breasting the sharp sea wind.

"I don't like that man!" Clotilde said as firmly as was possible in her childish voice. "Do you?"

Marsanne quickly recovered her common sense and

replied, "No . . ." But, as a young servant of the inn led the way with their luggage, she went on thoughtfully, "I wish I knew the full truth about him."

"He deliberately caused poor Monsieur René to be arrested. Poor Monsieur René was so shocked and—"

"Oh, *bother* poor René!" Marsanne cut her off rudely and then had to contend with her wounded feelings. "I'm sorry, Clotilde, but I don't want that Nicoletti to be following us to England either. Sir Philip tells me the rascal will be released in a day or two."

With a surprising show of independence Clotilde said, "Well, if it comes to that, I don't want your precious Sir Philip accompanying us to England. He's mighty suspicious you will allow."

In all fairness, Marsanne had to agree that the last word was unquestionably Clotilde's, and having won this concession, the girl kept up her stream of accusations against the Englishman until Marsanne was forced to hush her while she answered the innkeeper's questions about their stay at the inn.

"I should like your private parlor overnight. I'll pay the reckoning now. Will you please tell anyone who inquires that we sail tomorrow on the first tide?"

"As Madame wishes. Then Madame will also wish a dinner this evening. Shortly before sunset. We make our dinner hours later so that our illustrious patrons may taste the delicious seafood brought in during the morning."

Marsanne felt a little proud of herself at handling this business so well. It was also the first time a stranger with whom she did business had addressed her as "Madame," a title reserved for females over twenty. She must have seemed perfectly capable of traveling even unchaperoned. Unmarried females were not so independent in the society in which Marsanne had grown up.

When the girls were on their way to the "private parlor" Clotilde gazed fearfully at the weatherbeaten walls of the passage.

"The landlord looked like a pirate, didn't he?"

Marsanne shared her view of the swarthy fellow with his thick black brows, but she said nonchalantly, "No. Merely a smuggler, in all likelihood."

When they were alone in their parlor, Marsanne noticed Clotilde immediately starting to untie the soiled sky-blue ribbons of her own bandbox and said suddenly, "Don't unpack."

Bewildered, the girl looked up. "But why not, mamselle? I feel so dusty after that long ride. And I know I shall never get the wrinkles out of this pink skirt."

Marsanne had gone to the window and was studying the channel boat, a three-masted barkentine which gave every sign of sailing within the hour. Dockworkers were busy on the tipsy-looking gangplank and the sailors seemed to scamper all over the ship and even up on its crossyards, preparing to sail.

"Because we are going on board the ship at once. We are not waiting for the night crossing. Or for tomorrow when either one of those two rogues, perhaps both, will be back pursuing us."

Clotilde protested briefly, but was soon overruled and quieted. Marsanne summoned the young man who acted as footman, hostler and general scullery boy. He had a mischievous, open face and straightforward manner.

"Boy," Marsanne began with no nonsense, "do you have a fondness for tax men, officers of the Crown who make a business of detaining ladies because the brother of one of them occasionally carries a bit of English wool back after exchanging it for French silk?"

Clotilde gasped at such a tissue of lies, but the boy merely said, "Smugglers?"

"Gentlemen sailors."

He grinned, then sobered to assure her, "Them that

does the Crown's sneaking dirt, they're no friends of ours."

"This customs man knows we are here and will be upon us before the day is over, trying to make us betray my poor brother."

"Shall we slit his throat, madame?"

Clotilde stifled a scream, but Marsanne carried off very well the slightly superior: "Heavens, no! But we don't want you to let him know we are gone, or that we took the Dover ship this morning."

"But, madame, she sails in a few minutes. With the tide, and all."

"Then we must work fast." She counted two silver francs from her reticule and held on to them while retying the drawstrings of the bag. Without further hesitation the boy picked up portmanteaux and the three bandboxes while he kept a weather-eye out for the two francs.

"Soon's I've got you ladies on the deck, I'll run back and get the little trunk. Ought to be time enough."

"Good," she said. "Then we'll make it another franc. All paid when we are safely aboard with our trunk."

He did not take offense, apparently being used to his customers' mistrust. "Down the back stairs," he suggested, and the two women followed him obediently through the ancient, foul-smelling hall. "Out behind the kitchen through the stillroom. Nobody likely to see you at this hour."

Introduced by the boy from the inn, she bargained with the first mate, acting as supercargo of the *Sally Winkle*. He claimed her French money was unacceptable, but the innkeeper's boy offered to run back to the inn and exchange it for good English pounds, shillings and pence. In the end it was agreed that these ladies, and a half dozen other passengers, might occupy a small area of the deck space if they avoided the cargo holds, the orlop deck, and the crew's quarters. If they wanted to sit down, they must use Marsanne's neat little corded trunk.

Marsanne's biggest problem proved to be neither the escape nor the safe and timely arrival on the chaotic and shifting deck of the *Sally Winkle,* but Clotilde, who took instant exception to a wooden floor that moved under her feet.

"Oh, mamselle, I cannot! I cannot walk. Or stand. My head aches."

"Rubbish. We are still at anchor." Marsanne looked around, discovered she loved the motion of the ship. Then she said gently, "Why don't you walk about and look at the harbor? It is very exciting. See the activities on the docks. Or up in the—what do they call them? The shrouds."

"Shrouds!" Clotilde gasped. The notion very nearly caused the girl to return to Paris, but Marsanne maneuvered her around through the waist of the ship to what she confidently explained was the "larboard side."

"And out there is England."

Clotilde stared, beginning to hope.

A great rolling white bank of clouds concealed the low horizon, and without hesitation Marsanne pointed to it. "You see those white cliffs? They are near Dover which is not far from Cousin Sylvie's Sussex estates."

Holding on to her bonnet, Clotilde became so fascinated by this unexpected proximity to their goal that she forgot her fears for the moment. "Those lovely white things that look like clouds? They are the white cliffs of Dover?"

Having lied so many times this evening, Marsanne whispered an inaudible prayer for her immortal soul, then pragmatically and coolly turned to enjoy the cold, wet breeze and the crowded harbor with its many bare-masted ships.

Last-minute cargo came aboard along with a clutch of passengers, but all of Marsanne's attention was taken up by the activity of men at the anchor chains, the drawing in of the gangway, and—most glorious of all—the manner in which the sails billowed out high above her head. While she marveled at the swiftness with which the ship glided out of the harbor, Clotilde staggered about from taffrail to quarterdeck ladder, pale-faced and desperately clutching at everything in sight. Gently Marsanne put her arm around the girl and led her toward the rail . . . but Clotilde shrank back in horror.

"No, no. I might fall over."

"But, Clotilde, if you are sick to your stomach—"

"It isn't my stomach. It is my head. I have such a dreadful headache! And a buzzing in my ears. I can't bear this horrid voyage."

"Of course you can . . ." But Marsanne was beginning to panic at this impossible behavior.

A calm, confident voice which she remembered all too well suggested, "Miss Lefebre would be happier resting in her cabin." The Englishman had tracked them down in spite of all her precautions and bribes.

Clotilde was too sick to resent his sudden appearance. "I would, mamselle, I would!"

Marsanne wanted very much to know how Sir Philip Justin had managed to be on the *Sally Winkle* after her calculated effort to deceive him, but Clotilde's extreme discomfort was of first concern.

"I wish she might rest, sir, but the truth is we have no cabin." It was an embarrassing confession and his reply was even more humiliating.

"She may have mine. Come, Miss Lefebre."

Knowing Clotilde's distaste for the Englishman, Marsanne carefully followed them down the ladder, rescuing Clotilde's bonnet which had blown back on her neck, and picking up Sir Philip's crumpled handkerchief, which Clotilde had frantically clutched during the past several moments. The man was right. Clotilde felt much better when she lay upon the genuine fourposter bed in the captain's cabin with the curtains over the stern windows carefully closing out the bright silver light of the sky.

Clotilde was heavily bundled in several blankets, a coverlet, and her heavy weather-cloak, plus a hot brick wrapped in a sheet brought in by the galley-cook at Sir Philip's direction.

"Now, sir, please explain yourself," Marsanne demanded as they left the cabin and he was helping her up the companion-ladder.

"Very simple. Having seen how it would be with your friend, Miss Lefebre, I borrowed the captain's cabin. He is off on a voyage to the West Indies with cargo-halts at Dover and Plymouth and one of the Irish ports. The channel crossing requires all his attention. He was glad enough to surrender the cabin for a few hours and a few shillings."

Angrier at his deliberate evasion, she countered, "I am not interested in how you acquired the cabin but how you managed to appear on these decks at all. Clotilde and Monsieur Nicoletti swear you are risen from the dead. I am beginning to think that is the only explanation for your rapid appearances and disappearances."

"I am afraid the answer is going to ruin my supernatural aura: the landlord and his boy at the Dover Quai are in business with some friends of mine, so I discovered immediately what you were about. I had a feeling you might be taking the night packet. And, in fact, you did give me quite a chase to get on board before the *Sally Winkle* sailed. I nearly broke my leg running up the gangway."

"Bravo for you. Meanwhile, I wasted my bribe."

"Not at all." He dropped the three francs in her palm and closed her fingers into a fist.

Stunned, she accepted the francs as she acquiesced to the strong pressure upon her fingers; and then seeing the open amusement in his eyes, she was forced to laugh. "I suppose if you intended my demise you would have acted before now."

"Not necessarily. I am persuaded your death is precisely what Nicoletti intended, to separate you from your maid on board the packet, and then to heave you over into those waters below. Unfortunately, I have been unable to get proof of my suspicions."

"What a pity! Had I known it meant so much to you, I would certainly have encouraged him to throw me over, and in your very sight. You would have had perfect proof."

He pretended to ignore this sarcasm. "Don't forget, Nicoletti was excessively interested in the girl's sickness under the motion of the coach. You remember, he suggested that while she went below, he would take care of you on deck as you crossed the Channel."

"That is hardly a criminal suggestion." Nonetheless, she looked over the side and shivered. Now that they were out in the vicious cross-currents of the Channel she felt a strong sympathy for Clotilde's fear of those wild, churning depths. She grasped the rail tightly as the ship heeled under the assault of wind and wave. She felt the Englishman's fingers clasp her arm but pretended not to notice; as a *lady,* she should move away from his touch, and yet she felt much safer—now at ease—with him.

"Were you really sent by Mama to look after me?"

"I would have told you so earlier, if we hadn't been interrupted so much by your Clotilde, a born chatterbox."

"And you have come all this way to protect us? It was very good of you."

"Not precisely. I have business in England. The most important of my life. It was a lucky coincidence that Sister Veronique wanted to get you out of France . . . But tell me what you know about your Sussex cousins and their friends. I am slightly acquainted with the landowners there but wonder if we can trust them; or are they likely to produce some more like Nicoletti?"

She looked at him. His face appeared cold and sculptured under the bitter sweep of the wind; yet she now knew he could be extraordinarily winning. She had never admired coldly handsome men. She preferred . . . but she put a halt to the thought, because she'd never really known any man well. She could not remember any man she had *preferred*. And now Marsanne faced a frightening thought . . . could she be one hundred percent certain of him? And if she could now trust him, could she trust herself and the physical attraction for him growing stronger? She decided, in any event, that she could not honestly avoid admiring this strong man who seemed in control of almost any situation. And how could she not at least be attracted to such a man?

"As you probably already know," she now said to him, "I am going to my cousin, Lady Sylvie Lesgate. Actually, her first husband was Mama's cousin. She is very lively and social. And clever, too. At all events, she managed to win a fantastically rich English husband soon after Cousin Alexandre de Vaudraye died. Alex, as I understand it, was leading some emigré soldiers during the Vendéan rebellion. It is odd to think he was killed leading men against his own country. But he was a Royalist, of course."

Sir Philip said nothing to that, and she had the distinct feeling that he despised the long dead Cousin Alex. And perhaps all Royalists? It did not fit his English pose. She changed the subject suddenly, hoping to surprise him into revealing something about his past.

"What and who are you, sir?"

But he was always on guard. He even smiled a little at her naïve effort to trip him.

"I am an Englishman named Philip Justin who has spent the last twenty turbulent years in the Swiss Cantons with the lung sickness."

"I don't believe a word of it."

"My papers are in order. Would you care to examine them?"

"They'll find you out in England."

"Oh, no, they won't." Nevertheless, he refused to explain why. He pointed over her head at a small vessel, riding low at the stern, and borne along by a striped lateen sail, its triangular sheet billowed out with the wind. "You see that felucca? A smuggler making for the Sussex coast. Carrying French wines and silk, probably."

She stared at it, cupping her hands to her eyes to make out the occupants of the felucca. Dark figures moved about on the deck which had heeled over to a dangerous degree, but she could not make out the men individually. Seeing them, however, she remembered Paris and that day when she stood on the Petit Pont, watching a distant sailor who put her in mind of a smuggler.

"How odd! Mama had a visitor the day I left her at the hospital. She said the sailor was there to strip down the Napoleonic N's and replace them with L's for Louis. He was dressed like those smugglers. Only he had a red band or kerchief around his head. Did you see him?"

She thought she had startled him, but the ship was swaying so much it was hard to tell.

"I? Why should I see him?"

"But you talked to Mama that last day, didn't you? Otherwise, how would you know I took that particular Calais coach?"

"Very true. However, I don't recall your smuggler. We are making a fast crossing, thanks to this wind."

"I love it."

"Yes. I once loved it."

She turned to him curiously. "And not any more?"

He did not answer. He pulled her bonnet forward by the brim, warned her to tie the ribbons once more, and then studied her in a way she found disconcerting. She had no sooner anchored her bonnet safely than he reached out again. "It's quite safe now," she assured him, feeling that these gestures were a criticism of her looks. But he reached in under the bonnet brim and began to draw out wisps of her usually neat hair. She tried to stop him and he brushed her hand away.

"You are a very attractive woman. But Sister Veronique should not be your pattern-doll."

"What!"

"You are not a nun but a warm and passionate young woman, as I could tell the first time I saw your lower lip." She touched her lip self-consciously. "You look very fetching with your hair flying."

She was flustered and tried to cover this by a joke. "I must remember to be warm and passionate with Cousin Sylvie's Englishmen, so I may bring home a husband. I imagine that is expected of females my age."

"In that case," he said, "I am sorry I spoke."

While she was still trying to recover, he took the wisps of hair he had released and crowded every lock back under her bonnet. The flesh of his hand faintly touching her cheek excited her. She only hoped he did not guess as much.

She began to laugh and after a second or two, during which she found the light in his eyes luminous but unreadable, he laughed also.

Returning to the matter of his curious knowledge, she asked, "How do you know about smuggler ships? I thought smugglers were villains, cutthroats. But you seem extraordinarily familiar with them."

"Vaguely, yes." He leaned over the rail and tried to see through the clouds toward the fog-shrouded smugglers' felucca. "You see, the British excise laws protect the high tariff on liquors—brandy, for example. Yet the coastal people of Kent and Sussex have earned a livelihood for centuries by trade with France. Also, their chief customer during five hundred years has been France."

"And the British have been at war with France for most of that time."

"Precisely. The two governments have been at war. But not the seamen of the Sussex and Normandy and Brittany coasts. The French could get good money for English wool. The English made a profit on French brandy. You may imagine the true sympathies of the coastal English when I tell you their name for the smugglers is "The Gentlemen." Or the Free Traders. To these English, free trade saves them from paying the huge tax on French imports. And they are useful when a man has frequent . . . unofficial business between the two countries. . . ." He caught himself and stopped.

After that he remained impersonal, pointing out various flags on the vessels which crossed the wake of the *Sally Winkle.* An American brig, a Portuguese fishing boat, innumerable French and British ships making the crossing or Dutchmen coming down hard from the North Sea, driven by the swift currents.

"It's blowing up a rain," he said finally, staring up at the sky through the shrouds.

"There's another little smuggling ship." She leaned far over the rail, its wooden surface pitted by salt, and tried to make out the second felucca with a triangular lateen sail.

Beside her, he leaned over the rail to see where she pointed. "Sorry. No friends of mine. They may even be British Excisemen, officers of the Crown whose duty is to capture smugglers. Remember, the government loses enormous revenues every time the smugglers succeed in selling their cargoes. They are chasing the others—the smugglers—into port. They won't catch them, though. They don't have the speed."

A squeal from the deck behind them startled Marsanne so much she fell against the rail. While Justin caught her and restored her balance, Marsanne demanded furiously, "Clotilde, what do you mean by screaming like that?"

"Mamselle!" The girl lowered her voice to a panicky whisper. "He had his hand on your shoulder. He might have tossed you overboard. Don't you see? He could be the Binet man—"

"Clotilde, you are an absolute idiot! Come inside where

you can get warm. Your teeth are chattering." She apologized to Sir Philip. "I'm sorry, she only means to protect me, she's my friend. . ."

He said quietly, "I know. You need friends, mademoiselle. The little chatterbox may prove to be a better friend than those fine cousins of yours. . . Incidentally, those cliffs ahead mean we are nearing Dover. You had best be getting your things together. It will be raining by the time we go ashore."

Clotilde gulped and clutched at Marsanne. "Safe on shore! I was never so glad to hear that word in my life."

Marsanne looked back toward France, back over the long, choppy way they had come.

" 'Safe on shore.' I wish I could be as sure that Mama is safe."

She watched Sir Philip's face, searching for some reassurance. After a brief time, he said softly, "I'm certain she will be, mademoiselle. After all, she is widely loved for her good works. . ."

Marsanne appreciated the intent of his words, at the same time feeling he was perhaps trying to convince himself as well as her.

Chapter Six

At the English port of Dover, Marsanne settled passport matters and hired an ancient coachman, his open carriage and two bored horses to carry her and Clotilde that very evening to the Lesgate estates.

"I still say I could have found you a closed carriage. And I would be most happy to escort you," Sir Philip put in once more, but Marsanne remembered the long trip ahead in the darkness and preferred to make absolutely certain that she and Clotilde arrived without delay. She would be pleased—and told him so—to see him by daylight and in her cousin's house, and she was also a trifle put out when Sir Philip promised vaguely, "Soon, I hope. Meanwhile, my business takes me to London. I trust you ladies will enjoy your stay in England."

He brought Marsanne's hand to his lips, then Clotilde's, and having helped them with their luggage he turned and walked in the opposite direction.

This independence was strange and quite a novelty. Marsanne braced herself against the side of the carriage and held out one hand to help Clotilde, who teetered back and forth unsteadily before falling onto the seat and groaning. But Marsanne ignored her complaints.

During the first days of her journey Marsanne had been so haunted by the possible danger—perhaps from Nicoletti, perhaps Justin—that she hadn't time to miss her mother, but now the English Channel lay between them. For the first time in Marsanne's life she could not rush to Sister Veronique, who had always comforted and helped her.

As the old coachman gave the signal to start, and the dim lamplights on the outskirts of the port town vanished, Marsanne wondered where Sir Philip Justin had gone and what his pressing business might be. He had certainly parted from her with no more apparent feeling than he demonstrated in his polite farewell to Clotilde. Of course, she had to admit she had done little to encourage him, putting him off as she had.

The coachman gave a sharp, monosyllabic direction to the horses and the coach turned off the London Post Road onto a narrow estate road, full of deep ruts and carriage tracks.

They bounced up and down along the road but at the same time the mist seemed to dry up and they could enjoy the vague silhouette of this new world around them. They had passed through rolling downs that would have been monotonous but for the curious creatures, almost ghostly and sinister, which dotted the area. Clotilde clutched Marsanne. "Those things. Mamselle, they are moving this way!"

Marsanne tapped the coachman between the shoulder blades.

"Monsieur—I mean, sir, what are those creatures out on the downs?"

"Sheep, mum. Good Sussex sheep. You being Frenchies and all, you mightn't know we hereabouts produce the best wool there is."

"Yes, indeed." So much for the sinister, ghostly figures creeping up on them! At the same time, on one side of the estate road, the downs miraculously turned into an emerald green park, bordered in the distance to the south by the darkness of a copse.

The copse and a larger woods continued to border the south, but something loomed up on the eastern horizon, silvery in the evening light. Obviously, this long rectangular stone building of two stories and a series of attics was Sylvie de Vaudraye Lesgate's "little home" as she had referred to it during her Paris visit the previous year. The "little home" appeared at this distance more like one of France's royal châteaux.

At the same time the girls heard hoofbeats and the splash of water in the wheel ruts of the road behind them. The coachman looked over his shoulder.

"You ladies have friends in the Lesgate Deer Park?"

"My cousin is Lady Lesgate."

"So. But this fine fellow in his regimentals, this London dandy following us is not Lady Lesgate."

Marsanne sat up and looked around. The horseman tearing along toward the carriage was a soldier. Even in the overcast dark one could make out the red uniform, the shining accouterments, the splendidly athletic figure of a young Englishman.

Clotilde swiveled around. "It may be a highwayman. He is going to hold us up, I know it! Oh, this dreadful country!"

But Marsanne had less melodramatic ideas about their pursuer who rode up beside the carriage and with a lavish wave of one arm ordered the coachman, "Slow there, old man. I mean these lovely ladies no harm. Friend of the family, as it were."

The coachman relaxed, eyed the soldier and then the girls and shrugged. The soldier drew rein, leaned over to look into Clotilde's face and said with great enthusiasm, "May I salute your hand in welcome, Miss Vaudraye? By George, I'd no notion you were such a beauty."

Much too enthralled to correct him, Clotilde beamed as she extended her fingers, which he brought to his lips. Marsanne was a trifle provoked but could not help watching the scene with amusement. The young soldier went on happily, "I say, would you mind awfully if I rode with you to Her Ladyship's doorstep?"

"Well—I—" Helpless, Clotilde looked to Marsanne who asked, trying not to sound abrupt, "Who are you, sir?"

"Captain Roderick Fortenham, at your service. And yours, dear Miss Vaudraye."

Marsanne began to understand. "Ah. The bridegroom of my Cousin Amy."

"Future, mam. Future. Haven't quite brought her up to scratch yet. But I've been invalided out until this accursed thigh bone heals." He looked from one girl to the other. His chagrin made both girls laugh. "I say, I have done it now, mixing the two of you up. You are Amy's cousin."

Marsanne nodded.

He said in his winning way, "Don't suppose you'd consider making room for me long enough to hear my apologies."

It was all proper and charming, so very English, and after Captain Fortenham tethered his mount to the carriage and climbed in on Clotilde's other side, the coachman started up again and the captain began to remark upon the beauty of French women. But Captain Fortenham, whose service had been confined to the Portuguese and Spanish campaigns was ill-equipped to respond to Clotilde's volatile French and gradually found himself addressing Marsanne herself: "I am very much afraid I had a different impression. I thought—one hears so much about . . . French women. . . Miss Clotilde seemed more typically French—the little-charmer sort. At least, my friend René has always given me to understand that one can always . . ." He had gotten himself in too deeply and with every word was further insulting his French acquaintances. But his ingenuous efforts to please, and even his frankness, robbed his words of offense.

Marsanne knew perfectly well that this big bronze soldier with the manner of a blundering playful mastiff belonged to her Cousin Amy, and she should not encourage or make fun of his flirtation, innocent though it might be. She could understand, though, why Cousin Amy must find him lovable. Clotilde, however, was not swayed by such understanding and she put in unexpectedly, "Oh, monsieur, you must not speak so. Mamselle is a very serious lady. One does not talk to her in that way."

Before Marsanne could open her mouth in rebuttal, Captain Fortenham straightened himself in military fashion and apologized stiffly, "Mam, I can only beg your pardon again. We are here. Permit me to help you down."

They had drawn up before the long marble steps that fronted Lesgate Hall. A footman in Sylvie's green and silver livery hurried out through the long narrow center doors and down the steps. At the same time a stableboy shot into view from the distant stables near the copse, running along the pebbled drive that paralleled the front face of the building.

As Marsanne was lifted down from the carriage, it began to rain. At the same time, with sinking spirits, she heard sounds within the long front hall of the building and, through the windows, saw many figures parading that hall, figures whose presence told her she had interrupted a ball or entertainment of some kind. She groaned while Clotilde clapped her hands with pleasure.

"A rout. What fun, mamselle. I must change you immediately, so you will do yourself justice. Your deep blue satin slip with shot-silver overdress perhaps. And your silver chain with your Mama's miniatures."

Captain Fortenham had now lifted Clotilde to the steps and she did not hear Marsanne's short laugh: "I'll make a fine ball guest, all dripping wet."

With a flourish Captain Fortenham hurried the two females into the long marble hall. On the north end an elegant staircase fanned out into the hall, and the south end appeared to be a ballroom. Meanwhile, although the music of violins, tambours and other instruments came from behind the big hall, a dozen couples sauntered through the hall . . . ladies in jeweled Grecian coiffures and silk skirts over satin slips, males following the dictates of Mister Beau Brummel, the Regent's friend, all in stark black and white with a peppering of uniforms and some old-fashioned satin small-clothes.

Marsanne murmured to the attentive anxious footman, "I am Her Ladyship's cousin from Paris. Please do not disturb her. I suggest the housekeeper show us to a bed-chamber and Lady Lesgate may then pay us a visit when she is in better case to do so."

"Ay, mum. As you say, mum. But you was expected any time, and no doubt you'll want to join Her Ladyship's dinner musicale when you've made yourself comfortable and all."

"That is an excellent suggestion, but I think for now I should go to my room and make myself at least present-able. How it does rain in your country!"

"We've a fine wet climate, thank you, mam," the foot-man said proudly, and Marsanne concealing her smile went on up the steps with him while Clotilde trotted ahead exclaiming at the unexpected splendor of the gowns she saw in that parade of fashion along the marble-pillared hall that occupied three-quarters of the building's long west front. The footman took Marsanne to a lanky, long-faced and ferocious-looking female in housekeeper's black, who waved him away in a no-nonsense fashion.

"Run along, boy. You've done your duty. I'll take the poor young lady in hand now. Land, but you're a sight, miss! I'm Mrs. Grover, the housekeeper."

Confused by this brusque but not unfriendly chatter, Marsanne found herself dripping on an elaborate Persian carpet of exquisite blue patterns in a salon that appeared to be part of the upstairs hall generously widened to include windows looking out upon the desolate, rolling downs and the distant Channel. She started to make excuses but Mrs. Grover dismissed such wasted breath. "Won't be the first time. When she was younger, Miss Amy was always tracking mud through here—her and her horsey friends. Quite an athlete is Miss Amy. Not that it's like to help her with her gentlemen nowadays."

Captain Fortenham coughed and Mrs. Grover scowled at him.

"Well, it's the truth, Mister Roderick. You've said as much yourself, time out of mind. Did you meet your friend in Dover, that Frenchie, by the by?"

"Sorry, Grover. No luck. Half thought he was to come across in the day packet from Calais. But old René's been slowed somewhere."

"By a female, I make no doubt. I know these Frenchies," Mrs. Grover announced, adding with a hasty nod to Marsanne, who had clearly reacted, "I'm not including you, miss. Anybody'd see with half an eye that you're a lady. And I've mighty good eyes, I can tell you."

Marsanne cut in, "No, no. It's something quite different. Captain, your French friend, René . . . What is his full name?"

"Nicoletti, mam. Jolly chap. Met him in Dover not six weeks ago. He's by way of being an artist. Paints and turpentine and beautiful, that is, live models. But quite respectable."

Clotilde nudged Marsanne. "What did I tell you, mamselle? Respectable. Not a nasty assassin at all."

"Lord love you, no, mam. Old René's very popular with the ladies. Damned sight—sorry, ladies—a sight too popular with the pretty things."

"I believe," Marsanne remarked slowly, "that he told me he was an olive merchant, working for his father. . ."

The captain chuckled. "That's René, all right and tight. He was funning with you. But I say . . . does that mean you've met the good fellow?"

"Briefly, on the Calais coach."

"Great that you've met. Wonder what kept him. Must be a female. Just like René. Only one thing wrong—Amy seemed to find him interesting. Well, Miss Vaudraye, I'll leave you now. But do come down when you can. I'd like the honor of presenting some of my friends to you." He grinned at Clotilde. "And I know just a few devils who'd like to make your acquaintance, Miss Clotilde."

Marsanne said, "Thank you. You've been very kind. Perhaps another time. Good night, sir," while Clotilde smiled sweetly at him.

Marsanne was still puzzled about René Nicoletti. She might have dismissed her previous suspicions, believing they were promoted by Philip Justin for his own reasons, but even here with his friend Captain Fortenham, she had caught the Frenchman in a lie. Though he might not be the assassin hired by the Binet family, he was certainly not what he had pretended to be either.

Chapter Seven

Mrs. Grover led the way into the big chamber with its warm crimson-curtained bed and a fireplace which she promised to have lighted at once. Best of all was a splendid view of the Sussex Downs and English Channel on the horizon. It looked stormy, and the mere thought of the waves made Clotilde shudder.

Mrs. Grover bustled around the room.

"Now then you'll be wanting a hip-bath, I make no doubt. I best tell Her Ladyship you are here. She will be storming about, demanding to know why she wasn't told."

Suiting action to the word, she went off to fetch a hip-bath and Cousin Sylvie both, and Marsanne began to unpack. Once or twice she called Clotilde to her task, asked her to untie the bandboxes or to open the drawers on one side of the armoire, but Clotilde was too excited to hold on to anything.

"Did you see that footman, mamselle? The one who

came to the steps and met us when we arrived. So handsome. And taller than our gentlemen."

But Marsanne had her own romantic image to remember. Where was Philip Justin at this moment? Had he thought of her at all after their parting at Dover? She remembered his eyes, and his smile, as he'd walked away this evening. She said dreamily, "I wonder if he *is* English. Actually, we have many tall, blue-eyed men in France as well . . ."

Clotilde paused in gathering up the shoes, white hose, shifts and short pelisse she had dropped out of her bandbox: "That nice Captain Fortenham seems exceedingly English to me. But I think his eyes are hazel."

Marsanne sighed. "I hadn't noticed. Clotilde, is it asking too much for you to unpack at least one box without dropping things?"

"As you say, mamselle."

Marsanne's disposition was improved by the arrival of two young country boys carrying the big awkward hipbath and a maid with towels and a perfumed soap. The boys came back and left quantities of steaming water in every conceivable jug and bucket. While Marsanne bathed and the maidservant poured water over her back, she began to listen to the talk between Clotilde and a plain unobtrusive young-ladies' maid called Hattie Totter, who explained that since she spoke French she had been hired for the duration of Marsanne's visit. Clotilde and Hattie gossiped. . .

"Ay. Indeed, the Frenchie was here. Took a fancy to Miss Amy. He came on a visit with Captain Roderick. Made quite a commotion among all the ladies. Miss Amy even took time from her precious horses to dance with him."

"What Frenchman is that?" Marsanne asked, uneasily aware of the answer.

Clotilde explained, "Monsieur Nicoletti, mamselle. It is exactly as I thought. Everyone found him charming."

"Yes indeed, miss," Hattie Totter put in. "A painter, they say. He offered to make a sketch and then a painting of Miss Amy's favorite mount."

"Was Captain Fortenham jealous of his attentions to Miss Amy?"

Hattie said in a noncommittal voice, "I have not been here long enough to say, mam. I am told that the captain tried even harder to win Miss Amy's good opinion, but Miss Amy has a mind of her own, and naturally, she thought the young Frenchman was the more . . . appealing of the two."

"I would not have thought so," Marsanne put in.

Hattie shrugged. "They say, mam, the captain and Miss Amy have known each other since time out of mind. The captain is distantly related to the late Sir Peverell Lesgate and as a boy he often spent his summers here when Miss Amy was a child. They say Miss Amy was only three years old when Lady Sylvie married Sir Peverell."

During the progress of her bath, Marsanne's hair began to creep down from its temporary knot on top of her head and she shoved it up impatiently, calling for towels. These were being warmed by the fire, and when she wrapped herself in them and began vigorously to scrub her body dry, she asked, "Did Captain Fortenham not know the French artist before six weeks ago?"

"Six? I believe it was about that. After the Christmas celebrations, miss, when I was hired."

Just when the court of Louis the Eighteenth in France was being given the facts on Marsanne de Vaudraye's claim to the estate. Extraordinary timing, and she did not believe in coincidences. Anyway, thanks to Philip Justin's denouncing him as a Bonapartist, the Frenchman was not likely to be here tonight.

Since the evening was wearing on, Marsanne hurriedly

dressed in the blue satin slip Clotilde brought out with the silver-blue gauze overdress, and allowed her still-wet curls to be piled into the mode with silver ribbons. She could not but be pleased by the flattery of the maids and grateful for the loan of Hattie Totter, who proved so capable.

Just as she was leaving the room, she met Cousin Sylvie hurrying along the hall toward her. Sylvie de Vaudraye Lesgate was well into her fifties and actually a third or fourth cousin by marriage, making her Amy an even more remote connection. But as the last of the Vaudrayes they had all kept in close touch whenever war and revolution did not interfere. Sylvie waved her mirrored fan and when they were near enough for an embrace welcomed Marsanne with her characteristic charm.

Sylvie had never been pretty, but her wit and ease with everyone, her ability to make people like her, and to make them like each other in her presence, had been a rare one in the court of Louis the Sixteenth and Marie Antoinette. Her malice was not too cutting and there were those who had hoped she would replace the evil machinations of the Polignac clan with her own milder influence. Had this been so, it was possible that the disaster to the royal family might not have been so complete.

Marsanne, however, wasn't interested in twenty-five-year-old court history. She was too busy gaping at Cousin Sylvie's astonishing red-gold hair, which had surely not been such a color, even when she was a girl. It was coiffed elegantly, with one long curl nestling on her badly wrinkled neck, and Marsanne had to admit the red hair with Sylvie's golden gauze evening robe put her in mind of nothing so much as a bonfire burning against a vivid sunset.

As they embraced, Sylvie slapped her back with the mirrored fan, murmuring in her ear, "I know you will write to Cousin Veronique and say I am ready for

Bedlam, but one must take the shine quite out of one's rivals."

"You will always do that, cousin," Marsanne assured her.

Sylvie looked her over. "My dear child, if only I had your marvelous complexion and that silken hair. . . . You look like a dream. We must find you a husband while you are with us." She added teasingly, "After all, you are going to be a deal too rich for a single young miss. Did the deeds reach you before you left Paris? And how is dear Veronique? Poor girl. I fear she will lose that post she has held so long. If only she would be a little more diplomatic. Well, come along and let all these handsome young lads feast their eyes on you."

Marsanne tried but failed to keep up with each of her cousin's remarks, and then, too, they had reached the top of the wide marble staircase and she suddenly became aware that a score of Sylvie Lesgate's guests had congregated at the foot of the staircase where the steps fanned out so exquisitely. Behind her fan, Sylvie confided to Marsanne, "These stairs are my invention. Dear Peverell was used to the old dark Jacobean staircase, but nothing presents a female at her best like descending such a staircase as this. Providing, of course, she has the necessary air of confidence."

A large proviso, Marsanne thought, as she put one of her best silver sandals on the first step, wondering if anyone would notice that one of the ribbons tying the slipper around her right ankle was badly frayed. What ghastly business if she walked out of her slipper in front of Cousin Sylvie's friends. Hopefully they would be her friends too by the end of this visit, even though their government had been an enemy of hers.

The faces peering up at her and Cousin Sylvie were innocent enough. None of them knew what enemy occupation had been like, or what it was like to live under the rule of a man appointed for them by the enemy.

She said aloud, "I must stop thinking of 'enemies.' "

"Heavens, my dear girl, let us hope so. The English have accepted me. That proves their good nature."

Marsanne laughed, and those at the foot of the stairs saw her first at her prettiest. Captain Fortenham, looking more handsome and manly than she remembered, advanced to give escort to Marsanne and Sylvie. With head high, a bright smile and eyes sparkling, Marsanne met the captain who, with Sylvie's help, presented the guests to her, or reversed the process in the case of a local viscountess and the magistrate of the district.

The magistrate, General Winters, looked like an ancient dry leaf, but he brought her fingers to his lips, gallantly assuring her, "It's moments like this, mam, that make me glad we're no longer warring with a country that produces the most charming females in the world."

Rising from her curtsy she murmured her thanks, grateful to the old soldier even though she had heard the stir of resentment his words aroused among those present. Perhaps naively she had supposed only the defeated had a right to mistrust the conqueror. Now she wondered as she looked around at these faces . . . could one of these elaborately dressed dinner guests be involved in the Binet family's threat against her? Not likely . . . but still, she meant to be careful.

She would never remember the strange English names attached to all those unreadable faces around her and was relieved when Captain Fortenham insisted on showing her around the various salons, pointing out the distant markings on the downs from the southeast windows of the ballroom.

She found the mist-shrouded scene interesting, but it reminded her forcibly of the darkness around them in the empty ballroom; Sylvie's guests had either returned to the music salon or were joining others at the late supper provided in a summer salon next to the ballroom.

Captain Fortenham described the long strand to the

south beyond the Lesgate estates where the downs ended and the beach began. "Just past the copse which acts as a barrier. Below the copse the beach spreads out quite a distance. The property's been leased by an Englishman from the midlands. Newly returned from the Continent. Poor devil. They say he's been ill. Never saw any of our battles since Ninety-two."

"Heavens! A runaway?"

"Coward? Not from what they say. Lung-sickness. Had to lie abed for the past twenty-some-ut years."

She straightened. "The man who leased the very next property?"

He looked at her, having read something of her surprise in her tone. "Quite unexceptionable fellow, I assure you. Family's been known in English history since the Domesday Book. Justin. Sir Philip Justin. Knighted gentry for the past few centuries. Eldest son usually knighted for diplomatic prowess."

"Then he was knighted before he went to the Swiss Cantons for his health?"

"I should think so, mam. No question."

"How old is he said to be?"

"Hard to say. Those who have met the man recently say he is remarkably well preserved. But he must be in his late fifties, I should think. You know this Justin?"

"A casual acquaintance on the *Sally Winkle,* crossing the Channel."

He seemed struck by the coincidence. "Haven't met the chap myself. But that's the story. The ladies find him fascinating. Can't imagine why."

"Fascinating but unapproachable," Sylvie put in. She had obviously been eavesdropping. She joined them to add, "Fire and ice, I would say. Wouldn't you, Marsanne? A curious man. One doesn't know what to make of him."

Marsanne swore in French, apologized hastily, and while Sylvie's eyebrows went up the captain grinned. "No matter, mam. I like a lady who speaks her mind. It's one thing I've always admired in Amy, though I confess she speaks it rather too frequently. Lady Lesgate, do you think that girl will ever come up to scratch? Or must I give up the attempt and marry some . . ." Rather daringly before his future mother-in-law, he added, "Some lovely French miss?"

Marsanne pretended not to understand this flattery, but Sylvie did not seem offended. "Jealousy might be just the attack that will rouse Amy, my boy."

"Lord knows I've tried everything else, mam." To Marsanne he put in anxiously, "Lady Lesgate knows my feelings."

"Shares them," said Sylvie, with a nod. "Roderick, Amy's finally arrived. Spent the entire evening in the stables exchanging advice with a local smuggler who knows horses. She has dressed now, however, and is anxious to meet her French cousin. So, Roderick, come along in to supper with Marsanne on your arm and be excessively devoted. We have tried everything else with Amy. We'll give her a small dose of jealousy."

"A smuggler!" Marsanne suddenly recalled Philip Justin's talk of smugglers. Was it still another coincidence that he had leased an estate handy to smugglers, and to other lawbreakers, no doubt? She would be on guard, but all the same an idea had occurred unbidden: if Philip Justin was a neighbor, she would certainly see him again. Why hadn't he told her this? Then she remembered the supper and as they walked the length of the shadowy ballroom, hearing their footsteps ring hollowly behind them, she said, "I had best see to Clotilde. She must be starved. She couldn't eat or drink on shipboard."

Sylvie laughed. "My dear child, Amy tells me she left our new maid and yours well on with a hot supper. I imagine they are devouring syllabub and bonbons now."

The suggestion of supper appealed more and more to Marsanne as they joined the little groups in the summer salon. Captain Roderick fetched her a plateful of delica-

cies, many of which were unfamiliar to her—fresh-caught
seafood, prepared with seasonings. She was ravenously
hungry but tried to remember her manners, nibbling
buttered crab, oysters and other luscious morsels while
she listened to the captain's chatter and wondered why
Philip Justin had leased an estate nearby—before he knew
her or about her sojourn here—and if it had anything to
do with the fact that smugglers conducted their operations
on this coast.

Gradually, she became aware that she and Captain
Fortenham had aroused the interest of a girl at the far
end of the salon. The girl had been stopped by two gossipy,
bejeweled ladies and obviously wanted to be free of them.
She signaled to Marsanne who recognized in this short but
well-proportioned redhead the abrupt unsociable child
she had met once during the brief peace of 1802. Amy de
Vaudraye was as carelessly dressed now as she had been
then, but Marsanne saw that the carelessness was deliberate.

Amy rudely waved the women to silence and strode
toward Marsanne. Fortunately her plain bronze skirts of
heavy taffeta were unfashionably wide to accommodate
her leggy movements, but the entire costume resembled a
riding habit, and though out of place at a musicale looked
surprisingly well, if formidable, on her.

She reached Marsanne and the captain and elbowed the
latter unceremoniously out of the way. Marsanne hesitated,
uncertain whether her cousin would disdain any display of
affection. She need not have been concerned. Amy reached
out and hugged her.

"Dear cousin! How glad I am to see you. Mama tells
me you and I have much in common. You are no silly
pattern-doll. You do not waste time trying to make yourself over into what you are not. I see Old Roddy's been
looking out for you. He's a good sort." She glanced toward the captain, smiled vaguely as to an old and not
very intimate friend.

Marsanne began to wonder if there might be another and quite different man in Amy's life. René Nicoletti, for example. . . . Most girls her age would certainly have found the captain's attentions worthwhile. Amy exchanged a few reminiscences with her cousin, then excused herself and disappeared, clearly uninterested in Captain Fortenham.

"Off to see how that damned filly of hers goes," he explained. But he recovered rapidly and by the end of the evening when he said good night at the foot of Cousin Sylvie's staircase, kissed Marsanne's fingers. Then, to her surprise and faint discomfort, he held her hand a very long time, looking up at her. "Shall we meet tomorrow, do you think? My family's estates are in the North. Derbyshire. But since I was invalided home last July, Lady Lesgate has obligingly lent me the Dower House between the Lesgate Deer Park and the next estate. The one leased to Sir Philip Justin. Her ladyship hoped my presence would bring Amy up to snuff. But it doesn't seem to have done the trick. May I show you about the estate? You might borrow one of Amy's mounts. She is a bruising rider, by the by."

"I don't ride. I am sorry."

The astonishing information so affected him he had to consider some alternative and finally hit upon "a stroll about the grounds."

He was very kind and very sweet, but in her eyes he belonged to her cousin, and she managed to put aside the invitation "until the weather was no longer so rainy." That, she thought, would postpone any further private dealings until she and Sylvie discovered a way to bring the laggard lovers together.

By the time she reached the wide semicircle where the upper hall briefly became a salon with long windows overlooking the frozen downs, she heard Clotilde teasing and enticing the rosy-cheeked young footman who had welcomed Marsanne and Clotilde to Lesgate Hall.

Seeing her mistress, Clotilde sent her captivated victim on his way and joined Marsanne, whispering, "He is very sweet. And so good-looking!"

"He seems so," Marsanne said politely. Inside the warm, inviting room Marsanne began to unwind the silver ribbon from among the complicated curls of her hair. She found herself, abruptly, homesick for Paris, for her mother. Everyone here had been polite—Sylvie and Amy seemed glad to see her, and there had been no difficulties, but this was a very long way from her homeland.

"I should never have come to England, never left her alone. I feel it."

Clotilde was immediately alarmed.

"What, mamselle? Never come to England where you are so popular? Oh! We are not to leave already! There are so many . . . things to do here."

Marsanne laughed and promised her, "I won't take you away from all those interests you've found. I promised Mama I'd wait here until the estate was settled."

She went to the window, drew the portières aside and looked out across the downs. Far away on the horizon, beyond the violent Channel which cut her off, was home, and Sister Veronique. And Philip Justin . . . for some reason she thought of him when she thought of France. It was very odd. Perhaps it was because he had dominated her thoughts throughout the coach trip and later, on the Channel voyage. Hugging herself now, she wished she could relive those moments again.

Clotilde bustled over to the window. "What do you see, mamselle? Those horrid smugglers. Yes. I can see them now."

Belatedly, Marsanne turned her attention to the figures seen vaguely through the mist, below the rear terrace of Lesgate Hall.

Clotilde said wisely, "That man has a keg on his shoulder. He must be delivering it here. Albert—he's the footman you saw in the hall—says those smugglers are dangerous. But people deal with them anyway. Along this coast it's even patriotic, he says, because it's prohibited to buy at such cheap prices. Nobody likes the king's law that puts a high tax on goods from France, so they deal with those horrid lawbreakers. Look at the man with the red cloth around his head. Doesn't he put you in mind of someone?"

Marsanne remembered at once. "The sailor who was waiting to see Mama at the hospital in Paris. But this man is much shorter. Heavier, too."

Clearly, this was not the same man; yet even the idea of a connection between the two made her extremely uncomfortable.

Chapter Eight

The next three days were filled with entertainment . . .
more strangers forced by the laws of polite society to
accept Marsanne as a kind of appendage to their popular
hostess, but Marsanne knew she was regarded as an
enemy. More than once she accidentally came upon people
speaking of her. Nor did she feel entirely free with her
cousin Amy, who behaved oddly at times.

There was, for instance, the occasion she came upon
Amy hurrying into the house through a side door from
the stables.

The girl looked far more startled than the near collision
with Marsanne warranted. All the easy confidence of previous occasions was gone. The severe young sporting
female who cared nothing for the opinion of her mother's
guests had become nervous and fluttery, anxiously tucking
away a strand of bright copper-colored hair and then
continuing to brush her skirts with the flat of her hands as
Marsanne stopped her.

"I thought," Marsanne told her, "I would go for a walk on the downs. This sunlight is delightful. I had almost forgotten what it is like."

"Pay it no mind, cousin. Before you get back to the house it will be raining . . . Marsanne—"

The unexpected emphasis on her name surprised Marsanne.

"Yes?"

"Where is Mama?"

"With Mrs. Grover."

"Good, I don't want her to hear us . . . How much money have you?"

Marsanne was too surprised to think of any of the dozen questions that occurred to her later.

"Very little, I'm afraid. Only a few pence. I haven't been where I could change my French money, except the money I needed for the hire of the public carriage in Dover."

"No. You don't understand. It is precisely what I need. French money." At Marsanne's reaction, she explained hurriedly. "A friend of mine is in difficulties. He was delayed and could not take the Channel packet; so he must pay the fee again. And he needs money to repay a few debts in France while he waits. They won't let him leave without payment." She ran her hands through her hair, setting it all on end. "He needs the money so dreadfully."

Bewildered, Marsanne tried one more protest: "But a man, a mere friend! To take money from you."

"Don't you hear anything I say? I adore him. If he doesn't get the money, he won't come." She clutched at Marsanne's sleeve. "You're the only person I can tell. Mother would lock me up in a convent, if she knew."

"But how did you find out that he needs this money?"

"The supercargo of the French packet brought the news. My friend crosses the Channel often. He knows everyone. It's one way he earns an occasional fee. He does many things. He's ever so talented. My friend works as what is called an *agent provocateur*."

Marsanne was mentally counting the money she had brought with her. Before she left England she intended to buy Cousin Sylvie a splendid present to show her gratitude for this hospitality, and then she needed money to get back home to Paris. But this last detail of Amy's added to the rest seemed too much to believe. "You would give money to a man whose job is provoking people to betray their political opinions? It seems a detestable business to me."

Amy wrung her hands. "How can you say so? His job is to pretend to be a Bonapartist, supporting that villain Napoleon. This makes the real Bonapartists tell him all their secrets. Their plans to rescue their beloved hero from the island of Elba. Then he reports them to the authorities. That's all."

"All! These Bonapartists can be executed."

"Well," Amy said more reasonably, "they deserve it, don't they?"

"Until less than a year ago, the Emperor Napoleon was the legally constituted ruler of our country! He was not voted out of his office, you know." She stopped, realizing that political arguments meant nothing to Amy. But she also began to suspect the answer to her next question: "And his name, this *agent provocateur* of yours?"

"René Nicoletti. He's really a painter . . . so talented . . . and the lovely irony is that Old Roddy introduced him to me. But at all events he cannot make enough money painting, so he does anything he can."

Marsanne had a strong desire to laugh. If Nicoletti was an *agent provocateur* hired by the Royalist government of France, among other unpleasant things, then, thanks to Philip Justin, his recent fate was indeed neatly ironic. He himself had been arrested as a Bonapartist. Did Philip Justin know of his employment in the Royalist camp? Possibly . . . *probably*. Justin had an almost frightening way of knowing things. She pulled herself together, started to pour out her feelings about René Nicoletti:

"I must tell you, Amy, the man behaved in a most suspicious—"

"You have met my—friend?"

"Met him indeed!" Marsanne caught herself. She had no actual proof of Nicoletti's murderous assignment. She suspected him, partly because she had preferred to believe his enemy Philip Justin. She wondered what she would do if the man came to Lesgate Hall. She could hardly condemn him without evidence. Yet she certainly had no desire to provide that evidence with her own death—if he actually was doing the work of the Binet family.

"Well?" Amy pursued the matter. "Well, what did you think of him?"

"It's my opinion and that of someone else who knew his background that he is working for the people— who—" She saw the hardening of Amy's young features, the stubborn, unyielding look, and added, "I'm afraid I have barely enough French money to get Clotilde and me back to Paris. I haven't counted it recently, but I believe it will be a near thing."

Amy drew away from her. "You know quite well that you will be as rich as a nabob any day. But if you are determined to be a pinchpenny, I'm sure I cannot stop you."

"I am sorry," Marsanne said untruthfully. "But I daresay the young man will get his money elsewhere." She pullled up the hood of her old travel cloak before walking out onto the sunny moorland stretching east below the terrace. "I suppose it is safe to walk on the downs alone." She carefully concealed her purpose in this walk, which was to discover if Philip had returned from London to the house bordering on the Lesgate estate. From the beach beyond the downs she thought she might look up toward Justin's house and perhaps find some sign of his presence there.

"Safe for a healthy Englishwoman. There is no knowing how tedious one of you delicate Frenchies might find it."

Marsanne smiled at Amy's predictable pique and stepped off the terrace onto the grass. The wind caught her cloak and whirled it around her but she did not feel chilled. She welcomed the first vigorous exercise she'd had since her arrival. Behind her, Amy seemed to have second thoughts, and called out,

"If you see any of the Free Traders—smugglers, you know—pay them no mind. Mama does business with them and Old Thaddeus doesn't like to injure anyone he has custom with."

"Thank you," called Marsanne, "but I've no notion of pushing an acquaintance with them. If I see one, I shall play the wise coward and retreat."

Amy laughed and went into the house, having apparently already forgotten her grievance against her French cousin.

The downs stretched out before Marsanne like a straw-colored carpet, rolling up and over, around cliffs, sloping off to the lengthy strand of beach where the Channel had once flowed through the area, up to the cliffs themselves and the house Philip Justin had leased.

She saw a flock of sheep drifting over the nearest hillock, scattered now and gradually fading into the straw color of the brush that covered the ground. In a few weeks the spring weather would turn the brush green. There would be a strange, solitary beauty about the region then, but—to Marsanne with her memories of the eternally green parks of Paris, the woods of the Champs Élysées and Meudon where she was born—this coast seemed forbidding, even dangerous.

Again she wondered what her mother was doing at this precise moment . . . Remembering Amy's remark about the fortune coming to her, she wondered if some arrangement might have been made by now with the Binet family

—perhaps a division of the Vaudraye lands in Normandy. Would that end her suspicions and fears, first of Philip Justin, then of Réne Nicoletti? . . .

A man in loose dark breeches and a jerkin of lamb's wool suddenly appeared over the rise ahead of her, making his way among the sheep. Obviously the shepherd. His shepherd's crook was more like a walking stick with a ram's horn attached, but Marsanne's knowledge about sheep and their keepers was less than meager. Looking up at the dumb incurious little lamb who had wandered close to her, she winced to recall that her previous acquaintance with lambs had been purely culinary.

The grizzled, powerfully built shepherd looked down at her from a little mound which gave him an awesome height. She had an uncomfortable sensation that he might not be as sheepish as his flock.

"Ye be from the Hall, miss?"

She said pleasantly, "Yes. Miss Amy and Captain Fortenham invited me to walk on the downs with them to the next estate. They are behind me, there, on the terrace." She glanced back at Lesgate Hall in the distance. He said nothing, a fact which did not relieve her growing apprehension and she asked hurriedly, "Do the Lesgates run sheep on the downs as well?"

The shepherd looked down at her, his eyes half-hidden under the heavy eyebrows, but he answered calmly enough, "Ye like to come and see the salt marshes where they feed? It's that what gives our mutton a special taste. Come, I'll show ye."

"Thank you. Another time. Captain Fortenham will be here at any minute." She strolled around the rise where he stood, tried to see behind him. A helter-skelter sort of woods made up of many kinds of trees and brush she had never seen before separated the Lesgate Deer Park from the estate leased by Sir Philip Justin. It was an excessively overgrown copse, dark as night within. Beyond its borders she could make out a corner of the main building belonging to Philip. It seemed much smaller and older than the Hall and was a half-timbered Tudor house. Several workers were busy about the exterior, and she saw a stout female in an upstairs room directing a young male who scrubbed away obediently at the panes of a casement window.

The downs gradually merged into beach stand. She hesitated, wondered at her own daring and half-decided to go up to the Tudor house. But she had only taken a few steps across the beach when she saw two rugged-looking seamen come striding around the corner between Philip's house and what appeared to be the stables. The wind whipping in from the Channel slapped up against the men and one of them took a blue cloth from around his neck and tied it over his head, confining his disheveled hair.

There was no reason why a seaman in striped shirt and loose-legged pantaloons should be dangerous, but Marsanne's head was so full of talk about smugglers and other felons that she gave up her attempt to see Philip Justin and turning slowly, began to make a dignified retreat. The two lengthened their stride. The one with the blue headband and deep-set black eyes alarmed her by calling.

"Where to, lass? Since when does a comely wench run from Nate Tibbetts?"

His comrade carried on in an odious enticing voice, "She'd rather pick and choose old Searle, wouldn't she now?"

She knew they must be only teasing. After all, Lesgate Hall was almost in sight. They would not dare to assault a girl who was Lady Lesgate's guest, and she could not lower herself to the indignity of running, but she hoped to see the shepherd still standing on that little hillock in front of the woods with his flock. Although an older man, he had looked able to stop her snickering pursuers with that heavy stick of his if nothing else.

It was a shock to find him gone. He must have disappeared into the woods. The sheep were still there, however, so he must not be far away . . . She did not look over her shoulder. It would only have encouraged those two . . . They must be very close behind her. She could hear the deep wheezing breath of one of them.

Suddenly the steps to the Lesgate Terrace appeared around a rolling dune of dead grass and earth. At the same time Nate Tibbetts caught her cloak and jerked hard, almost dragging her off her feet. She cried out, as much in pain and anger as fright, and caught a glimpse of glittering black eyes and thick, high-colored lips. She shot her elbow back with all her strength, jabbing the mean fellow in the stomach. He grunted, cursed, and almost let her go, but then one of his hands pulled the hood of her cloak off and caught long strands of her hair.

Until now his friend had done nothing, but Marsanne, gathering her forces for a scream to bring everyone in Lesgate Hall, heard Searle's warning: "Take care. It's him!"

With difficulty, she raised her head and saw Philip Justin's tall, black-clad figure on the terrace above them. His gloved hands grasped the stone balustrade. Cousin Sylvie had called him "fire and ice." The ice was evident now—she had rightly suspected that Philip Justin could be a very forbidding man. She felt frozen as he moved from the terrace to the steps and down. He reached around her, forced Nate Tibbetts' hands away from her one at a time while the fellow stared at him. Freed, Marsanne moved out of reach and would have gone to safety on the steps, but she was held by the fear in Nate Tibbetts' eyes. A second later the heel of Philip Justin's hand slashed across his cheek and nose, causing a crunching sound. Marsanne closed her eyes, gritted her teeth, and hurried up to the terrace.

Dazed, Nate Tibbetts had struck back with a fist from which the strength had been drained; he missed his target and found himself being led away by his friend Searle. He held both hands cupped to his nose while blood flowed between his fingers.

From the open doors of the ballroom, Marsanne turned back once, then looked away quickly. In her entire life she had never seen violence . . . blood shed, the hideous sounds, the cold anger of men fighting . . . these were entirely new to her.

She went inside the empty ballroom and stood there, furious, not so much at the actions of the two smugglers, but at her own blundering. She had been warned about "Free Traders" but she had supposed they were merely dishonest seamen, not really dangerous. . .

Hearing a step on the terrace outside the open door, she had a sudden cowardly inclination to avoid Philip Justin until she could conquer her sudden irrational fear of him. For the moment, at least to Marsanne, he seemed to have placed himself in a kind of brotherhood of terror with these men.

Chapter Nine

She had her hands upon the two great doors that opened into the ballroom from the main hall when she saw Philip Justin's hand reach over her head to push closed the doors she had pulled open. She looked up. He seemed concerned. She wondered if this loss of his usual self-command was because of what had happened to her at the hands of men who were obviously known to him. Or was it because she'd made him reveal his connection with them?

She said abruptly, "You're acquainted with those creatures, aren't you?"

His eyebrows went up. Plainly, he had been expecting some maidenly wail about her ill-treatment. He looked as if he might smile but assured her, "They are business acquaintances."

"In short, you're a smuggler."

This time he did laugh. "No. But I use their methods of transport from time to time. They, on the other hand, find my protection and that of my estate handy. For the records, however, they are sheepmen."

She took a breath. "Did you break his nose?"

"I hope so. But I doubt it."

She flinched and glanced at the doors which he had forcibly closed almost in her face.

"I thought you were gone up to London. What brought you back?"

"Two things. I found that the men I was to contact were in this vicinity." She waited for him to open the doors, and he went on, "Aren't you going to ask me the second?"

"A rendezvous with those smugglers, I don't doubt."

He watched her for a long moment during which she stood uncomfortably under this intense gaze. Then he abruptly pulled open the doors and made a sweeping, mocking theatrical gesture. Out in the long hall, which looked majestic and cold by daylight in contrast to last night's glittering gallery of elegant strollers, he said abruptly, "You will have matters of your own to attend to. I only came to see how you were getting on. Will you present my compliments to Lady Lesgate? I did not see her when I came."

Feeling ashamed of her ingratitude and also flattered by the evident regard for her that had made him stop by, she turned and said quickly, "Must you go? I did not thank you for—for that business out there."

He smiled. "Yes. I wondered when you would remember your manners. Very likely, all Nate wanted was a kiss. I can hardly fault him for that." His smile remained but she thought his eyes took on just a shade of that chill ruthlessness she had seen when he struck the smuggler. "However, he knows better. They never bother the others here at the Hall. If Old Thaddeus had been there, he'd never have permitted it. Someone should have gone with you. Where is everyone?"

The great house did sound empty. Then she remembered.

"Cousin Sylvie is with the housekeeper. And Amy— by the by, Amy is expecting our friend René Nicoletti to visit the estate. He was here six weeks ago, painting a portrait of her horse. She seems to be infatuated with him."

"And he paints her horse! The ways of wooing are unaccountable." Though he spoke lightly, he was considering the implications in the presence of René Nicoletti.

She added, "Amy says he's a Royalist agent. He betrays Bonapartists by pretending to be their friend."

"Delightful chap." He nodded. "I know the type. But I hoped he would be kept out of our way for a little longer." He took her chin between thumb and forefinger. "Don't worry. I'll keep on the watch. And Thaddeus is a good sort. He will help."

She reminded him anxiously, "If Nicoletti has only known the Lesgates for six weeks, I wouldn't be at all surprised to discover the entire acquaintance was set up so that he might kill me, one way or the other."

His calm was contagious. "But we know him. We know our man now. That is a big protection. If you believe it will be too dangerous, however, I'll have you taken to some secure place. It is true that Searle and Thaddeus might persuade him to tell us his plans and who hired him, but I had rather not be quite so crude."

"No! Not that way."

"Unfortunately, we cannot be certain he is Binet's agent. Well, we must put some idea to work to protect you from him. I'll see if one of my . . . business friends can be put to work as his valet or groom when he arrives. That should keep him in sight at all times." He removed his hands from her face, asked gently, "Will you be easy now for a few hours while I make some arrangements?"

She found herself reacting in an uncharacteristically docile fashion. "If you believe I should." She had resolutely put her well-being in his hands and pushed away suspicion of him, his connections with the smugglers, the mystery of what he was doing in England, and, in fact, who he really was.

He seemed to be struck by her words. His expression softened. She thought how very different he looked when he was not on guard . . .

He lowered his head. He touched her lips with his so easily, almost playfully, that she had to acquit him of any serious intent. Nonetheless, the memory of this sensation lingered long after he had turned and opened the big doors onto the long marble steps and started toward the stables.

She was roused from her reveries by her cousin Amy on the fanned skirt of the great staircase, hissing at her with every evidence of secrecy:

"Sssstt! Cousin! Have you changed your mind, dear . . . dear cousin?"

Pretending she had not heard, Marsanne hurried out after Philip Justin, catching him on the gravel drive.

He masked his surprise quickly, took her hands. "If you had rather not stay at the Hall—"

"No. Quite the contrary. If I don't face the danger now, I'll be running forever. We must bring the danger here."

"Nonsense. We are not going to risk making you a target."

She explained then about Amy's request for money that would bring Nicoletti to Lesgate Hall. He shook his head, but she reminded him, "We can at least know what he is about if he will be under your eye at all times—"

"But he actually would not be. He would be in this house with you. . . ." His hands moved to her shoulders. "But you are right, let's have him here. Except he will stay at my house. Or, if he refuses, at the Dower House where his friend Fortenham stays. Between my place and the Hall. And they will have servants, naturally. A groom. A manservant. A maid. All of them people I trust."

She doubted that Nicoletti would be so obliging. "How can he be forced to stay there?"

"Why not? I'll speak to Lady Lesgate. I wager she will welcome the idea."

"And from there we might further force him to move. He might even be persuaded to confide in one of your men. Your man could pretend to help him . . ."

He looked at her suddenly. She read concern in his eyes. "No. It really is too dangerous."

"But am I supposed to go on fearing him, wondering when, or if? . . . We'll never have as good a chance. And this time you and I will be both on the watch."

He hesitated, finally agreed in part. "If I thought we could at least count on that addlepated maid of yours! We need someone with you at all times. I am only assuming Nicoletti is the Binet family's single weapon against you. I know that Nicoletti was seen in Rouen by the Binet family's neighbors in close conversation with the man who called himself the Binet boy's stepfather, a Monsieur Gris—he is our real enemy. I wish I might know better what the stepfather looked like, but no one seems certain. Ordinary. Average. Forty or older. Eyes light. And again: ordinary."

"Yes, but surely, if we see such a man we can be on the lookout—"

"My dear Marsanne, how many men match that description! I had hoped Nicoletti would be held by the authorities, but obviously the fact that he's employed as a Royalist *agent provocateur* saved him. A damned bit of bad luck!"

She urged him nervously, "Then it's better to do anything, take a chance with Nicoletti. I don't want to go on day after day wondering *when*. Let's settle this Nicoletti at once."

She could see that he too wanted to settle the Nicoletti matter and only hesitated because of her danger. She urged him again, pointed out that she could be on guard at all times against the young Corsican.

"Meanwhile," she reminded him, "I must have some French money for Amy to send him."

He smiled and slipped some coins into her hands. "Give these to Miss de Vaudraye. Tell her I regret my mistake in having him arrested and want to make amends. I'll play the blundering Englishman—that shouldn't surprise a Corsican too much. Meanwhile, I will have every docking watched at Dover. I want to be certain we know his every move. In the end it may be necessary to use force against him. He must tell us how to reach the man who hired him. I'll send someone over from my house at any hour. And you can trust Thaddeus."

She drew back. "Not one of your smugglers!"

His laugh reassured her. "Quite unlike Searle and Nate Tibbetts. Used to run sheep on the downs. And he still takes an interest in the local flocks."

She remembered the strong, grizzled shepherd she had spoken to on the downs. "I think I met him earlier today. I'm not too certain I trust him more than the others."

"You may," he promised her. "He is frequently in the kitchen here at the Hall. He is in love with Lady Lesgate's housekeeper. Now then, promise you will be watchful. And let me know at once if Nicoletti reaches the Hall before my men have found him. He must stay at the Dower House. With the gallant captain and my valet." Marsanne still looked uneasy, and he touched her cheek lightly with his forefinger, promising, "We'll have this fellow laid by the heels in no time."

"I'm sure it will take violence to make him confess."

"Leave that to me and my friends."

She stiffened at the hint of ruthlessness in that promise, and with mixed emotions watched him go.

"How very odd!" Amy's voice, close behind her, startled Marsanne.

"What is so odd?" Whatever her own fears, she resented someone else's criticism of Philip Justin.

"That a man his age should walk back to his estates. And he walks so rapidly! They say he has spent twenty years as an invalid. One would never guess . . ."

The tall figure vanished into the twisted dark foliage that formed a barrier between the two estates. Marsanne waited until the copse seemed to swallow him up. Then she turned and went back into the hall. Amy trotted after her.

"Cousin, you have not answered me. Dearest Marsanne . . . I am not a person who falls in love easily. I may never find another man who cares for the things I care for."

"If it's the money you are talking about, you may have it. Sir Philip knows your friend. He wants to repay him for a—mistake in France. He asked me to express his regrets and suggest that your René stay at the Lesgate Dower House where Roderick Fortenham is staying. Sir Philip is anxious to make his stay a happy one and then, perhaps, your René will forgive him."

"Oh, cousin! You are good!" Amy moved along beside her with eager strides. "And Mama doesn't wish René to stay here at the Hall because of me. But she can't object to the Dower House."

Marsanne gave her the little handful of French silver and gold Louis that Philip had given her.

"Wonderful!" Amy pocketed them.

"How are you going to get it to him?" Marsanne asked.

"The supercargo of the day packet."

Marsanne's experience with grand passions might be less than Amy's but she felt that her knowledge of human villainy was greater. "Can you—and Monsieur Nicoletti— trust this supercargo?"

"Yes, indeed. He owes René a great deal. Some past favors, I expect. He would not dream of cheating him."

Marsanne was unconvinced, but let Amy go about her frantic errand while she went up to her bedchamber. Clotilde came in with a borrowed box of silk thread reels to darn stockings and undergarments and demanded to know what Miss Amy was doing with a handful of French coins.

"For I vow, if they were English guineas, I am Queen Charlotte!"

Marsanne laughed at this highly British observation, which Clotilde had obviously acquired from her new victim, the footman, but then she remembered Clotilde's affection for René Nicoletti. It might go well, after all. Clotilde's friendship would assure him that Marsanne was not suspicious of him.

"They are on loan, Clotilde, and you must promise to say nothing. Mademoiselle Amy wishes to bring René Nicoletti to this area."

"Monsieur René here? Has he been freed then?"

Marsanne said he had, and added, "Charming fellow, to be sure, if he accepts money from a lady."

"Well—but—" Clotilde pointed out fairly, "we owe him that, after the scurvy trick your friend the Englishman played on him."

"It was only a mistake." She took Clotilde by the shoulders. *"Cherie,* I want you to do something for me." The golden curls leaped on the girl's head as she nodded. "I want you to come to me and tell me everything Monsieur René says or does. You will have a very serious, very important task. Do you understand?"

"Oh, yes, mamselle. I will tell you everything and you will prove to that Englishman how wrong he was about Monsieur René."

Marsanne dropped her hands, sorely tempted to blurt out the truth, but deciding just in time that it might be wise to leave Clotilde in ignorance.

"How clever you are, Clotilde! I'll leave it with you."

Clotilde was so set up by her new importance that she went to work at once on Marsanne's wardrobe.

"I will have every gown pressed. The housekeeper, that Madame Grover, says I may work in the room Her Ladyship's maids use. The irons are very light but good." She suited action to the words and tried to carry every gown at once until Marsanne stopped her and took away an armful of muslin, cotton and silk.

Together, they carried them all down the servants' stairs to the little room furnished them by Mrs. Grover, which opened off the servants' dining parlor. As Marsanne stepped out into the back corridor and passed the kitchen again, she heard a deep male voice murmur something she couldn't make out, followed by Mrs. Grover's matter-of-fact plain speaking: "Say what you will, the keg was short weight. I'd not trust your precious Searle. Or Nate, either, when it comes to that."

Marsanne stiffened and looked into the kitchen. The big, graying man she had mistaken for a shepherd earlier in the day was good humoredly discussing the two kegs—probably brandy—that he had unloaded beside the wide blackened hearth. So this was Old Thaddeus whom Philip had told her to trust!

From the shadow of the hall she watched him, decided Philip might be right. The fellow looked formidable but not repulsive and nasty like his associates. An hour earlier Marsanne had even thought of running to this man, this "shepherd," for help against the distinctly unpleasant Nate Tibbetts.

"Well then, mum," came Thaddeus' heavy voice, "I'll be bringing extra, but only for your good self, mum."

"Now, when do I drink brandy? What a tease you are! And don't eat that moogin or I'll box your ears! It's for Miss Amy's dinner. There, now, you've gone and done it."

Mrs. Grover seemed to be flirting with the big man. Marsanne passed the door and went on, amused at the discovery that the formidable Mrs. Grover could be won over by the charms of Thaddeus.

Shortly before she was to dress for dinner, Marsanne finished mending a shift and a petticoat. She took up the sewing basket and started out to the stairs to return it to the housekeeper, saw the hall clock and realized she must indeed start to dress for dinner. She returned to her room, considering what gown she would wear to the family dinner, when she was startled by a series of thumps, shrieks and thuds apparently issuing from the hall outside her door.

She threw open the door calling, "Who is it? What's happened?"

Footsteps sounded outside her door. Cousin Sylvie and two maids and a footman. No one paid any attention to Marsanne, who followed the crowd to the servants' stairs. At the bottom of the steep dark staircase she saw a huge bundle of bright muslin and silk gowns and beneath it, scrambling to get to her feet, was Clotilde. Marsanne elbowed several domestics aside, rushing down the stairs with Cousin Sylvie close behind her. She had never been so panic-stricken since her grandmother's death, for Clotilde was virtually one of the family now. Marsanne reached the girl and immediately tried to see where she was hurt.

"My arm! Oh, mamselle, my right arm!" she cried in French, cringing when Sylvie touched it.

Someone gathered up the dresses while Marsanne tried to make Clotilde as comfortable as possible and Sylvie ordered one of the maids to fetch in the butler who had experience with setting broken bones.

"*Cherie*, try to tell me, does it hurt anywhere else?" Marsanne asked anxiously.

Clotilde shifted her body, experimenting with various positions. "No . . . only my arm above the elbow—Oh!"

"Albert, carry her to one of the bedchambers on this floor," Sylvie ordered the young footman who had been flirting with Clotilde the previous evening. With the greatest care Albert lifted the girl.

"What on earth do you make of it?" Sylvie asked Marsanne as they led the procession behind the invalid.

Marsanne said guiltily, "It is entirely my fault. I should never have let her carry up so many gowns at once."

To everyone's surprise Clotilde's golden head turned and she peered over the footman's shoulder at Marsanne.

"No, mamselle. I didn't trip on the gowns. There were reels of thread at the head of the stairs, just under my feet. I couldn't stop myself. I slipped on them."

Chapter Ten

The butler surveyed his handiwork with pride.

"There she'll be, madam. Right as a trivet. Naught but bruises from the fall." Amid everyone's thanks, he bowed and retreated in glory, motioning the rest of the household to "get on with your work now, off you go."

Alone with the invalid and Marsanne, Lady Sylvie murmured, "My dear child, how did you come to be carrying reels of thread along with all those garments? You should have asked one of the maids to help you."

"Or me," Marsanne put in, puffing up the pillows to make them more comfortable for Clotilde, who had already begun to enjoy the attention. "Her entire arm will be black and blue. And her side and hip too, I daresay."

Clotilde sighed. "It was dreadful. You can have no notion, mamselle. I ache all over."

"Poor child!" Sylvie considered rapidly. "She must have a few drops of laudanum. It will ease her discomfort and give her a sustaining sleep."

"Yes, of course. Clotilde, you should have called me to help you."

The girl's large pale eyes gazed up at her, perplexed. "Mamselle, I was not carrying the reels of thread. They were on the stairs. Two of them. Or maybe three."

It seemed clear that Clotilde had dropped the thread on the stairs earlier when she came up to Marsanne's room with the little reels for repair work. Marsanne made no more out of the accident except to regret Clotilde's suffering, but it did occur to her that if she had gone down those stairs to return her mending materials as she originally planned, Marsanne herself would be the injured party.

The maid and Sylvie Lesgate were concerned, however, over other matters.

"Who is to dress you now, mamselle? And arrange your hair. You know it is always a trifle difficult, so thick and plentiful it is."

"What flummery! As though I could not dress myself! And as to arranging my hair—well, it is all a great piece of nonsense."

But this shocked Cousin Sylvie, who heartily agreed with Clotilde. "No, no, my dear. You shall have Hattie Totter."

Clotilde began to look jealous, and Marsanne assured her, "You shall give her all her instructions, *chérie*. I will send her to you for advice in every detail."

Relieved, Clotilde took her laudanum drops obediently and soon was resting in reasonable comfort.

Hattie Totter soon impressed Marsanne, being efficient without being obtrusive. Although she knew she was on her preferment, she did not let Lady Lesgate's frequent eruptions into Marsanne's bedchamber hinder her smooth work. She was quietly ready at evening's end with mulled wine to give Miss Marsanne a good night's sleep, and undressed her competently and without the fuss that Marsanne hated in her personal Abigails.

"But I shan't need the mulled wine, Totter. I'm much too ready for sleep after all the excitement of the day."

"Ay, mam," Hattie Totter agreed in her quiet way. She started out of the room, then hesitated in the doorway. "Beg pardon, mam. Seeing as you don't wish the wine, would it be agreeable if I drank it?"

"Certainly. Please do so."

Hattie Totter downed the little glassful, thanked Marsanne and wishing her a good night left the room.

By the end of forty-eight hours, Clotilde could report to Marsanne, "Totter's French is good. It will surprise you, mamselle, which makes it much easier to talk to her. And last night when I could not sleep she brought me hot brandy which was vastly obliging of her."

"Very. Still, I shall be happy when you are able to return to my bedchamber. I miss your chatter, *chérie.*"

Very much flattered, Clotilde insisted she could return to Marsanne that very night, at least to supervise . . .

Capain Fortenham came by then to ask Marsanne if she would care to be shown about the estate.

"You arrived this day seven-night, Miss Marsanne, and still you haven't seen the far grounds or the Dower House. Naturally, it would be highly improper for you to go out of sight of the Hall, but we may contrive respectably."

Marsanne smiled. "Anything else would be shocking in the extreme. So Amy has refused you again." Over the past week she and the dashing captain had become such good friends they indulged in a frankness which shocked even Clotilde.

"Really, mamselle, it is not polite to mention—"

"Later, Clotilde. Tell me later." Marsanne patted her hand and hurried away to change into suitable garments.

She came out on the long front steps to meet Captain Fortenham looking radiant in her smartest Paris pelisse over a matching gray gown, the whole of the outfit trimmed in cherry buttons, with full, cherry satin ribbons tying her bonnet just at the side of her chin. She was grateful to Fortenham, who took her hands in the most flattering way, remarking that she would put "other gels" —not to mention Miss Amy—in the dismals just to look at her.

"My friend," she said quickly—and gratefully, "when Amy comes to her senses, she will realize in short order just how much she loves you. It is only because she has been used to seeing you, that's all . . ."

He took her fingers and brought them to his lips before releasing them. "All the same, I begin to regret my little scheme."

"Regret?" She smiled and apparently produced too great an effect, for he blushed and said, "Damn—dash it! You make me regret more and more. It was a stupid notion."

"What is? You have me all in a quake, captain."

He lifted her over a tree stump and within the skirts of the dark, tangled copse that divided Lesgate Hall from Philip's property. She released herself. He begged her pardon and added, "It was my idea that—I knew Amy had taken a fancy to the artist I told you of, René Nicoletti. And I thought if he showed her he cared much more for you than for Amy, she might find him less . . . charming."

She had a premonition of what was to come. A ludicrous coincidence.

"So you sent for him to visit you."

"Exactly so. I knew he was sure to prefer a high-stickler, a well-mannered Frenchwoman, because Amy is only a girl, after all is said. Only I—I don't want him here hounding you now. But I've already paid the blunt for him to come."

She tried to restrain herself but ended by bursting into laughter at the rapaciousness of Nicoletti who managed to receive payments from half a dozen sources in order to arrive where almost no one wanted him. Then she saw that she had hurt the captain's feelings and changed the subject quickly.

"Do you see Sir Philip often?"

"Upon occasion. He rides into the city, and has visitors. Seems a popular chap."

More lightly than she felt, Marsanne remarked, "Popular with the fair sex, I daresay."

"Oh, gad, no! That is, there are females now and again, but in general, there is only one."

They had reached a gravel walk leading to a comfortable, two-story stone building with more recent half-timbering and while Marsanne wondered who Sir Philip's "the only one" might be, Captain Fortenham pointed out the Dower House was usually occupied by the dowagers of the Lesgate family upon the marriage of the first-born.

"The Lesgates frequently married the owners of the estate Sir Philip has leased, but with the last owner dead in the Spanish campaigns, his widow the condesa was only too glad for Sir Philip's offer to lease."

"The condesa?"

"A Spaniard. The Condesa Concepción Seaforde, who owns the property you see yonder. Her late husband Lord Barracleugh Seaforde was a Justice of the Peace of this coast."

"And his successor's dearest friends are a pack of unsavory smugglers!"

"Free Traders, mam," he corrected her cheerfully. "We don't precisely boast of dealings with—er—smugglers. Ah! Speaking of angels, we hear their wings. That'll be the Condesa Concepción riding with Sir Philip now."

Marsanne looked up quickly at the sound of hoofbeats on the road past the Dower House and what she saw told her very clearly why she had not seen Philip Justin of late. The latter reined in abruptly as he caught sight of

Marsanne and called her name. Beside him a black-haired
beauty of a certain age likewise handled her reins with
grace and ease.

Captain Fortenham called out with friendly informal-
ity, "Fine open weather for the time of year, eh, condesa?
I see you've been riding with your tenant."

Staring up at the condesa, Marsanne felt all the humiliation and jealousy of a commonplace mortal when faced
with the Goddess of the Night.

"Concepción," the captain called out, most familiarly.
He limped forward, cutting in on Philip's introductions,
"May I present my future cousin, Miss Marsanne Vaudraye? In France, because of their tiresome Revolution,
they removed the prefix to their name, but she is actually
a cousin of my own Amy *de* Vaudraye."

All this was highly unnecessary, as Marsanne could see
by Philip's impatience. However, the condesa spoke politely.

"Dear child, Philip has told me so much about you. We
were riding over to meet you this very moment." Smiling,
the Condesa Concepción Seaforde leaned down from her
high perch on the magnificent black mare and offered her
fingers to Marsanne, who did not curtsy. She was French,
and a revolution had wiped away such distinctions. She
raised her head, returned the lady's faint smile with one of
her own, and added for good measure, "I am ashamed
of dear Philip. He did not mention his beautiful landlady."

Both the captain and the condesa were taken aback
but Philip Justin, the one Marsanne had really expected
to shock by her rudeness, merely laughed and dismounted.
He went to Marsanne and said, teasingly, as he carried her
hand to his lips, "What can have made you look so
cross? I wish I might think you were jealous."

She tried to pull her hand away. "Rubbish. I have not
the smallest reason to be jealous."

He held her hand an instant longer before letting it go,

then lowered his voice and said, "I should hope not. She is old enough to have been your mother."

She tried not to look as satisfied as she felt and changed the subject. "The captain also sent for Nicoletti."

"Yes, I know," he said evenly. "I was riding over to . . . prepare you. He should arrive this evening."

Chapter Eleven

"Here, Captain," Sir Philip offered Fortenham *the* reins of his own bay mare. "Be good enough to escort the condesa to the Hall. I'll walk back with Miss Marsanne—"

"Oh, I say now! Wouldn't desert the lady like that," Roderick protested, glanced from Justin to Marsanne and then as the condesa's sleepy eyes opened a trifle, he added hastily, "not but what it won't be the greatest pleasure, mam. If you'll permit my escort."

The condesa beamed on him, looking as beautiful as a sleek black feline, and making Marsanne grit her teeth with envy. But the lady was gracious as well as beautiful. She assured her red-coated gallant, "We will let them make a so-tiresome walk while you and I gallop pleasantly together."

"Just so, Concepción . . . mam. By gad, there's nobody can sit a mount like you." He looked back at Marsanne. "You'll be all right and tight, cousin?"

Phillip Justin reminded him dryly, "I brought her

across France and the Channel, my lad. I am not likely to lose her between here and Lesgate Hall."

The two rode away toward the London Post Road where a short canter would bring them to the turnoff of the Lesgate Hall estate road. Marsanne was still watching them, marveling at the condesa's beauty, when Philip took her arm.

"Now then, how have things gone at the Hall since I came on you in Nate's arms?"

"If you assume I enjoyed the experience, let me assure you that I did not. Nor is he a friend of yours, whatever you may think. I heard him say—no! It was the other—Searle—who called you . . . With no affection, I assure you."

He laughed at that. As they walked along the gravel path parallel to the copse and toward the ancient Tudor house on the bluff above the downs, he said equably, "I can see that they might have called me *him*. It seems customary, in the circumstances."

Annoyed that he deliberately misunderstood her, she said, "It was the *way* they said it: 'Take care. It's *him.*' " She glanced at him and added, "You *seemed* quite angry. I think you terrified them. I suppose you are not in the habit of permitting your cutthroat friends to disobey you."

There was a hard light in his eyes now. "If you think I lost my temper only because they disobeyed me, you are very much behind the fair."

"Then why did you look so terrifying?" she asked with a fine show of innocence.

"If I terrified you enough to keep you from playing fast and loose with a bloody cutthroat—" he began, broke off and added firmly, "nor are those cutthroats my friends. Except for Thaddeus. He did me a good turn once. But only the prospect of healthy profits holds the loyalty of creatures like Tom Searle and Nate Tibbetts."

She saw that he was leading her around behind the Tudor house toward the rolling desolate region below it, which even on this windy February day was half-hidden by the foggy mist off the Channel.

"You appear to be taking me directly into the hands of your bloodthirsty friends," she remarked in amiable fashion. "Am I to be your peace offering to them?"

"You are a saucy baggage. I've a good notion to do just that. Throw you into their midst." He felt her body drawing a trifle closer to him and added, "However, I am much too selfish. And for God's sake don't be such a chucklehead as to ask for an explanation of that! I promised Sister Veronique not to compromise you."

She was reflecting whether she dared say "What a pity!" when he startled her by raising his voice and calling, "Is it you, Thaddeus? I see the mist is coming in. A pity. After such a beautiful day."

"Beautiful to you, mayhap," Thaddeus' deep voice answered as he emerged from the clutch of the fog, "but excusing the contradiction, sir, in our work we're none so fond of open weather. Down by Rye Sands last night there was a moon, as you may have noticed, and the excisemen was there a-waiting for Danny Cuttler's lads. There'll be some necks stretched after that night's work."

"The devil you say!"

Marsanne saw that Sir Philip was seriously concerned. It seemed odd, because she felt reasonably sure his livelihood did not depend on smuggling a few bundles of wool out and kegs of brandy in. She asked him, "You're acquainted with General Winters, a Justice of the Peace. Can't you help these people, the—ah—Cuttler men?"

Justin and the grizzled Thaddeus exchanged a long look . . . Justin said, finally, "I very much fear Cuttler's men are meant to be a warning. They did not pay proper tribute to the general. Thaddeus, mind you, see that the general receives his due payment in that excellent apple brandy he fancies."

"Ay, sir. That I'll do. I only wish I may persuade the lads. They're a mite on the edges, as the saying goes."

With deliberate care Thaddeus avoided glancing at Marsanne. "Nate's still nursing a bad nose. Burst one day when he was careless-like."

Marsanne winced.

"I'll be dealing with the general shortly. I don't want anything to interfere with the next few crossings."

Thaddeus nodded. "Ye'll be planning to return to them Frenchies, sir?"

Marsanne was suddenly tense. This might be the clue to Philip Justin's extraordinary interest in the transportation of the smugglers. His real business must be more important to him than brandy kegs. But why so secret? Why should this mysterious business be more secret or more dangerous than smuggling, which was punishable by a hangman's noose?

"That depends on many things. Meanwhile, take care, old friend. I'll see what can be done with the general."

He took Marsanne's arm. She went along but looked back curiously. She had not believed it possible but it was quite true. The fog was crawling in so quickly the smuggler chief had already become a hulking, blurry figure in the gray world of the winter downs.

She caught Philip studying her. "That is a very fetching bonnet. It shows you at your enchanting best. You seem to enjoy hiding your charms. I wonder why."

It was the kind of compliment to which there was no reply unless one were a great deal more sophisticated than Marsanne. It seemed to her that his eyes which could freeze one with their arctic blue gaze had now thawed out in a most flattering way. She was not used to this much warmth or praise directed at her and felt intensely conscious of him. He must have realized he was making her ill at ease and quickly reverted to the playful amused small talk.

"When does your cousin intend to bring you out? You should be all the crack in London. The Prince-Regent himself will undoubtedly flirt with you and if you are very good to me I may even present myself at Almack's in satin small-clothes, looking absurd, and dance the new waltz with you. Have you enough courage to waltz with me? Very shocking dance, you know."

"What fustian! As though I should be accepted by the exalted patronesses at that dreary Almack's. I am foreign. I am illegitimate, and I am twenty years old. Time to consider myself well upon the shelf."

He laughed aloud at that frankness, and then said something decidedly curious, coming from an English knight. "Twenty years old and on the shelf! Good God, my girl! You have not even begun to live. I was twenty in 1799, the year I did my bit to overthrow that damnably corrupt government the revolution had sunk to. Twenty. A glorious age. Those were the days! We helped bring order, and justice, and some modern institutions to—" He broke off.

To France.

She looked at him. His usually sallow complexion had a faint color. But surely the *coup d'état* of 1799 he spoke of had been the one that brought Napoleon Bonaparte to power and reorganized France. What had a man with the English name of Philip Justin to do with bringing the French government out of the chaos of revolution and its aftermath? Again she remembered how the Calais coachman had claimed Sir Philip spoke French like a native. He really must be in some far more dangerous game.

"At all events," she said almost casually, seeing that he had not intended to betray himself in that curious reminiscence, "I must soon return to Paris and see what Mama will do. She will be lost if they remove her from the Hôtel-Dieu. Another hospital, even an almshouse, might serve, but without people to care for Mama is lost indeed."

He said quietly, "Someday I will tell you about my first acquaintance with Sister Veronique. What a creature she is!"

" 'Creature'?"

"Superior to mankind. Most other 'creatures' are, you know."

She felt sure his cynicism had some deep-rooted cause, but still she was sorry to hear it. She wondered if he were capable of setting it aside, if he were capable of . . . love. Or had his past blighted the possibility of that . . . ?

Mist, by this time, had drenched her lovely new bonnet and she hurried her steps as Justin took a large handkerchief from his sleeve and obligingly dropped it over the crown of the bonnet. She thanked him for his concern and thought how nearly perfect he looked.

The exquisite happiness she felt was abruptly shattered by something that caught her eye and she looked skyward, beyond his head, to see what seemed a gigantic spiderweb materializing out of the fog and threatening to engulf her as well as Philip. He must have sensed the danger, because he lifted her abruptly away just as a huge cargonet came floating down to spread out on the hummocks of dead winter grass behind him.

"Ahoy!" a gruff voice called out of the fog. "Missed ye by a hair, sir!"

Marsanne was still shaking when Searle and his grinning companion Nate Tibbetts emerged to collect their net; Marsanne eyeing Philip saw that the mood between them was hopelessly broken thanks to the smugglers' not-very-funny joke. She was relieved, however, when Philip did not show his annoyance, and instead said casually, "You would do well to take better care of your nets unless you want to lose some pretty handsome profits. A keg of brandy would go entirely through that hole. You've caught it on a rock."

"Damned if we haven't," Searle muttered to Nate, whose dark face was still marred by a red scar between his eyes and across the wide bridge of his nose. This remnant of his encounter with Philip gave his narrow eyes and black brows an even more villainous cast and one that his toothy grin hardly improved.

"Ye hear about Danny Cuttler's lads?" Searle called as the rain spattered them in a more lively fashion and Philip hustled Marsanne along toward Lesgate Hall. Marsanne cringed inwardly at the meaning in Nate Tibbetts' loud taunt, "Mayhap we'll be needing a better protector. Seems like you don't count for so much with them law officers, after all's said. Eh, sir?"

And Searle's equally ominous remark: "Quiet, Nate. No need spillin' all that's in your head. Best later, with old Thad."

"Aren't you at least—just a little afraid?" Marsanne asked Justin.

"I'm exceedingly afraid." She glanced up at him and he added, "Afraid you may ruin that enchanting bonnet."

She laughed, and tried to persuade herself that Philip Justin was really clever enough to outsmart all his enemies. In the euphoria of her moment with him, she was almost convinced of it.

As they reached the steps leading up to the Lesgate terrace, Philip drew her close to the weathered stone wall. "I'm sorry to bring up the unpleasant subject of our friend Nicoletti, but I wanted at least to reassure you on one score."

"He should be here at any time."

"Yes, but he won't get far without the company of his valet, Mr. Hogue."

"Mr. Hogue! Who may that be?"

"A Bow Street Runner I've hired for the purpose."

"Aren't the Runners police of some sort?"

"Yes, but one may call upon them for investigative purposes. And Mr. Hogue, though somewhat undersized, is formidable I'm told."

"Well, so long as he doesn't turn out to be that wretched Binet family's stepfather."

He did not find this amusing and said gently, "Anyone may be. But I hope we are going to take him before he does you any harm . . . I've tried to think of everything—"

She looked up directly. "Why?"

He ran his forefinger gently over her lips. "First, if you must have the truth, because when I was a boy I fell in love with your mother. Later—well, we can't go into that now."

She was disappointed and said with a sharpness that surprised her, "Good day, Sir Philip. And I will try to repose confidence in your little Mr. Hogue. But there are times when I think I may count upon none but myself."

She went inside the house, alone, only to find herself dripping wet and amidst a bedlam of confusion thanks to the presence of the Condesa Concepción Seaforde, Captain Fortenham, and an attractive young man who bowed to her with the grace of a born courtier.

"My dear Mademoiselle Vaudraye, what pleasure! I had hoped of course to see more of you when I was so rudely detained."

René Nicoletti in full flower, with an anxious Amy de Vaudraye rushing down the great front staircase to meet him. She looked sharply from Nicoletti to Marsanne, and Marsanne realized with a sinking feeling that her cousin was indeed jealous. And being so, became in her fashion an additional threat—a potential enemy Marsanne hardly needed.

Chapter Twelve

Marsanne passed everyone so abruptly that the condesa felt it necessary to apologize for her. "What a pity! The young lady was caught in your dreadful rain. I vowed, I have never known a place where one is so often in danger of drowning."

"Now, Concepción," the captain teased her. "You made the same complaint of Portugal."

They were all in a jolly state except Amy, who passed Marsanne on the lower stairs hurrying on to meet Monsieur Nicoletti. Amy gave her cousin a dagger glance as they passed, muttering, "Someone might at least have told me he was here."

Marsanne stopped on the wide landing and looked back. Nicoletti, still smiling as though good nature were glued upon his face, made his skilled bow and raised the condesa's long slim hand to his lips. It was unfortunate that Amy was not better prepared. She had intended to go out to the stables and rub down her favorite mare, and

115

was wearing a singularly unattractive stuff gown that did not fit her properly—its pale faded pink might better have suited almost anyone than red-headed Amy. To cap the unromantic picture, she wore pattens on her feet in order to wander about in sloppy weather.

"Even I would know better than to appear like that before a man whose interest I wished to fix," Marsanne said to Hattie Totter, whose unobtrusive form appeared silently before her in the upper corridor. The young woman gazed boldly at Marsanne's attire, and Marsanne confessed, "I know, I know. I look quite as bad. And dripping wet beside all else."

"Yes, miss."

Marsanne looked at her and she blinked, adding hurriedly, "Not but what I mean to say, miss, you were caught in the rain through no fault of yours."

"That's better." Marsanne grinned and, untying her bonnet, went to her room with Hattie slipping along in her wake. "Incidentally, how is Clotilde?"

"Tolerably well, I believe. She is asleep now."

"At midday?"

"I believe the footman Albert was reading a most improving book to her and—"

"Inevitable . . . no one will ever accuse Clotilde of being a bluestocking. She will not even listen to Mrs. Radcliffe's romances."

Hattie Totter helped her off with her pelisse and went to get a flattering yellow silk daygown for her change. She asked casually, "Do you like Mrs. Radcliffe's novels, Miss Marsanne?"

"I dote on them. Not that I believe a word of them. Mad monks in strange abbeys pursuing helpless English girls, indeed! You should have seen those same English girls who came over to Paris as tourists after the armies of occupation! I'll daresay any self-respecting monk would run in terror from *them*."

Hattie smiled mechanically and began to button her into

a shapely gown. Marsanne studied herself in the long look-ing glass. Her first thought had been the hope that Philip would like her in buttercup yellow. Most men did. But then came the memory of their parting . . . Perhaps there was little to hope for. He had made it all too clear to her that something else was more important, that he would probably be too old to win her by the time he carried out his suspicious business. And, was this inaccessibility one of the major attractions of Sir Philip Justin? . . . She knew that if he were as easy to read as Roderick Fortenham or as unctuous as René Nicoletti, he would hold no fasci-nation for her at all . . .

"How long has that popinjay been in the house?" Mar-sanne asked as she picked up the silver chain of her mother's miniatures to slip over the high neck and close-fitting bosom of her gown.

"I believe the captain rode in with the condesa. He waited to see that the horses were stabled, and—"

"But Totter, I did not mean Captain Fortenham. I meant that odious Frenchman, Monsieur Nicoletti."

The maid said nothing to indicate surprise, but her fingers paused as she tied the ribbons of one of Marsanne's yellow kid slippers about her ankle. She said in her color-less voice, "I believe he arrived just behind the captain. A servant of some kind accompanied him to show the way, he said."

Ah, the Bow Street Runner, thought Marsanne, and wondered how Nicoletti had reacted to the idea that his nearest neighbor was his old enemy Philip Justin, the man who had accused him of being a Bonapartist.

Then with head held high she went out into the corri-dor and met Cousin Sylvie, who looked uncharacteris-tically nervous. "Marsanne, *chérie,* what under heaven is that dauber doing here? He caused havoc between Amy and Roderick a month or so ago. And my butler tells me he mentioned your name when he arrived."

Marsanne glanced over her shoulder, saw that Hattie

Totter, whom she'd begun to dislike, was well within earshot. So she said calmly, "I've no notion why, I'm sure. I met him briefly on the Calais coach, but I believe Amy had requested him to do a portrait of one of her horses."

Hattie finally left them at the head of the front gallery staircase, and as they started down Marsanne told her cousin in a low voice, "Mama was very concerned over the Binet family, as she wrote to you."

"Yes, indeed. But, my dear, you are safe in England now. You must forget all that nonsense. The Binets are far away in the Antilles. Martinique or some such place—where Bonaparte's wife was born, you know . . . and I hope you have not taken the young painter in absolute dislike, for I depend upon you to keep him away from Amy."

"Cousin, we . . . that is, I have reason to believe the Binet stepfather has hired someone . . . I believe it may be this Nicoletti."

Sylvie drew a long breath. "Now really, my dear, we must not insult a Lesgate guest, however unwelcome. Come along and smile, and be your own charming self. If anyone raises a hand to you, well . . . we'll make very certain no harm is done. But I give you my word, no person of that sort could ever be invited to Lesgate Hall."

Marsanne was angry but not surprised at Sylvie's easy dismissal of the threat. She merely said, "If anyone strokes at me, it won't be before a dozen witnesses. But as you wish, let us not talk of this any more."

"Certainly, my dear. Just as you say. That's really very sensible of you. And now it's time to entertain our guests."

Chapter Thirteen

Three days later, with the Lesgates' planning to dine at Philip Justin's, Amy went to Marsanne to confide a secret.

"It's concerning my wardrobe. I've tried to convince myself, but it's not the slightest bit of use. Cousin, I must and *will* have your opinion. Please do come to my room."

Marsanne, who had been writing still another letter to her mother, could not recall anything about a wardrobe discussion with her young cousin, but, curious, she dutifully followed Amy. When they reached Amy's sitting-room the girl had her maid, Moll Pierson, bring out two attractive gowns.

"Madame Treville, an emigrée, has her rooms in Rye, the hill town nearby, and Mama regularly employs her. She has patterns of my gowns, and I rode Titania over to her the morning after you mentioned the colors."

"The colors?"

"Marsanne! You must remember. You told me they

were my colors and no one should be permitted to wear them but redheads."

Marsanne vaguely recollected the conversation. "A new wardrobe? Amy, how exciting! Well, do let me see it."

Amy held up the gowns, one at a time as Moll Pierson brought them out. The first was a grass-green satin dinner slip with a demitrain, over which was worn a skirt of cobweb-thin lace open in the front.

Marsanne found it amusing that she who had never been considered beautiful nor fashionable, should be advising her cousin on the subject now. Nevertheless, she was able to say in all sincerity, "It looks wonderful on you. I can imagine how excited Captain Fortenham will be when he sees you."

Amy hesitated, looked at the lovely gown pressed against her youthful form in its rusty riding dress. She frowned. "Oh, but cousin, the fuss isn't for Roddy. The thing is, will *René* like it? I am persuaded he will, don't you think so, dear cousin?"

Marsanne felt herself unpleasantly caught. She did not want her cousin to waste herself upon a gallows-bird like René Nicoletti, but she was well aware that if she spoke too favorably of Captain Fortenham she would lower his chances even more.

"He will be blind if he does not adore you in that green. . . Really, I wish I owned one precisely that shade. It would be just the thing to please Captain Roderick . . ."

Amy, who had been signaling Moll Pierson to bring out the other gown, stopped and regarded the green dress without looking at her cousin. Her voice held just the hint of a question.

"I daresay Roddy would like you in green."

The second dress arrived, to be held up in front of her. It was a delicate straw-yellow and very flattering with the deep hue of Amy's hair. Marsanne expressed her admiration but did not again mention the captain, and by the time she was ready to leave felt she had failed miserably to turn Amy's thoughts from Nicoletti.

At the door, however, Amy startled and even encouraged her by remarking suddenly, "You aren't wearing green to Sir Philip's dinner, are you?"

"No. My blue-gray crepe. Why?"

"Oh. It will look lovely with your complexion and your dark hair . . . Did Roddy ever tell you he liked you in shades of green?"

"Heavens, no! He has never seen me in green."

Noting her maid's glance, Amy said quickly, "I—I think Roddy would like you in anything. You seem to have become great friends. Have you ridden together yet?"

"No. Nor will I. I do not ride."

"How—awful! Not that it will matter to Roddy."

All the same as Marsanne left she was certain the girl had been gratified by the news. Perhaps Amy would begin to appreciate the captain. Perhaps he would seem more desirable now that another woman found him attractive. . .

Marsanne considered it ironic that she was devoting so much attention to the tastes of René Nicoletti and Captain Fortenham when the only man she really wanted to impress was their dinner host, Philip Justin. She determined to devote more than the usual effort to arranging her hair, with the soft effect produced by black wisps framing her face beneath the narrow blue-gray satin ribbon that held her Grecian coiffure in place. When she appeared belowstairs to awaite the elaborate old Lesgate barouche and team she could not help noting, and being pleased to note, admiration in the eyes of their escort, General Winters.

Fortenham and Nicoletti were to meet the party at the Dower House beside the estate road to Philip Justin's house, but when Amy too received the admiring compliments of the general she whispered to Marsanne, "Surely they—I mean René—will like me in this green gown. The general has never complimented me before. I'm afraid he thinks I'm a hoyden . . ."

"Indeed," Marsanne assured her, "every male of the party will fall in love with you."

Amy hugged herself in happy confidence, but she threatened her mother's dream by the comment: "René will be so pleased. He wants me to be all the crack."

Sylvie exchanged a glance with Marsanne, who shook her head, and the harassed mother sighed but made no immediate objection.

Albert, the footman, held a deep pink umbrella over each lady's head as they descended the steps to the heavy regal carriage. Marsanne deliberately went last, and whispered to Albert, "Will you see how Clotilde does this evening? I want her to be happy here . . ."

Albert blushed, gave her his assurance by a brief nod, and wished her a happy evening.

She thanked him and went on, feeling little confidence that the evening would be as he wished for her. Her thoughts, her feelings were so intensely fixed on her host. More precisely, on his interest—or lack of it—in her.

By the time they were out on the drive the rain had begun to come down in torrents, blurring the view between the lines of trees bordering the drive.

"Poor John Coachman! And only this morning he had a cold," Sylvie remarked, devoting three seconds to his fate out there in the downpour before she calmly went on, "I do hope dear Sir Philip will have a lovely fire to warm us when we reach that ancient house of his. Or should I say—the condesa's house?"

"That tiresome old hag!" Amy muttered beneath her breath, but unfortunately she was heard by her shocked mother, who produced her fan and rapped the ivory sticks hard across Amy's gloved knuckles. "I will not have impertinence to your elders."

Amy countered: "Then the good woman shouldn't be making up to men young enough to be her sons. I saw her talking to Monsieur Nicoletti with great animation. He told me it was about those stupid Bonapartists, that she was talking nonsense about the return of the Emperor Napoleon. He said he thought she wanted money for a contribution to the cause or something of that nature. Jewels, I think. And for *that* cause!"

"Hmph." Sylvie shrugged and remarked to Marsanne, "He must have been lying. The woman is such a prattle-box. She hasn't a genuine political notion in her head."

Recalling the condesa's animated conversation in the green salon three days before, Marsanne automatically began, "But I heard her speaking very passionately on that very—" She stopped abruptly. Her own mother, after all, was an ardent Bonapartist and there were times when she suspected Philip Justin's rather mysterious private interests were similarly political and yet here she was risking implicating someone on their side . . . Prattle-box, indeed! . . .

"Yes, *chérie?*" Sylvie prompted her. General Winters also seemed to be hanging on her words.

Marsanne changed course quickly: "She spoke passionately about the—the smugglers. She thought they were impudent to her."

"How very odd!" Amy said. "It was my impression that the condesa had some sort of understanding with them."

General Winters nodded. "Purchasing brandy, no doubt. Old Seaforde played the same game. I'm hanging a few of the rogues very shortly myself—the Cuttler gang."

Amy put in, "Carrying messages, I think. I had the impression they carried messages for the condesa. But I've no notion to whom. Somebody in France, probably. I overheard Thaddeus in our kitchen one night. One of his men had followed him. I didn't understand any of it. But it was all very hush-hush."

The general yawned, begged pardon. "I'll look into the matter. Ah! Aren't we nearing the estate road to Justin's house?"

Amy nudged Marsanne. "I think I saw René at the window of the Dower House. It's beside the gates. He said he and Roddy would escort us right to Sir Philip's front door."

The team was given the signal and the coachman skillfully maneuvered the coach across the high road toward the two wrought-iron gate posts. Suddenly there was a pounding of hooves and a horse and rider thundered into view, headed directly for the coach and team. The coachman pulled off the road into the end of the copse, narrowly missing the outspread branches of an oak tree.

Luckily, there was little damage to the coach itself, and none to its passengers. Meanwhile Marsanne caught sight of the horse and rider galloping past. He appeared to be a tall gray-haired man wearing a tricorne and a gray cloak with at least a dozen capes flying behind him. For one startling instant she thought this rider was Philip. He did not stop, wheel about, or slow down, but thundered on out of sight.

"Amy! Marsanne! Are you hurt?" Sylvie asked as the general opened the coach door and Captain Fortenham and René Nicoletti rushed down the path to help.

The girls were unhurt, though Amy groaned because her hair had begun to tumble down and she clutched at it, hastily trying to put it right again. Marsanne, seeing her problem, whispered, "I'll rearrange it. Don't worry."

"Thank you, cousin. *Thank you!*"

René arrived just behind the captain, who had already caught Amy in his arms and suggested she let him carry her to the Dower House to await the closed carriage Mr. Hogue had been sent to fetch from Sir Philip.

While the general attended to Sylvie, Marsanne found herself being lifted down by René Nicoletti. He refused to set her feet on the wet leaves.

"No, no, mademoiselle," he protested, and went on in French, "you would stain those exquisite white slippers."

In pointed English she insisted, "It is my own concern if I do."

He set her feet on a narrow gravel path leading to the Dower House. "I wish you would trust me, mademoiselle. I have never done anything to make you feel such dislike."

"For one thing, monsieur, you seem to have an extraordinary effect upon every coach in which I find myself."

His dark eyes were briefly hidden by his long lashes. Then he looked up and with a peculiar half-smile said: "But, mademoiselle, there is another who is always present at your accidents. He was in France and he was here. Did you see the reckless fellow who caused the coach and horses to veer off? And very nearly killed you all?"

She moistened her dry lips. "What do you mean?"

"His entire appearance, mademoiselle. Did it suggest anyone of our acquaintance? The carefully queued white hair, the black tricorne hat. Even the gray riding-cloak." He raised his voice just as Amy shook off the captain's arm and started back along the path toward them. "Was it I who caused the accident? Ask anyone here . . ."

She felt the beginnings of a headache, a ragged little pain across her forehead—and she knew that the doubt he'd helped reinforce was at the root of the pain.

"You are being ridiculous. Let me pass."

He waved an arm and bowed broadly. "At your service, mademoiselle. There, my dear Miss Amy, how enchanting you look! That damned rider might have killed you." He took Amy's arm. The girl hesitated for a moment, obviously puzzled over the cause of his quarrel with Marsanne, then allowed herself to be led past the captain and back to the house. The latter, ignoring her, stepped off the path to rescue the silk reticule Sylvie had dropped during the excitement.

Raising her cloak above her head, Marsanne made her way carefully over the pebbles that littered the path and

concentrated on avoiding puddles. She didn't want to
think about the coach accident, even less about the identity of the rider . . . Nicoletti stopped abruptly. He
shouted, then shoved Amy aside and very nearly knocked
Marsanne off her feet as she went flying into Amy only
a second or two before a huge rotten oak limb, stretching
overhead, crashed across the path.

Just at that moment Captain Fortenham looked up and
—too late—limped to the rescue. "Good God! That
missed you by a hair, cousin Marsanne!" He helped her
regain her balance. Her ears rang with Amy's cry: "You
saved us, René! We might have been crushed to death."
And Marsanne was thoroughly shaken.

Captain Fortenham helped her to the Dower House,
trying to chide her into a happier mood: "You see,
cousin, we are well-suited. I limp on my right foot, and
you on your left."

She was aware for the first time that she had turned
her ankle, but she remained calm and when they reached
the shelter of the foyer in the Dower House she offered
Nicoletti her hand. "Please, sir, I am more grateful than
I can say."

While everyone dripped on the aged and well-worn
carpet, Nicoletti, with a graceful turn of his wrist, brought
her hand to his lips.

"And finally, may I hope you also trust me, mademoiselle?"

"Of course she does, René. You were heroic!" Amy put
in quickly.

Everyone seemed to be talking at once: "The nearness
of it!" . . . "I vow, I believed for a moment I should be
dead." . . . "It was nothing, Lady Lesgate. I simply turned
in time to—" . . . "Well, I'd say, my boy, it was a near-
run thing . . ."

For Marsanne, new doubts sprung from her earlier suspicion about Philip. Could he have been lying from the
first, and René Nicoletti telling the truth. She retreated to

an ingle-nook to calm herself. Suddenly the sounds of a
coach and team pulling up before the house made everyone move to the door. Lady Lesgate's man, who was still
busy calming his excited team, described the incidents to
Justin's coachman; then Marsanne heard footsteps, saw
the white hair and black tricorne hat of Sir Philip Justin.

She waited in the shadows. Would he be surprised to
see her unhurt? She suddenly recalled the description of
the Binet child's stepfather, her archenemy . . . tall, quiet,
with light eyes . . . Age? . . . forty to fifty.

She was deeply aware of the fact that when Philip
Justin entered, he acknowledged the others with only a
nod and moved directly toward her. And at the instant he
reached her she caught sight of René Nicoletti's eyes, his
upraised eyebrows.

Sir Philip took the hand, which she had not offered, and
held her fingers in his as he asked her, "How are you,
Miss Vaudraye? You were not injured, I hope. Your
coachman tells me all of you were badly shaken."

"We seem to have done better than the rider had reason
to hope," she said coolly. She felt more and more awkward
under his intent gaze, and while she could not deny the
feelings he evoked in her, she refused to allow this to blind
her to the danger of trusting him. Somehow she must
satisfy herself that he was the not the murder-bent man on
horseback. . .

She heard wth relief now Justin's coachman in the
doorway. "Will the ladies please step out one at a time
under this umbrella?"

Sir Philip held her back, and said with a troubled voice:
"What is it? Were you hurt today? Tell me!"

"Please. They are waiting."

"Let them wait. What the devil's happened?" His hand
went out again, tentatively. She could not bear this lie
between them, and looking up into his eyes she asked in a
voice barely audible to him, "Were you on horseback
today?"

She did not know what answer she expected but certainly not his quick, surprised, "Of course. What's this about, Marsanne?"

Sylvie called, "Cousin! Do come. It has stopped raining for the moment."

Marsanne raised her voice. "I am coming." She felt thoroughly confused and deeply conscious of him behind her, unmoving, until she had left the room.

Chapter Fourteen

The ladies, with General Winters, rode comfortably up to the Tudor house, where the Condesa Seaforde acting as hostess and looking elegant in Spanish black with jet bead trim and a high comb and mantilla greeted them at the doors. The ladies managed to deal with drips and drops, half-ruined coiffures and kid slippers with good humor. While they were being ushered through the low-beamed main hall with its crackling fire and long mullioned windows, the men entered, tossing aside various weather cloaks furnished by Philip Justin's servants.

Philip, who'd arrived on horseback, met Marsanne just as she was following the ladies up to arrange themselves becomingly in one of the large unused bedchambers. Realizing that he might grill her again about her feelings, she spoke quickly: "Have you spoken to Mr. Hogue about the rider who caused our accident?"

"Hogue knows his duty. He took his little cob and set off posthaste to overtake the fellow."

"Did he—" she almost lost her voice, she was so anxious to find out if Hogue had spoken to Philip here at the house before he set off, because if so Philip could not have been the one riding ahead of him in that gray coat and black hat—"did Hogue get permission from you first, here at the house?"

He frowned. "Hogue rode off after the fellow at once, when he saw that you were safe. Why would he return here for permission? As it happened—" he shrugged —"I'm afraid he lost the rider just beyond the toll-gate where the high road splits off to Dover."

And had he lost his quarry because that rider returned by a roundabout way to this house? It was possible. She drew away from him.

Still watching her intently, he added, "If the rider actually intended to kill you in the accident it was a ridiculous notion. There was little likelihood any of you would be seriously injured, and it hardly seems likely that he would try to kill six people, including the coachman and postilion, by such clumsy means."

He had taken her hands and held them gently, as if to lend her his strength and confidence. Her headache began to recede as common sense took over. Whatever her suspicions of Philip Justin, he was not a fool. And as he pointed out, only a fool would try to kill her by such a blunderbus method.

His thoughtfulness, however, did not fit his easy dismissal of her danger. "What are you thinking, sir? Was there more danger than you mentioned?"

"Not by that clumsy method. But there may have been another purpose."

She slipped her fingers out of what had seemed for a moment or two the warm safety of his hands. "I must join my cousins. They are expecting me."

He went to the foot of the old dark Tudor staircase after her and looked up. "And I think that purpose succeeded all too well. You no longer trust me."

She winced at the genuine feeling in his voice. A few hours earlier, how happy she would have been to hear it! Now she thought it was late to go back to that warm trust she had achieved earlier.

Having seen to coiffure and appearance, the ladies returned to the gathering downstairs. Sylvie had suggested that they should be shown about the house. Everyone looked at Sir Philip, who made no objection, but, Marsanne thought, showed no real interest either. He assigned the condesa as their guide and when that lady proceeded to usher them through one ancient room after another he merely trailed along after them without notable enthusiasm.

Marsanne herself wandered pensively along at the edge of the group. Several times either the captain or Nicoletti tried without effect to engage her in conversation, but finally they left her to her own devices. She lingered in a female withdrawing room, looking out at a group of men on the beach—she'd little doubt they were Justin's smuggler friends.

What was he up to? . . .

She turned away. It had started to rain again and she remembered the last time she had walked along that beach to the downs and then home to Lesgate Hall . . . it was that day she had discovered how much she cared for Philip Justin . . . She went through the side door now and found herself in a small unlighted bookroom. She instantly felt excited, wondering what books might interest Philip, whether they were in French or English . . . She stepped back into the withdrawing room, took up the branch of candles and returned to the bookroom.

Holding the candles high, she examined the first books but these leather copies of Shakespeare's tragedies and Christopher Marlowe's *Tamburlaine* proved only that Philip read the English language . . . nothing surprising about that. There were copies of Defoe's *Moll Flanders* and a set of Richardson's *Clarissa Harlowe,* which did not sound like the reading of the sophisticated Philip Justin, but on the shelves beyond were books in French. Among these was a large book between marbled covers, and glued within were old documents of the Justin family dating back to the period of Henry the Seventh.

She turned the heavy pages idly. Toward the latter portion of the book there was a letter from the royal family congratulating Sir Richard John Justin upon the birth of a son and heir, Philip Justin. She noted the date: 1758. Further along, young Philip Justin was congratulated upon his knighthood as a result of services to the Foreign Office. After that, a letter in French, dated September 17, 1779:

> My dear, it is plain that you were mistaken in choosing me as your life mate. Your politics, your puritanical character, your rigid attitudes make it impossible for you to accept a human being, a female, and a foreigner.
>
> Adieu, Love,
> Elise.

In 1792, a letter from a surgeon named Whippe congratulated Philip Justin upon his decision to visit the Swiss Cantons and recover from the severe damage to his lungs aggravated by the climate of his native England.

She stared at the letter, looked back at the letter mentioning his birth, considered the dates. A shadow crossed the page and she glanced around. She jumped guiltily. Philip Justin's tall figure seemed to loom over her. . . . "Well?" he asked quietly, "do they tell you anything?"

She hastily gathered her wits and borrowed his own lightness: "They tell me you are exceedingly well preserved, sir."

"Marsanne . . ." She thought he was going to make some kind of confession, but he broke off and instead asked, "You will not trust me then?"

Sarcasm and bitterness took over her sharp answer. "I

certainly should trust you. It is most improper to contradict one's elders and according to these papers you are fifty-seven years old."

He closed his eyes briefly, then managed a faint smile. "And you don't believe that?"

"I believe it! And since it is highly improper to find myself alone with a gentleman older than my father, I had better go and find my cousins. But, mind sir, *I do hate a liar!*"

She thought he would certainly make some defense now, but he stepped aside with obvious reluctance and let her pass him. Perhaps he too remembered their conversation three days ago when he had told her that he was twenty at the time of Bonaparte's coup d'Etat of 1799, which would make him thirty-six now. She'd had no doubt that was the truth. His face and hands, his strength, everything about him had indicated that he was under forty. That he should be a sick man of fifty-seven was ridiculous. Did anyone who accepted him as Sir Philip know how old the real Sir Philip really was? She thought not.

She reached the door still hoping to be stopped, to have him give her some explanation she could accept and certainly something that would assure her he was not the Binet family's emissary. Surely, she thought, he might point out that he had had many opportunities to remove her from the Binets' path, and instead had several times come to her rescue. But that was before she caught him in a clear lie about his age and therefore identity, before the man who so closely resembled him had ridden by on that horse. True, she had not seen the rider's face, but she'd seen the remarkable resemblance to Philip even before Nicoletti mentioned it.

Philip Justin . . . . *who* was he . . . what was his game?

Marsanne had by now been missed by the group touring the house and the captain came back to find her. She knew "Philip Justin" was behind her, and deliberately took the captain's arm, smiling faintly at him as they went off to join the others.

At dusk, the guests were escorted into the long dining salon whose windows overlooked the beach, a portion of the downs to the north, and the Channel in the far distance. There was an awkward moment when Marsanne found herself seated to her host's right, and though a part of her wanted desperately to stay close by him, she said quickly: "Cousin Sylvie, I believe our places are reversed," and Sylvie, liking the notion of exchanging seats, took the place at Justin's elbow, and Marsanne found herself beside old General Winters, who proved talkative and flirtatious enough to keep her mind off Justin.

It was not until the second full course had been served and the veal, the turbot, the vegetables and the roast goose were disappearing that Marsanne happened to turn her head and meet Philip's full gaze. She started and looked away quickly.

There was another trying hour of avoiding him before the evening finally ended. When the guests were gathering for departure Marsanne heard Justin's voice speaking her name quietly. She stiffened.

"I think Sir Philip wants to speak to you," the captain told her, not helping matters at all.

"The coach is here. We must go," she said abruptly.

And before she could be maneuvered into his company again, she hurried out through the rain to the closed carriage.

Chapter Fifteen

Lost in thought about "Philip Justin," Marsanne failed to notice Amy's new-found gaiety—her constant singing, humming and dancing did not strike Marsanne as strange until Mrs. Grover reminded Amy, "Young ladies who have not yet come out do not dance the waltz, as you will know, Miss Amy."

Which, of course, made Marsanne wonder at once what it would have been like to waltz with Philip Justin, to be taken into his arms, to feel the warmth of his hand on the small of her back, to step and sweep around the ballroom with all eyes upon them . . . or alone . . . to dance alone with him in some shadowed gallery . . . She said aloud, "Cousin Sylvie, what do you know about your neighbor, Sir Philip?"

"What, my dear? Oh, a man of unexceptionable family. Seems to have money. I believe he must have saved a pretty penny during those forlorn years in the Swiss

Cantons, but what else can one do there except save money?"

"Yes, but his family. You talk of his background. Have you ever seen any of his family?"

Sylvie paused over her tambour frame to frown in puzzlement. "We know of his family, of course. They lived in the west of England. All gone now, I understand. Only Sir Philip left. He comes and goes as he pleases, and since he leased the condesa's home he has been a flawless landlord. Matter of fact we seldom see him. He was in France recently, as you know."

"He told the barrier guards in Paris that he was returning from the Swiss Cantons."

Sylvie smiled. "You must have misunderstood him, *chérie*. I know he was here some weeks ago. Well, he must have been. Else how could he have leased the condesa's house? They are said to be wondrous close, you know."

Marsanne had not known, and found this distinctly unpleasant news . . . never mind if she had given up all hope of loving him. To keep her cousin's clever eyes off her face, she changed the subject abruptly. "I wonder why Mama has not answered any of my letters. I'm sure that is much more important than this tiresome Philip Justin. Or whoever he is."

"Whoever he—my dear child! All his credentials are perfectly in order. Thaddeus has had dealings with him since more than a year ago. But as to Veronique, you may be sure, if I know my cousin, she is busy. Forever busy. She makes me tired just thinking about her constant activities." She too wanted to change the subject, or had something on her mind that she considered more important than Cousin Veronique's lack of response. "Marsanne, doesn't it seem to you that Amy rides a deal more these days than before you came?"

"Heavens! Do I drive her out?"

"No, no. I should not have said 'before you came' but rather, before that Corsican painter came."

"He is doing a portrait of her favorite horse, I believe."

"Hm . . . I wish—Marsanne, you wouldn't keep a watch upon her, would you, my dear?"

"She would hate me," Marsanne said frankly. "And I cannot very well throw myself into her company."

She was therefore a good deal surprised when Amy approached her one afternoon, asking if Marsanne would join her on a trip to the Frenchwoman in Rye town who had sewn Amy's new wardrobe. Marsanne was delighted at the idea. She was beginning to find Lesgate Hall confining. "Do come, cousin," Amy said. "If you do not, I'll have Moll Pierson or that sneaking Hattie Totter of yours. You know Mama won't let me go alone."

Marsanne agreed with pleasure, and on that bright, sunny day under a rainwashed sky the two girls started out in the old gig used by the servants, with Amy capably handling the reins and in fine fettle, so fine that Marsanne began to be suspicious once again. She mentioned not having seen the "gentlemen" in two days and wondered what Captain Fortenham and Monsieur Nicoletti were about. Amy's reaction puzzled her: "He will be hurt. I'm most sorry for that. I must have behaved very badly to him. I didn't intend to."

"I suppose you mean the captain."

"Of course. Roddy. But you see he was always *there*, and I was forever coming to him when I was in trouble, or when I wanted to play games. He was not, I'm afraid, very mysterious, or masterful, or unpredictable or even interesting . . . He was just—*there*."

This hardly boded well for the captain's hopes, Marsanne thought.

Shortly after, they passed the entrance gates to the Seaforde estate, where Philip Justin lived. While Marsanne was thinking about Philip, she was startled by Amy's soft remark: "I suppose he must be there now, wondering what I ever saw in René . . . René isn't gentle. Roddy always treated me *too* gently—"

"He should have beaten you," Marsanne said severely. She was wondering suddenly if she had been as unfair to Philip Justin as Amy was being to her boyhood sweetheart.

Amy grinned. "Oh, even René could not do that. Matter of fact, he isn't big enough. Now, Roderick, if he chose to—but as I say, he is much too kind."

Marsanne continued to look back for a long time after they had passed the Dower House and the grounds where Philip might be at this minute, past the toll-gate separating the small country paths from the Dover high road and on to the little hill town of Rye. And looking back, occupied with thoughts of her own, she only gradually became aware of a rider following them. At first she expected him to catch up with the gig and pass it, but he remained persistently behind them, too far back to be identified.

When she could no longer contain her curiosity Marsanne said, "Can you imagine why anyone should be following us?"

Amy shrugged. "If he can pay the tolls, he is welcome to the road." She showed remarkably little surprise. Marsanne was beginning to suspect Amy might have other business in Rye town, and decided to dig for the truth: "It may be one of our friends. Perhaps Captain Roderick or Monsieur Nicoletti."

"Or Sir Philip?" Amy asked abruptly.

That upset Marsanne. Whatever she personally suspected of Philip, she did not want anyone to share her suspicions. Not, at least, until there might be proof of real villainy, proof, if necessary, that he was actually the Binet stepfather. Proof, in spite of everything, she acknowledged to herself, she really hoped not to find.

"Why Sir Philip, in heaven's name?" she responded finally.

"Because he is in love with you. Any but a fool could see that."

Startled, Marsanne laughed happily for the first time since the dinner at Sir Philip's house.

"I wish I might believe that." And then, half under her breath, "Or anything else about him . . ."

"What on earth do you mean?" Amy had looked behind her and now scowled. Clearly, she was looking for someone else and had forgotten the subject of Philip Justin. "I thought it might be—well, it isn't. Marsanne, have you ever been in love? So much so that you would sacrifice your name, your family, everything for him?" Before Marsanne could answer, she went on, "Perhaps it isn't love. It may be a kind of infatuation, a burning to have what is forbidden."

"You never loved the captain then?" Marsanne asked, relieved that Amy apparently had taken no notice of her unintended disclosure.

"Of course, I did. I love him today. But he is too . . . yielding. He always gives me my way. René is difficult. Foreign. Romantic. And he made me promise to—I would never dream that I could be disloyal to my family, or my cousin . . ."

"You haven't been disloyal to me. I am not the captain's keeper. If he can't win you, I'm sorry for it, but I don't feel that you need apologize to me over it."

Amy held the reins loosely while she looked at Marsanne. That long, appraising, sad look made Marsanne feel uneasy without knowing why. Amy said, "Do you really understand what I mean by being quite mad about a complete stranger?"

Marsanne understood very well and wondered if she herself suffered from the same complaint, but at least a consideration of Philip Justin told her that there were far greater depths to his character than to René Nicoletti. Depth of character might not invite trust, but in spite of all her suspicions she knew that Philip was enormously superior to the shallow Nicoletti.

"Have you thought, Amy, of how such a man as you describe—an unknown, difficult and foreign—would serve as a satisfactory husband and companion ten years from now? Or even five?"

"Oh, bother! I can't think of ten years from now. I shall be old and probably worrying my daughter over her romances."

"What? At twenty-seven?" Marsanne's amusement was contagious and Amy reluctantly smiled. It seemed to Marsanne that the girl was growing more and more nervous as they approached the turn-off to the little town once dignified by Queen Elizabeth as Royal Rye. She increasingly wondered what awaited Amy there, and why the young girl persisted in looking at her so oddly, almost repentant.

"Shall we be able to see the old tower at Rye? And the ancient gateway I've heard about?" Marsanne hoped that if Amy did indeed have an ulterior motive in making this trip she might confess it now and give her an opportunity to persuade her that she would be wiser to wait. But Amy only responded abstractly . . . "I've no idea, it depends upon several things . . ."

They saw the little hill town loom up suddenly before them, and Amy signaled the horse to begin the rough climb over the well-worn road. Marsanne spent the next few minutes absorbed in the charm of the little town, which had been one of the Cinque Ports during the Middle Ages and only fifty years before was the home of the notorious Hawkhurst gang of cutthroats and smugglers.

And now, she wondered, could there possibly be a "Philip Justin gang"? How absurd, she argued to herself, whatever secrets there were in Philip's life, they surely were far more serious, more complex than mere smuggling.

Amy turned off the steep street into a narrow alley that led to the stables behind several half-timbered row-buildings.

Madame Treville was a tiny curvaceous woman with jet black hair which gave her face a hard masklike look, but she met the young women with a soft smile of welcome. And she burst into enthusiastic French when she was presented to Marsanne. She hoped Marsanne would soon become a regular patron along with Lady Lesgate and Miss de Vaudraye.

"Truly, no, madame. Much as I admire your work, I have brought my wardrobe with me from France. I am sorry."

"Ah, no, mademoiselle. Your first gown is to be completed as a gift. You have but to choose the materials and the pattern."

Marsanne turned to argue with Amy only to find her cousin gone.

Madame babbled on. "Please do not be alarmed at Mademoiselle Amy's disappearance. She will return shortly. She is to meet someone and then return to you with this friend, I believe."

"Who is this friend?" Not that she didn't suspect.

"Mademoiselle would look divine in this white gauze with her exquisite complexion. And so appropriate as a loyal follower of His Majesty, Louis the Eighteenth. Perhaps golden ribbons in the hair, to further suggest the Royalist flag. White, you know, with gold *fleur de lis*."

Marsanne looked into the luxurious little antechamber which appeared to be a dressing room. To madame she said impatiently, "if I were to wear anything of a political nature, it would be violet."

Madame was at first taken aback at this frankness, then apparently decided that an expensive gown would make a lady out of even a follower of the deposed Emperor Napoleon.

"I understand, mademoiselle. I have heard that some of these highly placed in the Whig party sympathize with the Corsican Og—that is, with Bonaparte. Violet then, and the hair coiffured with violet ribbons." And suddenly madame asked her, "Are there new rumors that the Emperor may escape from that island? I imagine if he landed anywhere he would be shot at once by the citizens . . ."

Marsanne, who had scarcely listened to her words, was reminded suddenly of the mood she had seen in Paris, and more to herself than to the dressmaker murmured thoughtfully, "I wonder. I wonder if everyone is wrong, if he might not actually be met with open arms . . ."

Madame sniffed her opinion of that. "Indeed, mademoiselle! Now then, let me take your size. What a lovely figure for the round gowns! Exactly right. Like that poor Empress Josephine. We were all saddened by her death last May."

"Yes. All were saddened. Including the Russian Emperor," Marsanne said crisply. "Please tell me where my cousin has got to."

She wandered back through a little parlor toward the stillroom and then returned. "Madame, what did my cousin tell you about this precious gown you are to make for me?"

"Really, mademoiselle, have I offended? Although it is to be a birthday gift, it was necessary to discuss it with you. I fear it cannot be a surprise."

"And Lady Lesgate ordered it for me?"

"No. Her daughter. Mademoiselle Amy." Madame was beginning to lose her control. "It is true, is it not? You have a birthday like all young ladies?"

"Yes, madame. But my birthday was in January—two months ago."

She looked up suddenly as shadows crossed through the sunlight. A man on horseback rode along the steep, climbing street that ran past the front windows to the graveyard square at the top of the hill. His stocky figure was familiar. Marsanne said, "Excuse me, madame. I have a message for that person."

While the Frenchwoman gawked in amazement, Marsanne passed her and went out to the street. "Mr. Hogue," she called, "I need you."

The little man halted; seeing it was Marsanne signaling, he dismounted and walked over to her. "Mum?"

"I have a great favor to ask of you."

His heavy features lightened a little. "Well, mum, Sir Philip said you might be in danger and I was to watch them that comes near you."

Philip had not lied about that at all events. "Thank you, Mr. Hogue. But it is terribly important that I get a message to Captain Fortenham. Can you fetch him up? He must come here."

"Here, mum? But I'm not to leave you. It's my duty to see that you're safe."

"I'll be safe at Madame Treville's shop. I must write him a note at once."

Mr. Hogue seemed to find her firm in her determination. He pushed back his large sugar-loaf hat. "Don't know as I should, mum. This old nag won't make the trip. I'd have to fetch me another mount, and then there'd be the long ride back, and you'd be left here alone."

"I promise you to take excellent care of myself. Riding hard you should be back within two hours. And it's most important. But I must first write the note."

She waited only long enough to see a reluctant assent in his weathered face before she went into madame's shop to ask for paper and a pen. That lady did not know what to make of such conduct: a young well-proportioned woman who had little interest in an elegant new gown and a great deal of interest in a pen that needed sharpening, some very thick ink, and the back of a paper on which madame had been sketching the new full-skirted gowns all morning.

Marsanne wrote hurriedly, very much aware that if her suspicions were correct Amy and Nicoletti might arrive at any minute to use all their charm and talk her into joining them.

> My dear Captain,
> Forgive me the impropriety of this note. I believe Amy is to meet R.N. here in Royal Rye this afternoon. I may have been chosen to provide a chaperone for an elopement. Amy tells me your faults are your kindness, the way you let her march over you, your refusal to use a masculine authority, but that she loves you otherwise and always counted upon you.
> Need I say more? Haste is essential. She has left me in Madame Treville's shop, but if we are not there, Rye is very small, and I will do my possible to indicate where we have gone.
> I expect you to ride to the rescue, using all authority and overcoming any frippery objections she may make. I do not in the least doubt that you are more than a match for R.N.
>
> Your friend, Cousin Marsanne.

She folded the note, ignoring Madame Treville's remark, "You have no way to seal it, mademoiselle. How do you know that fellow out there will not read it?"

"Let him," said Marsanne, going back to Hogue. He took the folded paper and slipped it between the pages of an untidy black notebook with a half-torn spine, and slipped the book into the pocket of his tight jacket.

"You will hurry?" Marsanne begged anxiously.

"Ay, mum." He looked at her. She found something reassuring in that direct gaze. His eyes were pale and cold—unreadable—but she believed him.

He mounted and turned the obedient mare in the middle of the steep street. Managing to avoid a carter, several walkers and the local squire on his own ancient cob, he trotted back down toward the Dover road, taking up speed as he reached the bottom of the hill.

Marsanne felt at least temporarily relieved when she went back into Madame Treville's establishment and was even able to look on the violet gown with a sparkle of amusement. How the Royalists would hate that symbol of rampant Bonapartism, of loyalty to the exiled Emperor Napoleon! She had a great notion to let madame make it up.

She was relieved when Amy did not immediately return. She would have found it physically impossible to delay two lively people for perhaps two full hours. Instead, Marsanne agreed to accept the violet satin and killed at least forty minutes being properly fitted before she could break away and plead worry over Amy's absence.

Swinging her cloak over her shoulders, she went out through the back of madame's house and hurried up the street just below but parallel to the hill street. It stopped abruptly at the edge of the cliffs which provided the eastern border of the hill town just one street below the combined graveyard and public square that crowned the hill. Finally she caught sight of her young cousin standing at the top of a steep staircase that plunged directly downward toward a watery marshland leading to the English Channel on the horizon. Amy's red hair streamed out in the afternoon wind, which also whipped and gave high color to her smooth, faintly freckled face.

A moment after Marsanne caught sight of her cousin she saw that the girl was holding her hands out happily to greet someone hidden from Marsanne's view and evidently mounting the steps from the marsh below. Not surprisingly, René Nicoletti stepped into view looking as fine as ninepence in elegant fawn-colored breeches, well-polished topboots and a coat whose bottle-green color was a smidgeon wrong for his ruddy complexion. Amy was far from noticing it, however. He carried a greatcoat over one arm but ignored this when he took her hands. She looked gratified but resisted his attempt at a kiss.

Marsanne overheard her warm, slightly desperate voice: "Please, René. We must not until we are married . . ."

Nicoletti strategically retreated: "As you wish, my sweet. Do you imagine I would compromise your innocence?"

His protests had a theatrical ring but Marsanne was fair enough to allow that she might be prejudiced. After all, she was not the recipient. Taking a deep breath, she moved forward into their view. Amy was the first to catch sight of her and after an anxious start and a quick glance at Nicoletti, she called to her cousin, "Marsanne, do come and make me truly happy. I have been so nervous of telling you. I knew you would be out-of-reason cross with your fusty notions of behavior, but—" Amy looked adoringly at her suitor. "Tell her, René, how absolutely masterful you were—"

"How can he when you rob him of words?"

"Oh, but so sweetly," said Nicoletti with a special softness in his voice. "My love, we have not yet told your charming cousin why she had been—abducted, so to speak." Marsanne's dark eyebrows rose and the look she turned on him was not precisely warm. He proceeded rapidly. "Not for the world would I offend the proprieties, mademoiselle. When I asked my beloved Mademoiselle Amy to do me the honor of accepting my name, she mentioned the obvious fact that if we made a runaway match of it the humiliation of her family—whom I deeply respect —would be severe."

"And so you hit upon this happy arrangement," Marsanne put in sharply.

"Cousin, do not imagine we are so lost to what is proper that we are running away to Scotland. To that odious Gretna Green."

"Oh, no. You are in quite the opposite direction for that."

Amy hurried on. "We are going to France. Your very own country, cousin. You can't object to that. And you will be my chaperone to make it all correct. It was René's own idea. For my protection. He said he would flatly refuse to take me unless you were included to protect my good name until the ceremony."

Marsanne quickly decided on her tactics: "What?" she asked Nicoletti lightly. "You flatly refuse to take Cousin Amy across the Channel and back into France unless I accompany you there?"

"Precisely, mademoiselle. I have it arranged. A—an acquaintance of mine has reserved a bedchamber and private parlor for you and my Amy in Calais. It will be quite respectable—"

"This acquaintance of yours, monsieur—a very young gentleman. Like yourself? I should prefer an older gentleman. Say—between forty and fifty. A gentleman of average appearance. Not a dashing young Nonsuch like yourself, monsieur."

He put in eagerly, "Exactly so. My friend who arranged for your room—that is, I mean to say—your room and Amy's would just suit your careful notions of respectability."

The description would also just fit that of her deadly enemy, the Binet child's stepfather. This was certainly an original way to get her into his hands.

"And if I refuse?"

Amy was frantic "You would not be so poor-spirited! Marsanne, you couldn't!"

"What do you mean to do, take the night packet? People may recognize one of us. Many in Dover know your family, Amy."

"You misunderstand," Nicoletti assured her smoothly, "I have promised Amy that this will be truly romantic. So I have just now been at the business of hiring a boat to cross the Channel. One of those fellows who work about the marshes. A smuggler, very likely, but willing enough for a price. Rogue named Nate Tibbetts."

"Quite harmless," put in Amy. "He usually works for Thaddeus—a friend of our housekeeper."

"I know the man. I believe he has a fresh scar across

his nose," Marsanne put in. "But I don't know that I wish to go."

She saw the way Nicoletti's hand went tentatively to the large pocket in the greatcoat thrown over his arm, as if to reassure himself that a pistol was still resting there? She now felt reasonably certain that either on the Channel or in Calais the pistol within that pocket would be put to use against her and possibly against Amy as well.

Several notions occurred at once, not the least of which was the obvious fact that he could not shoot two females here in broad daylight almost within view of the towns-people walking about their business. On the other hand the fellow was quick and might simply hit her, and perhaps Amy too, on the head. He might have help nearby . . . she and Amy could wake up captives of Nicoletti and Nate Tibbetts in the middle of the Channel . . . If Captain Fortenham and Mr. Hogue would arrive in time, hopefully they might force Nicoletti to tell them how to find the Binet child's stepfather in Calais! The entire nightmare would end once Marsanne and her friends could find him.

If they could find him . . . and in time . . .

Chapter Sixteen

"The thing is," Marsanne began—*playing for time—"I* have nothing to wear. I wonder if I might purchase something from Madame Treville."

Saucily Amy put her hands over her beloved's ears. "If you mean your night-rail, cousin, do not worry. I packed one of your gowns, a robe and a shift with mine. You see, I thought of everything."

Poor Amy! Totally unaware that this grand elopement was a cynical device for executing Binet's purpose. That the dashing René was almost surely the man's hired agent, an instrument . . .

With one more excuse for delay gone, she must improvise. "Then I had best find my reticule and bonnet at Madame Treville's. What a pity I promised madame that I would select ribbons and gauze to match! I had best go about it."

"Really, dear, I think—" Amy glanced uneasily at her betrothed, whose temper looked to be near the explosion point. The fingers of his free hand flexed nervously. The other hand remained sinisterly concealed in the pocket of his coat. Amy went on, "We shall be late, we must go soon—"

"At once," Nicoletti inserted in clipped tones.

Marsanne knew that if she denounced him here before he had committed any act for which he might be punished, Amy would think him a martyr and he would not even be placed under restraints. He had to be prodded into something desperate. Marsanne only hoped he would not go too far in that direction before help arrived.

Nicoletti immediately started to usher Marsanne toward the steps. She winced painfully. "Oh, you are hurting me."

Amy was shocked and called Nicoletti to attention sharply. At the same instant Marsanne saw fury in her captor's face before he apologized, took his fingers off her hand and relaxed a bit. Marsanne had finally seen Nicoletti's real feeling for her and it ended any slightest doubt she'd had about him.

At this point Amy hardly looked as happy as an eloping young lady might be expected; Marsanne could only hope this mood would intensify over the next few minutes. There was still no sign of the captain but Marsanne had not given up. It was early evening and the staircase against the cliff was in shadows, but Marsanne could still make out far below the figure of a sailor standing in the deeper shadow against an outcropping of earth and rock.

Obviously because he did not trust her to cooperate, Nicoletti instructed Marsanne to go down the steps first, with both Amy and himself behind her. There would be no retreat. As there wasn't a stair railing of any kind, it made her a little dizzy just to look down those steps. And at the bottom would be Nate Tibbetts. She could now make out the red headscarf and the shabby, dark jerkin over a lighter shirt. She shuddered.

It occurred to her suddenly that there might not be a rescue, that Mr. Hogue had failed to locate the captain, that she was on her way to a singularly unpleasant destination, probably at the bottom of the Channel, and very possibly to be accompanied by her cousin. But she had by no means given up and considered the chances of slipping Nicoletti's pistol out of his greatcoat pocket . . . She looked up at him soulfully.

"It's so steep. May I use your hand to steady myself if I should feel faint?"

"You, cousin?" Amy put in, not altogether pleased. "I doubt you've ever felt faint in your life."

Damn! Amy's jealousy did not, however, prevent Marsanne from grabbing hold of Nicoletti's sleeve. He was getting into his greatcoat and her fingers very nearly reached the big patch pocket before he seized her hand and ordered her: "Now, mademoiselle!"

She started down the steps one at a time. Her knees shook and she felt that her long skirts might trip her. She had a ghastly feeling that she really might fall. Or be plunged down by Nicoletti's hand. Was that what he intended? Had she been wrong in guessing how he meant to kill her?

She descended four or five steps, trying to build up to her next move.

She turned her ankle deliberately, slipped the sole of her flat-heeled slipper over the next step and called out, "Oh, help me, *please* . . ."

In a panic Amy reached around past Nicoletti and caught Marsanne by the arm. Another few minutes were killed . . . Still no sign of the captain and Marsanne began seriously to fear that she would end up in Nate Tibbetts' "care" in spite of all her delaying tactics.

She climbed down, and through the darkness she could make out the smuggler's arms raised to take hold of her as she reached the marsh bed. She looked back up over her shoulder—pausing—until Nicoletti crowded her from above. A sharp salty wind swept across the marsh from the direction of the Channel, and Marsanne wondered if she might be able to run from the smuggler and Nicoletti along the base of the cliff toward what remained of the long sandy shoreline south of Rye town . . . In another few seconds she was within reach of the same man who had taken a fancy to her on the downs below Lesgate Hall. In the gathering dark she felt his strong fingers gripping her waist, and though she kicked out convulsively she was lifted down into his arms and tight against his body. She gasped—very nearly screamed.

In the semidark she could see his face. Most of his hair was covered by the red scarf. But she now recognized the vivid blue eyes, the well-shaped mouth of . . . Philip Justin. For an instant—while she tried to tell herself this was no hopeful dream in the midst of terror—she thought he might kiss her, his lips were that close to hers.

Another second, he was again his cool controlled self. He made a very slight sound asking for her silence, and she felt herself slipping through his hands until she stood on the soggy ground. He thrust her behind him and appeared to wait for Nicoletti while one of his hands went into the heavy-laden pocket of his leather jerkin.

With a rapid heartbeat, a mixture of excitement and dread, she watched Nicoletti lifting Amy down from the last step. She also realized that there was *still* no actual proof against Nicoletti, and realizing it, found herself, as if possessed, turning and beginning to run—slipping and sliding on the spongy earth.

Nicoletti pulled the pistol out of his coat pocket as Amy screamed, and Marsanne threw herself abruptly to the ground.

Chapter Seventeen

Philip just managed to knock the pistol out of Nicoletti's hand, diverting the ball wide. Looking over her shoulder now, Marsanne scrambled to her feet and Amy rushed up to help her up.

"He shot . . . he aimed at you . . . My God, he tried to *kill* you . . . Oh, cousin . . ." But as Amy hugged her cousin her voice broke down and the two stared at Nicoletti, struggling against the man Amy still took to be a common smuggler.

Marsanne raised her eyes to a point halfway up the steps, and Amy followed her cousin's stare. Captain Fortenham was coming rapidly down the steps, sword in hand, unintentionally if inevitably striking something of a pose.

"An accident, surely you believe me," Nicoletti began, trying to get to the captain. "Of course I'd no intention, my friend . . . mademoiselle, too, an old friend . . .

why should I shoot at her? . . . ask my dearest Amy, ask—"

"I *ask* you nothing, you gallows-bait," the captain cut in swiftly. "I tell you I'll have your head for this . . ." He looked to Philip, in whose hands the slight Nicoletti was struggling like an insect on its back. "Let Hogue do that, damn it! . . . My God, are you all right, ladies? Amy? Marsanne?" The captain swung roughly past Philip and Nicoletti toward Amy, who was now crying in near-hysteria, asking at the same time, "Why in God's name did he do that, cousin? Why would he try to shoot you?"

"Later," Marsanne said, and looked over Amy's head at the captain and pointedly nodded. Understanding, he stopped his run, took a breath, and took Amy firmly in his arms.

"You are coming home now, Amy, and I tell you, no more nonsense."

"What do you—?" she began, trying to pull back.

"And no more tears, please. We've had enough of it."

Apparently, Marsanne thought with satisfaction as she watched them, the captain had finally discovered the way to manage his sweetheart.

"Roddy, I'm sorry, I can't understand it—" and when tears again threatened, he told her, with a straight face, "No, tears are not becoming, they keep one from seeing your pretty eyes. That's truly a crime, my darling."

When she looked up at him, smiling now in spite of the tears, it was clear that the captain had managed his most important conquest.

The stocky Bow Street Runner had by now reached the marshy ground, and stepped into a furze bush as the captain passed with Amy, who turned her face away to avoid looking at Nicoletti. Marsanne, however, watched him closely, and could hardly believe what she next saw unfold before her . . .

The captain had boosted Amy up onto the steps. Mr. Hogue reached out to subdue Nicoletti, who suddenly relaxed, making no move to avoid the Runner, and Hogue and Philip—strong men both—incredibly managed to let him slip out of their hands . . . Nicoletti immediately sprinted away, and as he was passing Marsanne she extended her foot to trip him; then abruptly withdrew it as Philip called out sharply, "Marsanne! No!"

So her would-be assassin slipped by her, his elegant topboots barely digging heel marks in his haste. Mr. Hogue resolutely puffed after him, while Philip—still looking, Marsanne thought, very much like a pirate except for the queued tail of his white hair—appeared to start on the chase but stopped as he reached Marsanne. Seeing her shaking and understandably stupefied by the inept display she'd just witnessed, Philip reached out for her but she avoided his hands, whispering, "He wanted to *kill* me and you let him go. Why . . . ?

"Why did you let him go?"

"Why did you begin to run so foolishly?"

"But it was not foolish—well, perhaps, but I knew of no other way to force him to condemn himself. And then when he did . . . I can't understand how you could have—"

"And a brave, if still foolish girl you were. But I have only followed your lead. By letting him go, or seeming to, we have our only—at least our best chance of being led to your real threat, the man who hired our cutthroat fop and would doubtless hire others to take his place."

She let herself be drawn into the hollow of his arm, feeling the hard muscular protection.

"Well, I must say I don't see how it can help me if you let him escape across the Channel . . . which is what he is sure to do."

"Except he need not escape across the Channel alone. Mr. Hogue will be behind him the whole of his journey."

This news finally cheered her somewhat, and she allowed Philip to take her back up the steps, his arm still around her. She reminded herself, though, that very soon

she would have to find out the whole truth about him . . .
but right now she wanted to delight in his embrace, with
its comfort and temptations, as though it were the only
reality worth considering in her life.

"Did Mr. Hogue deliver my message to you as well as
to the captain?" she finally asked as they reached the most
elevated end of the town's High Street.

He smiled. "Yes, just as I was on my way to take Nate
Tibbetts' place on the marsh. Thaddeus had word of the
plot from Nate and came directly to me."

"And you deliberately let Amy and me go through such
a fright? Really, it is—"

"It was an unworthy trick, perhaps, but you were never
out of our sight—Hogue's or mine. Then you sent Hogue
away and I confess I knew some frantic moments when I
found Hogue had left you without protection." He looked
at her and she found it hard to avoid his eyes with their
message that she so much wanted to believe. "Come," he
urged, protectively but also as a command. "You need a
glass to relax you before the trip home. The George Inn
should be fine—"

She stopped. He had her in a pleasant but unquestionably firm grip, and with his free hand raised her chin and
asked gently, "Are you still afraid of me?"

She laughed sharply, feeling the start of nervous hysteria
after the events on the marsh. "If you could see yourself,
you would know why I might well."

He looked down at the stained leather jerkin, the torn
sleeves of his shirt, and worse, the loose-legged pantaloons with their hems torn off showing ankles scarred
with cross-hatchings above his clogs. He joined her laugh
but glanced once more toward his feet, then looked up
quickly. She caught herself wondering about those scars,
wondering if they weren't a part of the mysterious other
self that was *not* fifty-seven-year-old Philip Justin . . .

"The George Inn appears to be respectable," she told
him, "but you hardly look the part of a local squire."

"No, a simple sailor-lad. But your presence will lend me countenance."

"So it's finally out. That's why you saved me, to give you countenance—"

"Just so."

They laughed. He reached toward the inn door and for a moment she had the decided urge to yield, but caught herself up with the reminder that the question must be asked and she would only dread it more tomorrow or another day . . . "Not tonight, please . . . I had rather go directly home. I am very tired, surely you can understand."

He studied her face with an intensity that made her even more nervous. "I understand you most definitely need a small brandy. It will make you feel more the thing, and then I promise to bring you safely to your doorstep." He was watching her closely. "What is it, Marsanne?"

"Who are you, sir?"

He did not hesitate.

"I told you. Philip Justin."

She knew a second of painful disappointment—in spite of everything she had hoped to hear the truth. He could not miss the hurt in her voice. "I know. You are Sir Philip Justin and you are fifty-seven years old."

"No, my darling—"

"I have not given you leave to call me your darling, any more than I was that despicable René Nicoletti's darling. I don't even know you and I doubt if my mother knew you, except as this make-believe English knight—"

He no longer urged her toward the tavern, and though she shrugged to release herself from his arm which still encircled her she could not quite free herself. Could not . . . did not want to . . . ? She prayed that even now he would give her an answer she could accept.

"My darling—I'll express my feelings with or without your leave—Sister Veronique has known me from the time I was a boy of twelve, running errands for the man she loved more than any on earth . . . *your father*. The day you said goodbye to her at the Hôtel-Dieu I was waiting to see her, to escort you to your royal high cousins in England."

She stared at him, at the red cambric cloth bound around his head, and felt certain that at least this last part of his story was true. She raised one hand and touched the headband, and it seemed to her his eyes showed honest anxiety over whether she would accept his partial explanation. She said quietly, "Yes, I remember . . . Clotilde and I saw you waiting by the river door. Even when we mistook you for a pirate . . . But I still don't believe that you are Sir Philip Justin."

He glanced around and saw a pair of townsmen staring; they seemed intimidated by his glance and—opening the tavern door—edged behind him into the George. He led Marsanne into the shadow of the tavern wall.

"Listen to me very carefully, Marsanne. There are things I simply cannot tell you. But there is one truth, and you must believe it. I am Philip Justin . . . if you will translate my name into French, you have the name with which I was baptized—Jean-Philippe Justin. Sir Philip Justin," he hurried on, "was my father—though he never knew it. He died in Geneva about a year ago. I was informed of his whereabouts just before he sank into a coma. Since I found that I so closely resembled him, I simply took his identity to assist me—in my work."

"How dreadful that your own father never knew you existed!"

He flashed a rueful smile. "My mother was French. God only knows why they married. She was a shopkeeper's daughter in Paris when he met her. They saw nothing with the same eyes. And my mother would not compromise. Do you remember the letter you read from the girl who ran away from my father . . . 'Elise'?"

"Yes." She laughed in spite of herself. "I'm afraid I was jealous of her."

"You need not be. My poor mother died in Paris when I was nine, leaving me at first a street urchin. But when the Bastille was taken and the old order was overturned in France there was a place for me. A glorious time . . . just before the Terror . . ."

"Glorious?" Philip reminded her of her mother, so in love with a period Marsanne thought must have been a nightmare.

"Yes. It was glorious. It gave us all hope. As a commoner I suddenly found worlds open to me. I needed not to belong to the nobility or the clergy. I could serve the government, serve the great men who were molding a new nation, a democracy . . . unheard of in our tired old Europe. Your father was a courageous political artist, a very kind and generous man." He added thoughtfully, "I am now almost ten years older than he was when he died . . . I actually took some wine to him and his friends in the prison that April day. I never saw a braver lot. They actually sang and joked, even at the very end . . ."

She closed her eyes. The tears like pinpricks came in spite of herself. "So *that* was why Mama always hated April so much."

He said nothing, waited. She knew by his tension, by the way he looked at her that her acceptance of his identity meant a great deal to him. Still, if he had been a revolutionary, and was now involved in something he called "dangerous" . . .

She tried to make her question light, bantering, but the tightness in her voice betrayed her. "And now you are planning another Guy Fawkes Day? You are about to plant gunpowder and blow up the Chamber of Deputies, or whatever they have in England?"

"No, my sweet perversity, and that is enough for you."

She persisted with, "I assure you, my mother would have preferred the man she loved to be unlaughing, unsinging and very much alive."

He said nothing to that but moved his arm, raised his

other hand, and she found herself pinned against the brick wall of the tavern.

"Now, see here—" she began indignantly.

It was probably the glow from the tavern light but she fancied his eyes burned as he told her, "Whether I joke or sing to suit you, I assure you, I am very much alive."

And promptly proceeded to demonstrate as his lips harshly silenced hers. She felt as though that curiously leashed power of his had suddenly escaped its bonds and was devouring her.

Loud, drunken laughter now rippled over the square as two sailors, a woman in tow, staggered toward the tavern door, and Marsanne, reluctantly, broke away from him.

"My cousin will be expecting me . . . please take me home—"

"Very soon, all too soon . . ." His voice was slightly hoarse, quite unlike the man who was forever in control, but now as he kissed her again, gently this time, there was great tenderness in the touch of his lips, as well as in the warmth created by it. Feeling as if in a dream, she expected the perfect ending, his confession that he loved her. It did not come. She felt herself released.

When she took her first step she stumbled and he caught her arm, smiling in good humor now. All the same, she noted with satisfaction that he was breathing fast.

He stopped abruptly and looked around into the dark streets emptying out of the churchyard square.

"What is it?"

"I rode here with Hogue. He won't be riding back, of course. He's following Nicoletti, as I told you. That leaves us with two horses, one rider, and one lady who does not ride."

"But if I had a lady's saddle perhaps I could—"

He laughed. "I can imagine. No, Hogue rode a fine heavy stallion. The good creature will carry us, and we will leave my mount for my stableboy to retrieve."

In front of him on the huge bay stallion, his arms holding her secure as well as the reins, she knew it was not the time—nor place—to ask the other question burning in her mind—had he been the man on horseback who caused the near-accident on the road to the condesa's? She realized she was afraid of any answer that might make her feelings for him inappropriate, that might in fact end with her losing him. And, of course, the nature of whatever special mission seemed to drive him so was still completely unknown to her.

There was surely one permanent benefit from today's events—now that Nicoletti had shown himself, she was at least one important step closer to safety. And if Hogue could trail him to the real enemy, the Binet child's stepfather . . . Well, just to think of Nicoletti gone from these shores was at least a great relief.

Though little was said on that ride back to Lesgate Hall, Marsanne doubted even then that she would ever forget —and surely never wish to—the moonlight road, the warmth of Philip's arms, and the conviction she felt when she glanced at his face, etched in silver light and shadow, that for the first time since their meeting on the Calais coach he looked to be a man content, human and loving . . . that for this short time he seemed to have laid aside whatever terrible compulsion it was that drove him.

They were met on the Lesgate estate road by several horsemen led by Captain Fortenham, who was delighted to find his "cousin" Marsanne and his friend Sir Philip safe and sound. Among his troops were Lady Lesgate's stableman and General Winters, who though rather obviously had been imbibing too freely of Her Ladyship's smuggled brandy, insisted that in his capacity as keeper of the peace of this district he must lend his authority to the search.

Marsanne's first impulse was disappointment, even annoyance, at the sight of these well-meaning rescuers, but she was well pleased at Philip's muttered, "Damn, this seems the end of our few minutes alone . . ." making clear he felt as she did.

When they reached the long steps of the hall the general wanted to lift her down from the big stallion's back, but Philip extended his arm across her body, his hand warning away the general, then himself lifted her down before dismounting. He walked with her to Cousin Sylvie and Amy, who were waiting nervously on the steps. Both women clustered about Marsanne, who patted *their* backs consolingly while she prayed that Philip would at least not leave without wishing her a good night . . . The abrupt sound of hoofbeats and the sudden stir of pebbles on the estate drive told her, however, that he'd ridden off without another word, that she still must take a lesser position to his damnable precious cause. . .

She had one consolation which she hugged to her in the midst of her depression: his last words to her when they saw their "rescuers": "This is the end of our few minutes alone." At least he had wanted her then.

Chapter Eighteen

Marsanne was swept rapidly indoors by her anxious and curious cousins, who followed her up to her bedchamber and there questioned her while Clotilde fussed over her ruined clothing and badly skinned knee. The silent, ever-efficient Hattie Totter fetched up cloth for a bandage as well as a small glass of Lady Lesgate's brandy to soothe Marsanne's nerves.

After she'd been properly attended Amy insisted on bringing a tray to her, and having persuaded her mother to leave them alone, she confided sadly, "I will never forget how dashing he seemed, cousin. Such a horrid little man! But after he had persuaded me to elope in that odious way, he changed so . . . I couldn't believe it. So crude and brutal! And when he deliberately tried to shoot at you—"

"Don't think of it," Marsanne advised as she took another bite of cold York ham.

Amy lowered her voice. "I didn't tell Mama, nor did

Roddy. She thinks René was merely trying to abduct us. Roddy has been so splendid! I'm really very pleased."

Marsanne grinned but wisely offered no additional praise to that which the captain's conduct was rapidly accumulating from Amy.

Amy then confided after a slight hesitation but with no diminished enthusiasm, "Mama hinted that at our Spring Ball day after tomorrow the announcement of the betrothal should be made."

Marsanne asked casually, "And you resent being pressed to the betrothal so soon after—"

"Oh, no! It is a perfect time. No one will suspect René was anything more than a silly flirtation, which I am persuaded was indeed all he has been to me . . ." She looked at Marsanne as if expecting contradiction but received none.

"I see. Very sensible. He is indeed, a splendid-looking man, and so masterful . . . I do envy you."

Amy blushed with pleasure and shortly afterward went off to her own bed in excellent spirits.

Marsanne's own emotions were less easily satisfied. She could only console herself with two thoughts as Hattie Totter snuffed the candles: she appeared safe for at least a while from the Binet vendetta, and she had the memory of Philip's embrace. There was desire in that embrace and a very real, if unspoken, love. She was certain of it. . .

She closed her eyes intending to experience Philip's tenderness in her dreams but was brought back when Clotilde, who was lying on the smaller bed in the room, called out through the darkness, "Mamselle, may I confess a secret? Mamselle Amy is not the only one to be wished happiness tonight."

"What on earth do you mean?"

"I too am in love . . ." She could not mistake Marsanne's sigh and added defensively, "It is different this time, I assure you. Truly different. Albert wishes to marry me but—"

Marsanne sat up. "Tell me, can there be any objection? He seems a highly desirable young man."

Clotilde clapped her hands, and agreed. "He is, and such a very respectable man as well . . . not in the least like the gentlemen and the soldiers I knew in Paris."

"Then what can be the objection? I'd say you are a very lucky girl, Clotilde."

"But don't you see, mamselle? His post is here. He is English. He doesn't even speak French. If I marry him, I must stay here with him."

"Oh." Marsanne had been so concerned with her own affairs that she'd not really thought through the idea of Clotilde marrying an Englishman. It was a blow, for in spite of Clotilde's preoccupation with males she was a friend and often amusing companion. Sometimes a loving and devoted one too. And Marsanne had a sudden vision of what the return to Paris would be like without both the man she loved and her companion.

"I think you must ask yourself how much you love Albert. When I love—" she stopped, began again "—if I loved a man, I would place that love before anything else." Yet she also knew she had been enormously relieved to learn that the man she loved belonged to her own people, her own country. "Clotilde, I love you dearly as a friend and a sister. But you know quite well that you had rather be in Albert's company than in mine."

"Mamselle, you're so understanding!"

. . . I only wish I understood the man I love as well, Marsanne thought, and closed her eyes at last.

She did not see Philip during the next two days. The household was full of plans for what Amy now incessantly referred to as "my betrothal ball." Like most of the other unmarried young females invited to Lesgate Hall, Marsanne planned to wear her best white ball gown in spite of Madame Treville's unexpected and faithful delivery of the violet satin.

But she changed her mind on the morning of the ball

when General Winters and a number of his cronies rode over with the captain and began discussing rumors that the Allied Congress meeting at Vienna might remove the "Corsican Ogre" from the island of Elba near the Italian Coast to a forsaken rock in the South Atlantic . . . some place called St. Helena.

She thereupon quickly decided she would wear her colors for all to see. Since it was now forbidden to fly the Tricolor in France, she only wished she had a ball gown of blue, white and red to flaunt her allegiance with as well.

When she was being dressed for the betrothal ball that afternoon Clotilde found nothing inappropriate in the delicate violet hue of her mistress' satin underdress or the matching gauze overskirt. It graced her figure in a way that made Clotilde exclaim over her "beauty."

"Indeed, mamselle, you will break the heart of every male at the ball, including the future bridegroom. Isn't it so, Hattie?"

Hattie Totter said quietly, "Do you wish me to arrange the violet ribbons through your hair à la Grecque, miss?"

"You don't think it is rather too much?" Marsanne asked dubiously, for there were already several tiny violets embroidered on the ribbon. However, the entire costume was of exactly the same delicate shade, and if there had been no political significance in the violet flower itself, the gown and ribbons would have been highly proper. In the circumstances, though, there could be no doubt she was a living advertisement of the Bonapartist sympathizers, and just at a time when the person of the exiled Emperor Napoleon was the subject of discussion throughout Europe.

Hattie said, "The color is unexceptionable upon you, miss. I see no reason why it should be too much."

"I meant the politics of it . . ." Nevertheless when Marsanne studied her image in the long looking-glass, having carefully worked her elbow-length gloves into place, accepted the silver gauze shawl around her nearly bare shoulders and taken up her mirrored fan, she was impressed herself by the image reflected there. She had never, she decided, looked . . . so elegant.

By the time she arrived at the head of the staircase, the long hall fronting the house had been transformed into a strolling gallery for the exhibition of the ladies in their most elaborate guise. Thanks to the influence of Beau Brummel on the gentlemen of the English court, she noted a preponderance of the male guests present in the elegant austerity of black and white, but the older gallants still wore satin small-clothes, and one or two wrinkled Eighteenth-Century gallants still affected powder and patches.

Feeling too conspicuous now with her colorfully proclaimed Bonapartist politics, Marsanne moved as quietly as possible down the great staircase, but the beautiful Condesa Seaforde, in the company of two smiling gentlemen, looked up, laughed delightedly and applauded Marsanne.

"Bravo, mademoiselle. The violets *indeed* return with the spring."

Beside her one of the Englishmen protested but laughed as he did so. "My dear condesa, a little caution, if you please."

At the same time Marsanne was almost blinded by the Spanish noblewoman's overabundance of jewels, from her tiara to—actually—a ruby ring upon one toe that was revealed by her evening slippers. It was exactly like the shocking post-Revolutionary days described with some relish by her grandmother.

Another group reacted more predictably. General Winters, busy giving several cronies the benefit of his opinions as to why the Congress at Vienna did nothing but argue, dance and make love to clever . . . uh, women furnished by that subtle rogue Comte Metternich, Austria's brain and spokesman, took notice of the sudden united admiration on the faces of his audience and turned to see what had distracted them from his discourse.

"Exquisite creature!" exclaimed one of the gentlemen— loudly enough to make Marsanne blush. "French, of course."

General Winters gasped, exclaimed in an equally ringing voice, "French, undoubtedly, the impudent strumpet!"

Marsanne's back stiffened. She scarcely heard the shocked befuddled defense of her by the general's friend: "I say, general, that's a bit rough. Poor creature can't very well help her birth, you know."

And another put in, "Really, old fellow! Pretty little chit, for all of that."

Marsanne could only be thankful that Amy chose this moment to descend the stairs, looking scrubbed and charming in her virginal white. The attention went at once to the belle of the evening, and the ladies sighed appropriately when Captain Fortenham came to the stairs, his limp slightly more pronounced with his nervousness, and offered an arm to his betrothed, his eyes shining.

At Marsanne's ear the condesa murmured, "God knows he has earned the girl. Such fidelity . . . !"

And Marsanne allowed herself the fantasy of a magic moment such as this when Philip would come to claim her . . . She moved back now to make room for Amy and the captain, who promenaded along the gallery receiving the congratulations of their friends, and was close enough to hear comments from unfamiliar voices around her . . .

"What can one expect of French females? You know what they say . . . I heard that our Allied troops in Paris . . . Well, but *violets,* mind! Who does she fancy she is —Bonaparte's wife?"

A male voice protested weakly, "Hardly more than a child, m'dear. Naughty puss to be wearing Bonaparte's color, but it's not her fault the Little Corsican chased us the length and breadth of the continent for twenty years."

"Chased you! That is not very patriotic."

"True all the same, m'dear."

Marsanne moved away, found herself within the circle of the condesa's pro-Bonapartists, who also made her uncomfortable because they seemed to contribute to her own family disloyalty.

This subject, however, was soon abandoned in favor of a matter even more shocking. Lady Lesgate had announced that the new German Waltz would be danced tonight. Mothers with daughters who had not yet been presented at Court or at a Coming Out sought each other to exchange opinions on the propriety of the matter. It all ended with general approval, for no mother wanted her daughter to sit back among her elders while other young ladies whirled about—held shockingly close to their partners.

It was the wish of Marsanne's life to waltz in Philip's arms, but he did not seem to be present tonight. She had been taught the German Waltz on instruction of her late grandmother, the Vicomtesse de Vaudraye, a lady always up to the mode in every way. The furnishing of a suitable partner for this titillating dance in which a lady found herself within the arms of a male during every round and whirl of the dance had not, unfortunately, been a matter the delightful vicomtesse could control. Marsanne stood aside from the fluttering chattering girls and tried to concentrate on other matters.

One thing struck her as odd. The condesa and her Bonapartist friends seemed remarkably excited, more so certainly than a country ball would seem to explain. A conspiracy of some sort seemed to be at work here tonight . . . Suddenly she wished she knew how to play piquet, whist, or some other game of cards, for the gentlemen gathered at tables in the music room looked quite content and removed from political controversy.

As partners were chosen to open the ball, Captain Fortenham led out Amy, who looked truly glowing with a pride and a grace that her cousin never had noticed before. The condesa was taken by General Winters in spite of their startling divergence in politics. A titled gentleman noticeably lacking in chin had Cousin Sylvie on his arm, and Marsanne now began to suspect she herself would be the only female left against the walls. Several men seemed about to approach her, then drew back. She could only suppose it was her flaunted Bonapartist violets . . .

However, one of the condesa's Bonaparte-sympathizing Englishmen, a short stout young gentleman, came to fetch her, introducing himself as "George Baldridge, ma'am, the—er—Honorable George Baldridge . . . Shall we?"

She curtsied, smiled, accepted. In the long ballroom they took their places in the set that was forming. The freshly washed and polished crystal lustres with the mirrored walls reflected a brightness that dazzled Marsanne. She was still looking about with interest when the Honorable George said, "No one will say I lack courage now, Miss Vaudraye."

"Really?" she asked, with a slight edge to her voice, wondering if he would boast that only the brave dared dance with her.

"Oh, quite. Several of us had our instructions not to choose the lovely French miss," he said, and flinched a little at her fiery look.

"General Winters, no doubt."

"Lord, no. Prosy old bore, besides being a Tory. I'm a Whig, myself. No, no. We had our marching orders from your admirer. Said he would hand me a facer I'd long remember. But I see he's not around yet, so I can demonstrate my courage without being struck to the floor by his very punishing left."

Privately she was pleased by the intimation that her

"admirer" had jealously forbidden others to choose her for the dancing, but she said, "I cannot imagine who this mysterious admirer may be, sir. He has not received my permission, I assure you."

" 'Pon my soul, ma'am, I'd no idea. But may I say—he seems to think so."

They were separated by the movements of the dance, which left Marsanne to speculate nervously until they went down the dance again when she casually said, "You have not told me the name of this insolent fellow who instructs everyone concerning my dancing partners."

"Haven't I? Good Lord—beg pardon, ma'am! I thought you knew. Your gown . . . the violets . . . It seemed clear you dressed so in order to please Justin. Sir Philip being . . . ah well, let's not talk politics. . ."

She was so pleased she took little interest in the politics, but suddenly it occurred to her that if Philip Justin was a Bonapartist in the present circumstances, with his emperor in exile, this might explain the "task" he'd set himself. She'd noticed that most people who followed the emperor seemed to place this devotion before any other. For a moment she hated Napoleon Bonaparte and his extraordinary hold upon those who served him. . .

"Sir Philip and his precious politics mean less than nothing to me!"

"But—but your gown, those charming violets . . ."

"A coincidence. Nothing else."

She saw that she had done more than surprise him. She had caused him to betray his own Bonapartist sympathies to someone who might very easily bring disaster to him and others. She waited until the music ended, then assured him, "Sir, I spoke hastily. I am French. I was reared under the Empire. My sympathies are with you and your friends."

He thanked her but she wondered if he would again trust her. She was sorry for that, but sorrier by far that Philip was still absent.

After that she was pleased to be chosen for the two next dances by Captain Fortenham, who talked charmingly of his happiness in having "brought his Amy into line." From that moment Marsanne found herself flatteringly sought and had little time to regret—or resent—the absence of the man she'd come, at times in spite of herself, to love.

Just before the German Waltz commenced, the Honorable George Baldridge urged his stomach through the little group surrounding Marsanne.

"I say, Miss Vaudraye, have you the courage? Lady Lesgate has given permission, so long as your chosen partner is an old friend."

Marsanne suddenly heard a familiar voice say, "None older than myself surely," and found herself being led past her other admirers by the one she'd wanted at her side more than any other.

She would try to restrain herself, however, until she learned what excuse he would offer for having only just arrived at this late hour.

Chapter Nineteen

She was sharply aware of his presence—his touch—and when his arm encircled her waist as they reached the floor she felt herself actually tremble before raising her eyes to look at him for the first time.

What she saw now took her breath: Tonight he wore black and white and the snowy folds of his cravat against the black of his coat were as startling as the virile brightness of his eyes against the white of his queued hair. There was none of the once habitual coldness in his smile as he looked down at her.

"I meant to be here for the opening of the ball, my darling, can you forgive me?"

"I have still not given you leave to call me darling."

"Haven't you? I wonder where I had the idea. I do beg your pardon . . . my love."

"Nor have I given you permission to call—" She broke off, biting her lower lip to hide her laughter.

"What shall it be, then? 'My darling' or 'My love'? Or perhaps—"

"You are being nonsensical." All the same, she laughed delightedly.

When the waltz ended there was great excitement, laughter and much chattering, punctuated for a startled Marsanne by Philip's saying, "Now, let me explain, my darling," and led her off the floor, pretending not to hear the remarks and greetings from friends.

"Are you cold?" he asked, further startling her.

She had no idea what to say—she was certainly not cold while she remained in his half-embrace . . . and then she understood as he opened the doors to the east terrace, which overlooked the downs and the faint Channel lights far off on the horizon.

Peering into the half-dark, she whispered, "Someone is out there."

He laughed shortly. "The lovers, I expect—Mademoiselle Amy and her captain. Well, let's try the next salon."

"The supper is spread there." She readily admitted to being "famished," and seeing his amusement, added sensibly, "If you wish to speak with me it's far easier in a crowded room where people are concerned with their own affairs. You may, for example, explain to me over those lovely lobster patés why you told the Honorable George you would give him . . . I believe you called it a punishing left . . . if he danced with me."

He laughed. "I said I would give him a facer. I am sure the punishing left was his notion."

"Must I remind you, sir, that I am not your property."

She had been right. The long formal dining salon was now crowded, and when he answered her there was such a rumble of voices she felt that no one but she could possibly hear him.

"Do you mean to break your mother's heart?"

"Am I to understand your entire pursuit of me is to oblige Mama?"

He appeared to think this over. "I love your mama, no question. But I am afraid I can't imagine asking her to share my life. Or my bed, for that matter . . ."

She felt certain that her face must have reddened. No gentleman had ever made such a direct remark to her. She tried to recover, acutely aware he was mischievously watching for her reaction. Before she could say anything, however, he had put his finger over her lips. "Hush, now. You need not decide at once, you shall have as long as you like. Shall I say something further to you . . . to sway your decision just a little?"

"Don't trouble." Had he or had he not proposed marriage to her?

He began to heap delicious bits of food—patés and jellies, fine slices of ham and mutton—on a plate for her, remarking casually at the same time, "I wish your mother might see you at this moment. She would say—" he presented her with the plate and fork—"as I do, that there never was a lovelier lady, that you are surely above my touch."

"But you have touched me," she said quietly.

He drew her away to a corner.

"Marsanne, darling, something *is* about to happen, and very soon . . . My task will be finished as soon as I deliver an important series of . . . of objects to certain parties in Paris. Then, if all goes as we hope—as we expect—I will be entirely free to ask you to be my wife."

"Lady Justin?" she asked, provocatively innocent.

Now that she was certain of his intentions, she would like to have shouted her answer before the entire party, but being certain, she also could afford to tease a bit in revenge for the doubt he'd made her suffer. She turned her fork, considered the lobster paté and said slowly, "Very well. I promise—"

"My darling . . ."

"—to think about it."

Though his eyes seemed to smile he took the plate out

of her hands and kissed her. The buzz of conversation around them slowed and gradually ceased. Appearing more in control of the situation than he felt, Philip returned the plate to her hands and suggested, "Try the mutton. It's local."

She burst out laughing, then remembering a matter that had haunted her for days, her mood abruptly changed as she asked, "Philip—*why* has mama never answered me? The only letter I've received is dated the morning after we left."

He looked around, waited until those nearest the corner had shifted away and resumed their own flirtations. In a carefully lowered voice he said, in French, to Marsanne, "You must know that your mother has been active with the Bonapartist clubs in Paris. We are expecting a very important event any day now. Sister Veronique is undoubtedly involved in it. So it would be extremely difficult for her to send letters to England. You see, don't you, my love?"

She started to object but he took hold of her wrists. "Marsanne, I will tell you something, but you must not reveal it to anyone . . . you understand? *Anyone!*"

She nodded, feeling terrified.

"Well, then, I hope to be back in France tomorrow night. Shortly after, I should be in Paris. I will see Sister Veronique at once and send someone back with a message to you."

"Thank you, Philip, you are so good, and when I think how I—"

"I love you, my darling, and I tell you when I think how a year ago I never imagined it possible I would love anyone . . . But never mind. What matters is now, and that when my task is finished I will come back and fetch you home to France . . ."

She looked at him. "I believe this 'task,' as you call it, whatever it may be, means more to you than even your love for me, isn't it so?"

He considered her thoughtfully. His reply was slow, not a facile, and false, compliment, and his eyes glowed with a warmth she'd never seen there before. "Had you asked me a month ago—the night we shared the coach out of Paris . . . and I tell you I desired you even then—"

"Did you? I would hardly have guessed it from your manner in the coach."

"I did." He smiled, but with that gentleness she found marvelously new, as if she had uncovered another side to him. "But now, these last few days . . . that awful hour when I wondered if Nicoletti would have murdered you before I could get there . . . I knew then that you meant more to me than even this business that had occupied my mind like a burning vengeance. And I say thank God for it. You've made me a very different man, my darling . . ."

"Well and good, and yet I shouldn't like you to change too much, sir. After all, I did fall in love with the original, that horrid man who studied me so coldly on the Calais coach."

"And when I think I have been trying to change only to oblige you!"

The musicians were tuning up now, and as he looked in the direction of the ballroom, he asked, "Shall we?"

"I shouldn't. Cousin Sylvie will say it is shockingly bad form for us to be seen as partners in an entirely different dance, so soon after the waltz."

"Shocking, indeed, but we are not English. We will not let their customs crush our French spirit."

She grinned. "Vive la France!" she cried, trying to wave her mirrored fan but dropping it as the plate nearly went the way of the fan. "Heavens," she whispered anxiously, "I must have drunk too much champagne."

"Nonsense!" He set the plate aside, took her arm and they returned to the ballroom.

As the evening wore on, Philip relinquished her to other partners but much to her satisfaction did not himself dance again, and she could see him, tall and trim, standing alone with hands clasped behind him.

It was near three in the morning when the dancing ended and the guests began to depart—mostly parents with eligible young daughters, but the parties broke away afterward and Marsanne, whose white silk slippers had been worn down until they appeared slightly ragged, stopped to say good night to Philip at the foot of the great staircase while her arm was being tugged by Amy, who kept whispering. "Do come, cousin. I must tell you how heavenly it was. He is a new man, my dear Roddy is. And a very good dancer, as I've always known, of course. Oh, do come! Aren't you tired?" She yawned elaborately.

It was maddening—Marsanne longed to be taken into Philip's arms before they separated for the night, and yet the moment Philip tried to draw her into the shadowy semicircle below the turn of the great staircase, one of the footmen carrying a candelabrum with candles flickering as he moved paused in the false notion that he pleased these two embracing lovers by illuminating their kiss.

"Damn!" Philip muttered, releasing her.

She touched his lips with her fingers, and he kissed them. She again marveled that such a man could love her, and with a wave to him followed Amy up the stairs. On the half-landing she heard someone call Philip's name and looked over the marble balustrade to see two of the condesa's friends join him in the corner, which was in shadows again, the footman having moved on.

Amy yawned widely. "Oh, cousin, I am so tired and so happy, I shall take a drop or two of laudanum and sleep until noon. I suggest you do the same. It will see you through many dreams of your dear Sir Philip."

Clotilde and Hattie Totter were also on hand as Marsanne assured her cousin she would do as she was advised. Meanwhile, seeing Clotilde with her golden curls crushed under a night cap threaded with pink velvet ribbons,

Marsanne remembered that Clotilde too had her romantic evening.

"How did you get on with Albert?" she wanted to know as Hattie helped her to undress and wash.

"The most delightful thing, mamselle! We are to be married in April—such a delightful month! And then we shall have our very own apartment in the Hall here. A bedchamber and a sweet parlor. A delightful room. And I am so, so . . ."

Marsanne hugged her. "I know. You are delighted. And so am I for you." She went back to stand while Hattie helped her remove her gown over her head. Then she took water from the carafe, started to pour it into the cut crystal glass but Hattie offered her the usual glass of mulled wine.

"How many times have I refused this?" Marsanne asked, smiling and accepting, as she went to the chest in the powder closet. Opening the half-empty vial of her cousin Sylvie's laudanum—she'd never used the stuff before—she carefully measured out two drops into the wine glass. The notion of even this slight amount made her faintly uneasy, but she realized that the extraordinary event she'd gone through and indeed anticipation of those to come could well bring her a sleepless night which she could ill afford. Her cousin Amy might not be the levelest of heads, but in this case she doubtless made good sense. She drank the wine and dismissed Hattie with thanks. The maid curtsied and left.

"How lovely you looked tonight, mamselle," Clotilde murmured sleepily. "Did you enjoy the wonderful supper they served in the dining salon?"

Marsanne smiled to herself. "I think I did. I don't quite remember. I was being kissed."

"Mamselle!"

"I was so excited I dropped my fan. And then I—Heavens!"

Clotilde sat up abruptly. "What is it, mamselle?"

"I dropped my fan and never recovered it. The fan grandmama gave me for my eighteenth birthday. Her very last present to me. The fan with mirrors. Oh, I wonder if it's still there."

She thought for a minute or two, then went to the door and looked out into the hall. Hattie Totter was gone. She didn't want to disturb Clotilde, already in bed and nearly asleep. Besides, no one else would know where it had dropped. There was a side table. A chair. The fan must have dropped between the chair and the walnut table.

Marsanne took her robe, tied the green velvet ribbons around her waist and stepped into her white silk evening slippers.

"Mamselle, you aren't going belowstairs this time of night!"

"I'll be back immediately. I'll snuff these lights and take the bed-candle."

No one was about as Marsanne crossed the long hall to the deserted dining salon. She slipped into the room, made her way between abandoned small tables, followed the length of the baronial dining table itself until she reached the wall of the music room with the door ajar nearby.

As she'd suspected, her fan had fallen between the chair and side table and now lay against the wall. She yawned as the laudanum drops began to take effect and knelt and fumbled along the floor until her fingers reached the fan. One of the mirrored panels was broken, and she clasped the delicate fan to her bosom, remembering well the happy day the old vicomtesse had given it to her.

A voice rang clearly from the music room—the Condesa Seaforde: ". . . and that should make it at something about six million in the worth of these jewels . . ."

Marsanne forced her sleepy mind to a sharp awareness. The next voice she recognized as that of her chubby friend the Honorable George Baldridge.

"If His Majesty should land prematurely Jean-Philippe

here must be permitted to use these jewels to bribe the Emperor's way through France."

Marsanne raised her head, listened breathlessly. The next voice she knew to be that of her Philip: "Very few bribes, condesa . . . gentlemen. The Emperor is firm on one thing. He must be genuinely supported by the people's wish. He will not allow himself to be imposed upon them as Louis the Eighteenth was last year."

Marsanne moved silently nearer to the doorway between the deserted dining salon and music room and listened.

"Now, see here, Justin, we've decided to trust you with the gems for the purpose of restoring the Emperor. Is that what gives you these fine crotchets?"

Philip explained quietly, "We count upon—no, we believe that the people will rise to support the Emperor. If they do not, all the bribes in the world will be ineffective. Our intention with those jewels and those we have collected for the Cause elsewhere is to use them for the reestablishment of a legitimate government in France, a government headed by the Emperor, the Peers, and a Chamber of Deputies chosen by the people's will. Otherwise we'll have what the Allies foisted on us, the remnant of a discredited family."

Marsanne gasped. This was dangerous treason against the present government that indeed had been forced upon the French by the Russians, Austrians and British. It further chilled her to realize that her mother too had this dangerous if splendid dream of a government supported by the people rather than by the foreign powers. She herself had worn a violet gown and professed a Bonapartist sympathy, but she'd not felt nor shown this kind of burning faith . . . Perhaps she was of the wrong generation, or simply too practical.

All the same she was intensely proud of the man she loved whose "task," it turned out, involved him in nothing less than the most dangerous and quixotic adventure she could dream of. And her mother. Did this explain the long period that had gone by without a word from Sister Veronique? Whatever Philip's dangerous politics and her worry over his safety, she was relieved that he would at least have an opportunity to learn of her mother's whereabouts.

There was more discussion about the plans of the conspirators, but Marsanne could scarcely keep her eyes open and cursed those two drops of laudanum, wanting very much to find out just how dangerous Philip's role in this adventure might be.

He was saying now, "I have every name on the statements, have I not? Well, I am more than ever anxious to complete my task as soon as possible."

The Honorable George Baldridge laughed. "Ay. No mistake. Had merely to watch you whirl about the ballroom with Miss Marsanne in your arms tonight. Lucky devil! Are congratulations in order?"

"Very much, thank you. The moment His Majesty returns to the Tuileries, I am free. You will never know, condesa, and you, messieurs, what a change mademoiselle has made in this misanthrope you see before you."

Marsanne stopped yawning, delighted by his words. She got to her feet, swayed sleepily and clutched at the side table. She must get out of here. By holding on to the various pieces of furniture in the room she moved toward the double doors, swearing that never again, no matter the occasion, would she take a drop of laudanum.

One step. Another. One step. Another. By the time she reached the staircase, there was a terrible buzzing in her head. She put her hand up, rubbed her forehead and heard the fan drop with the tinkle of another mirror broken off the sticks. She leaned against the balustrade, trying to decide whether she wanted to laugh at the perverseness of the situation, or cry.

Trying to control the noise in her head, she stopped,

picked up the fan and then climbed the rest of the steps to the half-landing.

Then she collapsed. For the few minutes she remained conscious she thought, it *cannot* have been only two laudanum drops . . . there must be another Binet agent . . . and in this very house . . .

She fumbled for the balustrade. The candlestick rolled down the steps and flickered out. Marsanne fell into a deep sleep.

Chapter Twenty

She had never in her life been so maltreated. Shaken, slapped, her head raised and then gently set back against something warm and solid—a man's shoulder?—and worst of all, forced to swallow vile salted water and loathesome oily substances that made her stomach revolt, she felt the cruelest thing these tormentors did was to let her alive. How much better to sleep peacefully.

It was curiosity and deep-seated courage that finally made her gather her wits together and realize that some-one of considerable strength was holding her up, helping her to walk, keeping her alive.

She heard herself mutter indignant complaints and opened her eyes. The light of a sunny morning struck at her defenseless eyes and she closed them quickly, insisting "Why will you not let me sleep when I wish to?"

"That's my good girl!" someone announced cheerfully. She was certain it was Philip's voice. Confused, she opened her eyes again with great care and frowned up at him.

"Oh! It's you, and in my bedroom, this is dreadfully improper, I must . . ."

He laughed and remarked to someone beyond her vision, "She is recovering. She insists on chattering." He kissed the top of Marsanne's tousled head. "Keep chattering, darling. Chatter and take another step. And another. Now, as you were saying?"

Clotilde's happy giggle attracted Marsanne as the girl rattled away in French, "Monsieur found you on the stair landing last night when he and some friends left the ball at a late hour. It was dreadful. We thought you were dead. Lady Lesgate says he saved your life."

"Well, he very nearly ended it in the process. I always suspected he was a villain!" She just managed a smile as she said it, and then with an effort looked over his arm and around at the bedchamber she shared with Clotilde. Amy, dressed for the morning, sat on the edge of Marsanne's bed, kicking her feet nervously. Seeing her cousin glance at her with a smile, Amy jumped up and started to her.

"You are yourself again. Oh, cousin, we were so worried! If I'd known you never took laudanum I assure you I would never have suggested it. Mama is furious with me. If you died, she said, it would all be my fault. But dearest, I had no notion you would take a whole vial of the drops . . ."

Philip got between them and, with some firmness cautioned Amy not to excite Marsanne too much: "Easy does it, ma'am. How do you go on now, my darling?"

"Very well. Indeed, I do! But Philip—"

There were steps out in the hall and Cousin Sylvie came in, fluttering almost as much as her daughter.

"*Chérie, chérie,* thank God you are yourself again! I'll never forgive myself. I should have warned you that laudanum is not to be treated as—as a mere tisane."

"But I didn't, Cousin Sylvie. I was most careful."

Sylvie shrugged and smiled, as one does to soothe a

child. "That surgeon from Dover is still in the house. Poor man, up all night. At all events, I may now send him on his way?"

Philip looked into Marsanne's eyes, liked what he saw there and agreed, "Yes, yes, I think she will do very well now."

Marsanne put in, "I am feeling more myself. But I mustn't be seen like this. Does everyone know Philip was here? And me in my gown and—and—"

"Really, Marsanne," her cousin reminded her with French practicality, "Sir Philip has explained that as soon as he returns from a business trip to France you are to be married. I am persuaded that no one would think the less of you because your betrothed saved your life while you were in your night-rail. Then, too, we need not tell anyone."

"Exactly so, madame," Philip assured her, in the best of spirits in spite of his long night's vigil.

His good spirits were contagious, and Cousin Sylvie's relief was compounded by her pleasure in the romance between her cousin and their distinguished neighbor. Hours later, Marsanne finally sent Philip home to get some sleep before he met with his political friends, and Cousin Sylvie began to discuss her future.

"Such a handsome man! But, *chérie,* you are quite certain you will be happy married to one so much older than you?"

Marsanne, her mind still tired and a little hazy, popped out unthinkingly with, "I see nothing aged about a man of thirty-six."

Sylvie appeared stupefied but recovered valiantly. "Forgive me, I thought—I suppose someone must have told me that he was nearly thirty when he went to the Swiss Cantons before that interminable war with France."

Unable to avoid this fact, Marsanne lied with great facility. "Ridiculous! He was a mere youth. And I would marry him if he were eighty!"

"But are you certain your dear mama will approve of Sir Philip, an Englishman?"

Marsanne smiled at a memory. "Oh, yes. I know now she intended it from the moment we said goodbye that day in Paris." The happy memory faded as she picked at the coverlet under her fingertips. "Cousin, I am so worried! What can have happened to her?"

Which brought Sylvie, Amy and Clotilde to a united effort at cheering her, but when she was alone at last and could rest without the persistent attentions of well-meaning friends, she dreamed of Sister Veronique and by degrees her dream gathered in Philip Justin so that when she awoke in the evening and found him sitting on her bed, holding one of her hands in his, it seemed a competely natural part of her dream.

"Mama will like you."

"She does like me," he assured her, grinning at her.

"Heavens! What conceit!" But she could not help laughing. What he'd said was, after all, so entirely true. Then her frayed nerves betrayed her and she whispered, "Philip, please tell me why I have heard nothing from Mama."

He did not brush aside her concern, instead promised her, "I will leave for France tomorrow night, and I give you my solemn word I will find her."

She was looking directly into his eyes as he went on, "Marsanne, I want you to believe something. Of all the millions living upon this planet, I care for very few human beings. You are first, and Sister Veronique is second. The others are—" He considered and shrugged. "I have political loyalties I regarded as the greatest in my life. They took me from starvation in the streets after the Revolution. They gave my poor despised and blood-drenched country a pride and dignity that we all could share. A government, a code of laws. Public works. Hospitals decently run. We had our own representation in the Chambers of Deputies and Peers that he created. We never had that before. You grew up under that government."

Her fingers fluttered nervously in his grasp. "Yes, but you see, I can't care about governments, or even about Napoleon who gave us those things. It's my mother I care about."

"And now you and Sister Veronique have come between me and those old loyalties." He leaned forward and kissed her pallid lips, his mouth lingering warmly, giving her enormous comfort. When he moved back he tapped her hand gently. "So rest, my darling. I mean to find Sister Veronique, even if the heavens fall."

The housekeeper Mrs. Grover bustled in with Clotilde, ordering Philip, "Out now, sir, begging your pardon. But this young lady needs her rest. Such a foolish business, taking laudanum! However! You, Miss Clotilde! Do you have the water for Miss Marsanne's washing? Now, Sir Philip, that'll be all for you tonight."

It was disappointing to have to say good night in front of both Mrs. Grover and Clotilde, but when Philip kissed her again, lingering long enough to earn another scolding from Mrs. Grover, and then waved a good night to her from the doorway, she felt so comforted she was able to sleep almost at once.

She slept straight through the night and by mid-morning was insisting she had never felt stronger and must be allowed to get up, dress and go wherever she liked.

With a rustle of silk Cousin Sylvie moved across the room, patted Marsanne's hand and said in a heartening voice, "Dear girl! When you are feeling more the thing you must come down and meet our new guest—your new guest, as a matter of fact."

Marsanne sat up excitedly. *"Mama* has come!"

"No, but a friend of hers. The lawyer she hired to obtain your inheritance. Maître Louis Reynaud arrived this morning. He came over last evening on the night packet.

And he tells me he carries the king's own seal upon the papers you need."

Amy, who had rushed in to celebrate the news, laughed and clapped her hands delightedly. "Think of it, cousin. You are as rich as Croesus—whoever he was."

Marsanne changed the subject quickly. "I must talk to Maître Reynaud immediately. He has seen Mama. He can tell me how she is, why she hasn't written . . . I will dress and go down to meet him. Clotilde, will you ring for Hattie Totter?"

Her cousins started to leave the room. Then, as Clotilde touched the velvet bell-pull to summon Hattie Totter, Sylvie told Marsanne, "Sir Philip asked me to get your promise. You will never again take that drug. My dear child, what possessed you to take so much?"

"But I didn't!" She heard her voice raised in anger, and glanced over to see if Clotilde were paying attention and would spread the word that her poor mistress was now hysterical. Clotilde, however, was daydreaming and had paid no attention to them.

Sylvie smiled in relief at the girl's restored health and said to placate her: "Very well, just as you say. Only you must promise me never to take even one drop again."

That was easy enough to promise and she did so. She could not forget yesterday's stomachache, the headache, and she certainly would never care to endure the fear again. She added anxiously, "Did Philip say he would see me again before he leaves for France?"

"You could not keep him away if you tried. He will visit you this evening before he sails, though I told him you might be too tired."

"Cousin!"

"But," she added mischievously, "he seemed very set upon it. One would think he was off on a life-and-death mission!"

Marsanne only nodded and smiled weakly. But other

thoughts persisted . . . *Only two drops to cause all this commotion?* It was inexplicable. . . Too much to be done now, though. She would see Maître Louis Reynaud, who must have just come from her mother. It had certainly taken him a very long time, it had been more than three weeks since Sister Veronique wrote that first note saying she expected Maître Reynaud the next day.

Clotilde finally reported that Hattie Totter did not seem to be anywhere available. The young woman, Clotilde added, had sat up all of the previous two nights, waiting to be called in case she was needed to attend Marsanne. Then Maître Reynaud's arrival on top of Marsanne's illness had upset the household, and no one knew quite what to expect, so Marsanne dressed herself. She set about wearing a plain gown and exercising as much as possible. Her stomach muscles still felt sore—as if someone had stomped on them.

In a short time, however, she was ready to go down and see the French lawyer. She found a tall, thin, graying man in the green salon with Cousin Sylvie. He arose and bowed stiffly as Marsanne entered but looked to Sylvie for an introduction.

"Marsanne, *chérie,* your dear mother's highly competent legal adviser is here with your long-awaited deeds and papers to the Vaudraye estates. You must be very kind to him. He and his papers have made you a rich young lady."

"It is not solely my work, Your Ladyship. The seal of His Majesty King Louis has some weight, I daresay," and he brought Marsanne's hand to his lips.

While Marsanne was thanking the lawyer, whose cold eyes, she decided, must be a mark of his profession, Sylvie rambled on . . . "Dear King Louis! He was my friend, you know, when he was here in exile. But now I begin to think I should have also befriended that new exile, the Emperor Napoleon. Marsanne, this gentleman tells me there is great unrest in France, particularly from the army and the lower classes. They want their beloved Bonaparte back again. And I do like to be in good standing with all parties. One never knows, don't you agree?, when such friendships will be useful . . . as in the case of King Louis. Poor man. How fat he has grown to be . . . !"

Marsanne smiled politely, thinking how the news from France would suit Philip. "Really? There is unrest over the Bourbon king?" Her mood changed as she looked at the lawyer. "Monsieur, I am exceedingly anxious. When you saw my mother in Paris, was she well? I assume you saw her at the hospital. The Hôtel-Dieu."

The lawyer's grave eyes regarded hers for a moment, then he seemed to recall. "You ask about Sister Veronique, I take it. Yes, she was quite well."

Marsanne breathed more freely. "And she is safe then?"

His eyebrows faintly raised. "But of course, mademoiselle. Why should she not be?"

"I didn't know," Marsanne added quickly. "It's just been so very long since I've heard from her. I can't understand why she has never written."

Seeing that the lawyer had no more news of Veronique, Cousin Sylvie changed the subject, insisting that the lawyer should remain the night at Lesgate Hall before going on to conduct his other business with the French Embassy in London.

Beginning to tire after her recent ordeal, Marsanne watched sleepily as the lawyer was shown to his room by Hattie Totter, who had now arrived on the scene, stifling a yawn herself but apparently efficient as ever.

Marsanne spent the rest of the day either lying down on her bed or getting up to walk about and ask herself why, if her mother was truly well and had seen Maître Louis Reynaud only a day or two previously, she had not written . . . She must have received Marsanne's own notes asking what had happened—pleading for some word of reassurance from her. . .

Nor were Marsanne's spirits raised when she found that during one of her naps Philip had called to find out how she was, and had been advised not to disturb her.

Shortly after dinner that afternoon Marsanne returned to her room to change for the evening's social activities— it was Lady Lesgate's belief that any visitor fortunate enough to be permitted to sleep at Lesgate Hall must expect entertainment and other guests.

By the time Amy came to fetch her, Marsanne was feeling quite herself and could agree heartily with Amy's sudden turn to the rightabout in praising all the splendid qualities of Roderick Fortenham. She seemed to have totally forgotten René Nicoletti, who by now must have reached Calais, and even met with the Binet stepfather. . .

As the two cousins left Marsanne's room they met Maître Reynaud in shirtsleeves advising Hattie Totter about his needs, including the hour when he would require the warming pan applied to his bed. Even the lawyer, Marsanne thought, suppressing a smile.

Amy murmured to her, "He doesn't much look as though he might wish to dance, which is a blessing, I must say, for I am still tired. After your experience I shall be frightened to take even my usual drop or two of laudanum." She looked at Marsanne curiously. "Truly, cousin, had you no notion that half a vial of laudanum could kill you?"

Marsanne was anxious to be understood and refrained from losing her temper. "But I did not take more than two drops. I swear it. I took out the vial—it was half empty, and I carefully counted two drops into the glass."

"Impossible! Your maid said the vial was full when she saw it in the powdering closet."

Marsanne stopped abruptly. "Who told you that?"

Bewildered, Amy said, "Clotilde herself, of course. Or was it the new girl?"

Marsanne went back into the bedchamber so fast the door banged back and forth. She called to Clotilde, who had just tied an enchanting blue ribbon through her curls.

"Yes, mamselle?"

"Did you tell my cousins and the others last night that the vial of laudanum was full when I went to pour the drops?"

Clotilde blinked innocently. "Yes, mamselle."

"Why?" Marsanne could not believe the cold clipped sound of her own voice.

"But—but—was it not true?"

"How did you know it was full? You couldn't have seen the vial. I was standing in the doorway of the powdering closet across the room. And the vial of laudanum was in my hand. Clotilde, you could not have seen whether it was full or empty."

Clotilde looked and sounded ready to cry. "I never said I saw it. I never said that. It was Hattie Totter who saw it. During the night she told me that mamselle must have taken half the vial. By mistake."

Marsanne snapped, "Then she is wrong. It was only half full when I took the two drops."

Amy had now arrived and, overhearing them, looked startled. "But if you only used two drops, how did . . . ?"

"How did the rest get into my wine when I only put two drops there? Yes, that certainly is the question, and I am beginning to think I have an idea of the answer."

Without explaining further, Marsanne hurried out of the room and meeting one of the maids in the hall, sent her for Mrs. Grover, the housekeeper. Amy followed in confusion. "What will Mrs. Grover know?"

"How Hattie Totter came to be hired at the Hall."

A male voice startled both girls as the French lawyer emerged from his bedchamber correctly attired for the evening. "Pardon, mesdemoiselles. Do I understand that one of you has had an accident?"

"I did, night before last," Marsanne spoke up.

"I see."

Marsanne realized now as he stepped into the candlelight from her room that he had been about to speak with her privately but was prevented by her cousin's presence and the conversation between the young women. He waited for Amy to start downstairs, then turned to Marsanne, who told him she was waiting to speak with the housekeeper.

He hesitated, but once Amy had gone he said in his stiff way, "I believe I have not spoken to you as I should. I thought it was for the best. You are young. Your mother knows very well what she is about, and you can do nothing here in England."

She started anxiously. "What do you mean?"

Maître Reynaud retained his careful, legal demeanor, but she saw that he was uncertain, obviously unused to emotional problems.

"I am expected downstairs. I shall go down and speak with you later when you have done with the housekeeper. I should not trouble you at this time, when you are still a trifle unwell, I daresay."

He had already started away when she called to him frantically and ran after him. "No! Please tell me. What do you know of my mother? Something has happened. You must tell me!"

She felt even more terrified when he turned back, took her hands in his dry stiff fingers and cleared his throat before trying to put her off with: "It was nothing, really. You are not well, and I have disturbed you. I beg your pardon, mademoiselle. It was simply that I . . . Frankly, I am a mere man of papers. Legalities. I do not deal in the life and death of—that is—in the lives of human beings. Only their wealth, their land and papers . . ."

"Tell me!"

Looking thoroughly ill at ease he tried another tack to soothe her. "You are assured that Sister Veronique is innocent of any wrongdoing? She has committed no crime?"

"Of course. Can you imagine my mother, Sister Veronique, hurting anyone? She has saved hundreds of lives."

"Then there is nothing of which the government can find her guilty. So you need have no concern over her arrest."

Staring at him and trying to concentrate on the full horor of his disclosure—he could not understand it if he knew nothing of her mother's politics—Marsanne felt the room and the lawyer's gray face spin around before she once again got hold of herself and with an enormous effort asked calmly, "Did you see her arrested? How long ago?"

"Due to the riots I have had some difficulty in reaching the coast. Then, too, there was the problem in Paris over receiving my passport papers. But I assume your mother will have been released long since."

"How long since? When was she arrested?"

"The very day I spoke with her in mid-February. But of course, she is free by this time."

"Oh, God! Almost a month! She might have been—" She could not say it aloud—*she might have been executed by now.*

"But, mademoiselle, do not agitate yourself so. King Louis is not an ogre. He does not punish Sisters of Charity for no cause. And you say yourself that Sister Veronique has committed no crime."

"No crime to concern the Prefect of the Seine. But a political crime. My mother is an active Bonapartist sympathizer. You must understand now . . ."

"Ah! That puts a different face on it. Still, who would have betrayed such a saintly woman?"

Marsanne had been thinking as calmly and sensibly as she could. "That Binet family, in Martinique. They would hate her. And the Binet child's stepfather has been in France. He even shot at me on the quai near the Pont Neuf. I make no doubt he or one of his agents is responsible for my poisoning last night."

"Mon Dieu! What have I come into? Such savagery, it is unbelievable." He looked startled as well he might, but after a little thought he added in his dry fashion, "All the same something certainly can be done for your mother. I am not without connections in the king's councils. I can say quite honestly that the duc d'Angouleme himself owes me a favor. As you know, his wife is the late Queen Marie Antoinette's daughter. I might write a strongly worded letter which some acquaintance of yours might deliver—"

"Acquaintance! I shall go myself of course . . . and this very night."

He began by trying to dissuade her, but while he was failing at this she proposed something even more to the point. "You must return with me, Maître Reynaud. With your influence you could save my mother. But not by a letter which might never reach the duc. Please, monsieur . . . Please, for her sake."

She thought he was beginning to soften, though it was difficult to tell. This lawyer was not a very demonstrative man. Finally he said, "I have been asked to assist in obtaining an estate for an emigré connected with the French Embassy in London. There was no date set, however. Another week? I daresay . . . After all, my profit in your estate has been a fair one." His thin lips parted with what seemed his version of a smile. "I myself proposed my own share. Still, my time is valuable . . ."

Eagerly she seized upon his hint. "But of course you must be repaid for your trouble. You may propose whatever you think appropriate while we are on our way. Tonight!"

It occurred to her even as she spoke that she might be journeying to France tonight with Philip. But once they reached Calais each would have to go his own way. Philip and his Bonapartist "task" represented every danger to Sister Veronique. Marsanne, with Reynaud's help, would need to try to prove Veronique innocent of Bonapartist sympathies. There must be no connection with Philip and the Bonapartist clubs of Paris.

"All the same," she said aloud, continuing her thought, "I must tell him what we plan, what we must do."

"Who is this that you must tell?" Maître Reynaud asked.

"The gentleman I am to marry. His estate runs beyond the Lesgate Deer Park."

The lawyer took out his huge waistcoat watch and examined its face. "There will be very little time if you insist on the night packet."

"But it will take only a few minutes to reach Sir Philip's house. Half an hour at the most if we take the downs to the house. He is also leaving tonight for France. We can share his carriage to Dover."

He had some preliminary, fussy objections to this, but he must have recognized in her a stubborn adversary and soon agreed with a thoughtful nod.

She went back to Clotilde, who was mighty curious about her long and excited conversation with Maître Reynaud. When she explained to Clotilde what she must do the girl's shocked protests warned her of how it would also be when she explained her hurried departure to Cousin Sylvie.

"But, mamselle, you cannot make such a journey without a female companion. It would be most improper!"

"I am not only going, but I am going within the hour. I will make part of the journey with Sir Philip. If he permits me to return to Paris in the company of an old gentleman like Monsieur Reynaud then surely Cousin Sylvie can have no objections. He can save Mama. Think of it! Three weeks since she was arrested. Anything might happen to her. I quite literally haven't a minute to lose."

"What is this? Another piece of misfortune?" Lady Lesgate asked, having come up to announce in despair that the maid Hattie Totter had apparently gone off, taking all her clothing with her.

Which seemed solid proof to Marsanne that the woman had indeed tried to poison her and now knew herself to be found out. "It was she who poisoned me last night," Marsanne told them. "She is working for that Binet family —my enemies."

"She must be mad! I'll send guards to look for her and will notify General Winters immediately . . . *Marsanne,* what are you doing?"

The matter was explained to Sylvie while Marsanne hastily packed a portmanteau, and she was still arguing against the entire notion when Marsanne fastened her case, threw her travel-cloak and hood around her and kissed a sobbing Clotilde. She embraced her cousins as she started down the stairs.

"If we are lucky, cousin," she called over her shoulder, "Mama and I and my husband will all come to visit you next time."

"I hope Sir Philip will talk some sense to you tonight, *chérie.* He and this good Maître Reynaud can save dear Veronique and accomplish everything perfectly well without you."

"I conscientiously believe that is so, madame," the lawyer agreed. "But as mademoiselle seems so distraught we must leave persuasion to her betrothed."

Marsanne silently thanked him for making no more trouble. As they stepped out onto a terrace swept by Channel winds, Marsanne turned, wondering when she would see her cousins again. She again hugged Amy, who told her, "I know you will save dear Sister Veronique, and meanwhile be assured we'll attend to that awful Hattie Totter."

"God be with you, *chérie,*" Cousin Sylvie called.

The wind blew their voices away as Marsanne hurried over the downs, the lawyer trailing with difficulty behind her. "A moment, if you please, mademoiselle. If you please . . ." He was carrying her portmanteau, which was not so heavy but very awkward.

She apologized and slowed to a rapid stride. "It's only that I am so anxious." She saw that he was headed a trifle southeast—toward the marshes—and called his attention to it. She added, more to herself, "And not too far from here I was nearly murdered by Nicoletti—"

He stopped. "Who is this Nicoletti?"

"One of the Binet assassins. But he has scuttled back to France. You need not be afraid of Nicoletti."

"I am not afraid, mademoiselle, I am merely cautious."

The wind had gone down and the fog began to gather in little puffs so that she had to remind him again not to venture too far out onto the marshes. "Unless you mean to walk to France." Suspecting he might still be afraid of roving assassins, she added, "Men like Nicoletti are not the real threat, you know. It is their employers."

There was surprising force in his crisp response. "I find the René Nicolettis of the world despicable. They hire out to kill for a few francs and not content with being hired assassins, they prove to be cowards as well and run away. Despicable!"

It was like the splash of boiling water upon her flesh. In spite of the fog and the chill of the night, her entire body felt flushed from the shock of his words. She hoped to God he had not noticed what he'd said, but in her panic she took several moments to answer him—all the while a question hammering in her brain, over and over:

Not five minutes ago he had asked who "Nicoletti" was. How then did he know the first name?

She said finally, "We turn to the south here, to avoid the estuary and the marshes."

For a moment there was no answer. Then his voice, dry and calm as ever.

"What a pity your ears are so sharp! That was a stupid blunder of mine, was it not, mademoiselle?"

Chapter Twenty-One

She thought he probably did not plan to kill her here. It was too near Philip's grounds. He must have intended to get her closer to the water and then drown her—which would explain his persistent effort to urge her toward the marshes and one of the Channel's small estuaries. Playing to this thought and the last-ditch hope that she could somehow put him off-guard and run for help, she murmured in a shaken, tearful voice, "I've no idea what you mean . . . please, nothing matters now except to save my mother . . . in simple justice, sir, *please* . . ."

"Do you think I am a fool? The new government betrayed my stepson's rights. To overlook us entirely for a granddaughter of the old regime! Was *that* justice?"

"You say you are not a fool, and I believe you. Then you would not hurt me now with help just over the rise," she lied.

"Not quite so near, mademoiselle. You wished to go to France. Very well. I oblige. This way, if you please."

A dagger's sharp point cut through her clothing to a spot between her ribs, and he urged her on with it. He had discarded her portmanteau, and she had little doubt he would use the dagger if necessary. "No, no, to the east, mademoiselle, toward that sloop in the estuary just on the edge of the marsh."

"I can't see it." She started in pain at a jab from the dagger's point.

"Through the fog there. You may see the lantern-light at the mast now."

She saw something else as well. The storm-lantern was shuttered on three sides, but in its light Marsanne could make out the profile of a seaman in blue headscarf, loose pantaloons and short jacket. She recognized the smuggler, Nate Tibbetts, just as Reynaud called out to him.

"Ahoy!"

Nate turned and grinned in the lantern-light, the scar across his nose casting a faint shadow over half his face. Marsanne slowed her steps as her feet began to sink into spongy ground where the marshes spread inland from the sea. Her companion took her arm in his free hand and supported her over a watery pothole. Since he'd not let her drown as he well might have, she decided to try to develop a spark of communication between them.

"Monsieur, you were exceedingly clever. What have you done with the real Maître Reynaud?"

He caught his foot in a bit of muddy furze that had blown off the downs. For a breathtaking instant she thought she would escape, but he gave her arm a wrench that nearly pulled it from its socket. He answered with a mirthless laugh, "In the eyes of the French courts I am Maître Reynaud. The unfortunate old fellow was a misanthrope with few friends and fewer relations. He had retired. Ideal for my purposes. Few people in the world would know him well enough at this late date to expose me."

"Certainly Mama would never have known. And his

reputation worked well for you. How long ago did he . . . disappear?"

"Let us say I have been Maître Reynaud, come out of retirement to practice the law, just since old Joseph Binet died. A pity, I assure you, mademoiselle, that all this should be necessary. I am not by nature a violent man."

Heaven defend the world if you were, she thought bitterly. She remarked in her forced conversational tones, "Your stepson's wealth really meant so much to you?"

"Yes, indeed, to *me*. Why else would I marry a widow with her own brat?"

"I see . . . of course, very sensible." They had reached what appeared to be a floating dock of rotten boards and she stepped out in a gingerly way, all the time wondering if the estuary water was deep enough here for her to plunge in. It seemed obvious that she was to be taken out to sea . . . No doubt Maître Reynaud would express shock and horror over her unfortunate accident. "Washed overboard" was not an uncommon fate.

But, surely, if there had been no fog Philip's house could be seen from here. Was it possible that one of the servants in that house, or one of his free-trading friends might notice the mastlight? Still, much good that would do . . . dozens of boats sailed in and out of these waters every week—and more often by night.

All the same when Reynaud shoved her toward Nate Tibbetts she remembered that house on the bluff above and proceeded to scream as she fought to be out of his arms, kicking hard as she could and raking her nails down the smuggler's cheek. Nate's hard slap caught her across the chin and throat as she was dumped unceremoniously into the boat, her hands protecting her head but the rest of her body taking the fall. Nothing, however, silenced her. Shrieks that threatened to tear her lungs were her last resort. Not even a kick from Nate's wet boot could silence her.

Through the noise she could hear Reynaud complaining in French, "Hurry, hurry! I see a light there at the head of the estuary. The devil! Is it moving this way? Can't you keep her quiet?"

Marsanne drew herself up, fighting, as Nate's big hand covered her mouth, pressing his fingers and thumb into her flesh. She got out one more cry before her furious efforts were muffled. A coil of rope dropped across her legs. She felt the little boat move out from the ancient wharf.

Arguments now broke out between her two captors, but the Frenchman recovered first. "Quiet! We are a pair of wool traders, where's the bale you brought with you?" He was drawing off his cravat, and now as the smuggler removed his hand from Marsanne's mouth he bound the cravat tightly between her teeth and tied it behind her head.

Trying at the same time to untie the cravat, Marsanne could see very little except the engulfing fog, but she did not miss the anxiety in Nate Tibbetts' voice. "It's headed this way, Frenchie. Best be ready. Looks like three of 'em. Should we shoot?"

"Let them think we are unarmed. Wait until they put by their weapons. Is your pistol ready?"

"Ay. And you?" To Marsanne's relief he took his fingers off her ankle and felt for the pistol at his belt.

"Reynaud" whispered to Tibbetts, "Do you recognize them?"

The lapping of water came closer. Marsanne tried to raise her head again and work at the knot in the cravat but her bruised fingers were numb. She did manage, though, to make out the fore-and-aft rigging of the other boat as it approached, moving slowly between narrow marshy banks. The attention of her captors was so closely fixed on the oncoming enemy that neither noticed the creaking of the wooden planks on the small pier behind them.

"Here, what's this, lads?" Nate called out, his forced-hearty voice floating eerily through the fog. "Give 'way there."

"I've the way, as you may see," came the reply. "Is it Nate Tibbetts, I'm thinking?"

Marsanne's heart thumped with excitement. The voice sounded very like Old Thaddeus, Philip's freetrading friend.

Nate took out his pistol, trying to conceal the shining barrel with his hand. "Ay, friend Thaddeus. We'll take the outer tack. Stand, ho."

"Sorry, Nate. You're needed tonight for a haul. We'll be heading out on the tide."

As the boats drew up port to portside like floating ghosts, Nate glanced at "Reynaud," then called out, "I've my hands full, I need help. How many are you?"

"Me and the Dutchman de Hooven. Give him your hand. Lower sails. It's back to the dock till we get the master aboard."

As an ugly, powerful-looking man beside Thaddeus stood forward and appeared about to leap into the waist of the sloop, Marsanne caught the flash of "Reynaud's" pistol and quickly reached out to push him off balance. She did not succeed but the pistol's aim went wide, its shot followed the next instant by another that sounded like an explosion . . . from *behind* Marsanne.

She could not imagine what had happened. She tried to raise herself but fell back, watching "Reynaud" either plunge or fall overboard into the dark, choppy waters. In full panic Nate dropped his pistol and cowered away from the Dutchman, who battered him in the stomach and then paid no more attention to the groaning man.

As the boat nudged back beside the dock Marsanne tried once more to get to her feet and heard Thaddeus cry in astonishment, "It's her! It's the master's Frenchie. Don't you worry now, miss. All's well . . ."

As she tugged at the cloth still cutting into her mouth she heard Thaddeus calling out, "Master Philip, they were a-carrying off your mam'selle . . ."

The boards of the dock creaked under running feet, and just as Philip reached her the giant Dutchman untied the cravat at the nape of her neck. Her mouth was dry as bone and her tongue felt paralyzed, so that in spite of herself she groaned when Philip lifted her out of the waist of the boat and pulled her to him. He was holding her so tightly she could barely get her breath—a condition she was not about to complain of now.

Philip looked down at her, badly shaken. "Two nights ago it was poison. Tonight—abduction. My poor darling, what will you get into next, I wonder?" Over her head he said to Thaddeus, "Who was the fellow I shot, the one who went over the side? He was about to send a ball through you?"

Thaddeus, who had brought in his own craft, now hauled in the lines on the sloop while Nate Tibbetts hugged his battered stomach. Realizing that no one else was in a condition to enlighten Philip, Marsanne told him in a hoarse voice, "He is the Binet stepfather, what if he should escape . . . ?"

Philip immediately instructed Thaddeus and the Dutchman to turn the lantern on the estuary waters, after which the Dutchman took off all but his breeches and dove into the murky water while Philip removed his voluminous travel cape and wrapped it around Marsanne.

But she protested, "Please don't delay, Philip. They can look for him, make certain he is dead. I *must* get to France tonight . . ."

"What? After all you've been through? I think not!"

"I must. Mama has been arrested as a Bonapartist agent. Reynaud may have lied but I don't think so. It's all that could possibly explain her not writing to me all these weeks. I simply can't stay here. In Paris I can surely help her in some way . . ."

"I'll find her somehow," he assured her, "but you need rest, and I'll take no nonsense about that."

"Look at me in the lantern light, dearest, and you will find I am less fragile than you thought. Now then, while you look for Reynaud I'll go to your house and make myself presentable for the voyage. And, Philip, if you refuse to take me, I'll make the journey myself."

He squeezed her so tightly she cried out. "You will *not* go alone. In fact you are not going to be alone again." He called to the man in the water, "Dutch, you and Thaddeus keep looking for the fellow. We'll sail on the tide as planned. And Thad—do as you like about our friend Nate here."

"How did you know we were out here?" she asked, trying to put out of her mind the likely fate of Nate Tibbetts.

"Easily. You have, thank God, a most penetrating scream, and I was also watching at a window for Thaddeus and the ship."

By this time they had reached the Tudor house. They entered through the big medieval kitchen, where the candlelight revealed Philip in the outfit he customarily wore when working with his smuggler friends. He saw her stare and told her, "You needn't look so disapproving, my love. You are about to become a freetrader yourself."

She was then taken through the lower floor to his pleasant, masculine bookroom, which she was surprised to discover played a role in the smuggling forays—she noted various pirate-looking garments about, some of which appeared to be made for a slim, very young man. Watching her pick it up and inspect it, Philip explained, "Thaddeus' grandson. He sometimes sails with us."

He left her to change while he went about the house, making last-minute arrangements for the long journey. When he returned with the red headscarf concealing most of his white hair, he found Marsanne looking very "ship-shape," as he announced with some pride.

He took her by the shoulders, touched her forehead with his lips and confessed, "This is the first time I've kissed a cabin boy." Then, having summoned his stableman to stay with her, he ordered Marsanne to wait on the bluff outside the house until he and his crew located the body of the unlamented "Maître Reynaud" . . . She knew she would never believe he was dead until his body was actually recovered.

But by the time Thaddeus called "tide's in" from the marshy end of the dock, it was clear to his companions that they would have to abandon the search. Philip came up the bluff to get Marsanne. "You make a very fetching cabin boy. Also a most unhappy-looking one. You aren't beginning to regret the voyage, are you?"

"No, no. I am excessively anxious to reach Paris, only . . . do you think Reynaud is dead?"

He considered for a moment before replying, and she knew he had been about to lie but now decided to be frank with her.

"God knows, darling. He may have gotten back to the marshes. He may even be there now, watching us. But at all events he cannot fool us again. We know him now. And I am not going to chance leaving you alone again."

She loved being so close to him, knowing how much he cared for her, but she could not forget Sister Veronique or the threat of "Reynaud" still alive, despite Philip's sensible attempt to put that in perspective. As they walked down through the foggy dark toward the twin lanterns on the boats, Marsanne took some comfort in the thought that she had at least, as she now believed, solved another of her mysteries:

"I have no doubt it was Reynaud we saw on horseback that day, dressed to resemble you, Philip. Monsieur Nicoletti made quite an effort to accuse you. But Reynaud is tall and thin like yourself and might well have deliberately made himself look even more like you. We only saw him from the back as he passed our coach at the Dower House. A white wig and clothing like yours . . . and Hattie Totter worked for Reynaud—I'm certain of it."

"And who may Hattie Totter be?"

"The maid who brought me the wine with half a vial of laudanum in it." Seeing him shake his head, she added smugly, and without further explanation, "I should have been a Bow Street Runner. I seem to have solved all the crimes."

Thaddeus met them at the dock. "Sorry, sir. He's either drowned or he's a damned good swimmer."

Philip nodded. "No more time now, we must sail on the tide." He lifted Marsanne down into the stern of the sloop. As he did so Thaddeus confided in a low voice, "Mr. Hogue in Calais says to tell you Nicoletti is still waiting at the Dover Quai Inn for some-ut, sir."

"Obviously for his employer, this Reynaud. Nicoletti hasn't seen Hogue? He doesn't know he's being watched?"

"Not so, Hogue says."

"Good. But the sooner we get there the better. He remains a threat until he knows we've found out his employer, who he'll then realize can no longer be of use to him."

"And Hattie Totter is still free," Marsanne put in, trying to find a place to sit that was not taken up by bales of wool.

Philip explained to Thaddeus, "Another one of Reynaud's hirelings."

The Dutchman's quick reminder stopped their talk. "Tide's running."

As they sailed out toward rough water the Dutchman and Thaddeus reported how Nate Tibbetts had been sent to join the remnants of the late Danny Cuttler's band of smugglers and despite what the fellow had done to her, Marsanne was relieved. She kicked now at a box at her feet that smelled of fish, and was about to make a joke about stubbing her toe against it—then broke off, silenced by the suspicion that this box could well contain those jewels secretly donated by the Bonapartist sympathizers to be used for their hero's cause.

Her mother's rescue was the most important thing in the world to her, but she also realized the enormous implications of this attempt Philip was involved in to restore Napoleon Bonaparte.

She huddled close against him, warmed especially now by his close embrace, and by the thought that he felt as she did.

Whatever their future, she believed she had already known the happiness of a lifetime.

Chapter Twenty-Two

Crossing the Channel in a small sloop was quite a different experience from that voyage Marsanne had found so pleasant on the large sailing vessel, and as it met the choppy cross-currents head on, Marsanne worried she would disgrace herself by becoming as sick as Clotilde had been on the ship coming to England.

"Like my daughter's boy," Thaddeus suggested when he discovered Marsanne's difficulty. "You move about, ma'am, think of the sky or of seeing your sainted mother. Just don't look down into the trough of the wave."

"Just when we are comfortable, you send her away from me," Philip complained, but he got up with Marsanne and—though the little ship listed badly under the assault of the Channel wind—held her in a safe grip with one arm around her while they made their way past the bales of wool. Marsanne, at first terrified of being washed overboard, gradually managed something approaching sealegs. Watching Philip, who seemed so at ease, indeed at home on a slanting deck, she asked him how long he'd been going to sea.

"Since I was old enough to join the French Navy," he told her—lowering his voice when they were sheltered behind the hatch opening into the cabin in the waist of the ship. Peering into that cabin Marsanne found it too was filled with items to be traded to the French. She remained in the shelter of the mast and the cabin, her face taking the spray but finding it exhilarating after the first symptoms of nausea had passed.

"And all those years you were there when we heard of the battles and the victories—"

He laughed shortly. "And the defeats? We were never as lucky at sea as on land." He drew her over to a bale of wool and they sat down, Marsanne proud of her ability to keep her balance now even though the little ship had heeled over to an alarming degree.

She looked at the big Dutchman and then at Thaddeus. . . "It seems a long way. From the French Imperial Navy to Sussex freetraders."

Philip followed her glance, waved a hand in a kind of salute to Thaddeus, who grinned at him from his place at the tiller. "I was captured when the powder magazine of our ship blew up off Cape Mola, and woke up to find myself headed for the British prison hulks. Do you understand what they are?"

She nodded, horrified by the image of the man she loved starving and freezing in such a hole.

"Sometimes rotting hulks run aground. As prisoners we lived almost exactly the lives of the rats that kept us company when they weren't feeding on us. We were moved several times, but I assure you there were no improvements. I did manage to escape twice . . ." She stared at him, and he hurried on to finish his story. "I was returned—third time lucky, they say. They were moving about a dozen of us by sea . . . they'd removed our irons when the poor devil chained next to me died, and I went over the side and swam ashore. Thaddeus there, with one of his men, found me nearly drowned and saved my life."

She smiled her gratitude at Thaddeus, then said, "And you became a smuggler in return?"

Philip gazed at the choppy seas. The fog had closed in again and the water was calmer. "Not exactly. I became a smuggler to get back to France. I'd done reconnaissance work earlier in Spain and Portugal for the Emperor and I knew His Majesty personally. You may imagine how I felt learning that he had been forced to abdicate only a few days before my escape."

The Dutchman bellowed out now, "Lights on the larboard, have a care!"

Philip and Marsanne got to their feet, and Marsanne felt her heart in her mouth as a huge hull of a brigantine loomed up, passing so close that their sloop received a specially generous baptism of salt water and spray. She nearly cried out, but was quickly silenced watching how calmly her companions accepted this near miss.

She sat down again, her laughter strained, and forced herself to resume their conversation as if nothing had happened. "Tell me, how did you happen to find your father when he died in Geneva? And why did you disguise yourself to take his place?"

He glanced over at the box of "fish-tackle" near Thaddeus's feet, then took Marsanne's hand as he returned to share their seat.

"Credit the ex-Prefect of the Seine for that," he told her. "Raoul Joubert was a devout friend of the Emperor. He'd done his best to maintain the loyalty of the prefecture toward the Emperor, so of course he was the first to be replaced by the Allies. But he had discovered something we might use. He knew I had a father. I didn't. He knew the man was dying in Geneva. And when he saw me, he said I was finally in luck . . . My hair, you see, had turned white during the four prison years. My father also had white hair and our faces were strikingly similar."

"And before that you never knew you had a father?"

He smiled wryly. "Not a legitimate one, certainly. But then, as I've told you, Sir Philip Justin never knew he had a son. At all events, he was in a coma when I reached him. He died the same night." She closed her fingers around his and he looked down at them.

"I felt nothing," he continued. "I followed the advice of Joubert, bribed my father's surgeon and became Sir Philip Justin. My father was buried as 'Jean-Philippe Justin, French citizen.' And I returned to Sussex on my mission, bought this sloop for Thaddeus and the lads and leased the condesa's house . . . I had known her in Spain when she was the mistress to the French general I took my orders from when I was ashore. I suppose in a way it seems an adventurous time—though it hardly seemed so when I was living through it . . ."

He studied their joined hands again and raised her fingers to his cheek. His face still felt cold, but the gesture told her what she wanted to know of his feelings. She guessed from all the odd little jumps in the story of his life that his special work had been as a spy—a patriot— one of a special breed of people so in love with an idea or a country or a leader that they could devote their lives to their cause . . . which justified everything . . .

Having forgotten that she was now a "freetrader," Marsanne expected the little sloop to sail into the Calais harbor and dock near the packet boat or near one of the great deep-water ships. Instead they sailed off the rich green French coast for an hour before approaching an obscure harbor filled with small fishing vessels and several sloops like their own.

Here they were met by several local citizens, including a French customs official who was obviously in their pay. While Thaddeus and the Dutchman unloaded their cargo, Philip rented a gig and a strong, sturdy nag and set off for Calais with Marsanne, who immediately began steeling herself to confront her enemy René Nicoletti.

By this time she was almost accustomed to her odd male clothing, having found the loose-legged pantaloons surprisingly commodious when she'd needed to climb in and out of ships and gigs and such. Philip looked at her, grinning at the sight she made with her garments now as water-stained as his. She raised her chin and gave him back an insolent, mischievous smile.

She felt somewhat less confident when Philip took her toward the dark, almost deserted taproom of the Dover Quai Inn. As they left the alley he reminded her that she was Thaddeus's grandson and before she could draw back in dismay he stuck his palm into a muddy runnel in the street and slapped the mud over her face. She wiped off some of the dirt but enough remained so that along with her headscarf she convincingly looked her role of a young cabin-boy.

In the taproom Philip ordered a mug of Blue Ruin "for myself and my mate here," but as the barmaid went off to fetch the Dutch "gin" he advised Marsanne, "Don't drink it down all at once." She assured him, "I'm not likely to."

Suddenly in a panic she whispered, "You left the fish-hook box behind in the sloop."

"Have I?" He gave her the dunnage bag he'd thrown over his shoulder and said, "Hold this, mate, whilst I get a grip on the mug."

As she lifted the bag she understood; its cloth contents did not entirely disguise the wooden container she called the "fish-hook box." Much relieved she returned it to him, and taking it by the long draw-strings he slung it casually over his shoulder as he inquired if the innkeeper was about.

The tapster's girl, who'd been trying to flirt with him, shrugged her ample shoulders. "He's off to market. Be back before dinnertime. You a friend of his, m'sieur?"

"He knows me. Has an Englishman been hereabouts lately? Stocky, middle-aged?"

She gave him a curious glance. Marsanne, who suspected he was talking about Mr. Hogue, listened anxiously as the girl swiped a greasy lock of dark hair out of her eye. "Him? An odd one, that *Anglais*. He comes late at night and buzzes gossip with the master. I think they talk about one of the guests abovestairs."

"A Frenchman?"

"A Provençal, I think. Or Corsican." She tossed her head coquettishly, including the "cabin-boy" in her flirtations. "Very handsome, that monsieur in the room abovestairs. But afraid of something, refuses to see anyone else. He even demands to have his meals served in his bedchamber. He says he's waiting for an older gentleman from England . . ."

"What sort of older gentleman?"

"Tall and thin, he says. Gray hair and eyes."

Marsanne and Philip glanced at each other, and Marsanne said under her breath to him, "Nicoletti may still expect help from 'Reynaud.' In which case he'll refuse to talk to you, or to Mr. Hogue."

"He will talk, I'll see to that," Philip promised.

The barmaid stared at him briefly, then quickly turned away. Marsanne found the "Blue Ruin" undrinkable, but went through the motions of bringing the mug to her lips.

When the barmaid was out of earshot Marsanne whispered anxiously, "Your landlord's boy once helped Clotilde and myself escape from you during our last visit . . . Are you truly certain the landlord is your friend?"

His eyes lighted with a memory that seemed to amuse him as he reminded her, "You forget, he then ran to tell me where you had gone and what ship you had taken."

"True, true," and she added with mock solemnity, "what a sinister fellow you are, to be sure!"

To Marsanne's discomfort, the tapster's girl this time appeared to have heard her remark. Marsanne nudged Philip and they moved away to a corner of the long room near the hearth.

"But what if neither Mr. Hogue nor the landlord returns

soon?" she said urgently. "The longer we are delayed here, the longer it will take us to reach Paris." The image of her mother, imprisoned, ill-treated and hungry, without opportunity to get word out to friends or her daughter was a constant pressing reminder.

"Yes," he agreed. "We can't spare much more time. Nicoletti should confess and testify soon enough if he believes Reynaud was captured and gave us the evidence against him—which finally, darling, should remove him as a threat. But meanwhile, what am I to do with you?" He looked about and noted two burly, dark seamen had come into the taproom, though they seemed to pay no attention to him and the "cabin-boy" beyond a first cursory glance. They spoke in a Breton dialect almost impossible to understand, but their tone was unmistakably full of anger. Philip listened closely.

"What is it? What are they saying?" Marsanne whispered.

Philip pressed her hand for silence. "Later."

The Bretons were clearly deep in discussion of some serious matter. When Marsanne indicated she couldn't stand the suspense any longer, Philip maneuvered her into the far corner. "Don't say anything. Understand?"

The edge in his voice upset her, but she also noted an excited gleam in his eyes that helped offset it. She nodded, and waited.

"The Emperor has landed on the Mediterranean coast of France," Philip told her in a tight, quiet voice. "Near Antibes. He had only eight hundred of the Old Guard along with a few families. He ordered no shots be fired. No violence."

She could scarcely believe it. "But . . . only eight hundred men against the King's armies?"

Philip struggled to contain his enthusiasm, which could give them away to the Bretons.

"He knows his old soldiers. He must believe they would

never lift a hand against him. It seems the people of
Cannes, in spite of their Royalist governor, have opened
their city gates to him, and the garrisons of Grenoble and
Lyon—at Lyon, mind!—have apparently gone out to him,
the people are running to march with him . . ."

"The Bretons don't seem to like it," she observed.

He glanced their way. "Brittany and Calais have always
had English ties. We expect that . . . But come, now."

"Where?"

"I'm going up to Nicoletti, but I am *not* going to leave
you alone again. You'll wait upstairs in the hall . . ."

Mightily nervous over the confrontation, she nonetheless was pleased not to be left in the taproom, where a
closer inspection of her might reveal the woman behind
the cabin-boy camouflage. Philip stopped now in front of
the barmaid and asked where the Corsican gentleman
might be found.

"He won't see you," she warned him.

"All the same, I'll try."

She shrugged and said in a bored voice, "The door at
the back of the hall on the right, next the servants' stairs,"
but as Philip and Marsanne left the taproom her eyes
followed them with keen curiosity.

As they went up the ancient, sturdy front stairs separating the taproom from a private parlor, Marsanne reminded him, "When Clotilde and I escaped from you we
used the servants' stairs and came out into the alley."

"Well, no more of that. You may be sure I'll keep you
with me next time."

And for all time, she thought hopefully. . .

The upper floor was dark, and until Marsanne became
accustomed to it she had to rely on Philip's remarkable
ability to see his way in what was virtually a black hole.
When they reached Nicoletti's door Philip scratched on
the panel in the fashion of the inn's serving men.

"Monsieur?"

No answer.

He tried again. "Monsieur? A message from Maître Reynaud."

"That should fetch him," she whispered.

After a third trial he edged Marsanne away from the door. "Stand clear, he may panic and fire when he sees me—"

"No!" she whispered, but obeyed him, imagining she heard the cocking of Nicoletti's pistol behind that door. And watching Philip take out a small black pistol from under the cape slung over his left shoulder hardly reassured her.

"Don't worry, I won't fire. We need the man's testimony."

He tried the door with his free hand. It was not locked or bolted, though it squeaked a trifle as he pushed it inward. René Nicoletti was not in sight. The room smelled of strong spirits, even from the hall where Marsanne waited. She looked around the open door, saw the broken brandy flask in the middle of the floor and the wide stain in the threadbare carpet. And she watched Philip move into the room with his light quick step.

He looked around at the heavy ancient armoire, kicked the doors open but found only a greatcoat and an elegant shirt hanging in forlorn splendor. The room contained an unlighted fireplace, a table, a narrow bed with no posts and a big uncomfortable settle with its back to the window, which was open and provided a view of the alley as well as rooftops and chimneypots.

Since Nicoletti had obviously escaped by the window, Marsanne now moved into the room, wondering how much this would delay their journey to Paris. Philip had started to the window. He got around the high back of the settle, pushed it to one side so that the view of the floor below the windowsill was exposed. Suddenly Marsanne heard him catch his breath. She moved quickly to the settle, and looked down.

René Nicoletti lay stretched out on the carpet, an arm still reaching for the window, a leg twisted as if he had fallen trying to climb out over the sill. His eyes were wide open—staring and blank.

"Did he fall?" Marsanne asked in a small voice.

Philip turned the dead man's dark head, mutttered, "I think not. He had help in his fall. There is a bullet hole above his ear. Certainly not Hogue's work . . . Nicoletti would never have let Hogue in to see him. So that leaves the one man he was waiting for . . . Reynaud."

"Then Reynaud escaped after all," Marsanne said uneasily, then forced herself to look. She had thought there would be more blood. The dark trickle had formed a pool scarcely bigger than a louis d'or.

"Reynaud must have worried Nicoletti would betray him, given half a chance. With that possibility now taken care of . . ."

She could have finished the thought for him, especially since she had been sharing it. . . "There is only our word against his for him to worry over. But surely—"

Too intent to notice the creak of floorboards in the hall, she was doubly startled to hear the piercingly loud voice of the barmaid in the doorway as she spoke to someone behind her.

"You see, *Monsieur le Préfet?* They insisted on forcing their way into the poor young man's room. I even heard the little one there say to that one with the gun in his hand . . . 'What a sinister fellow you are!' And now . . . well, do you need more, monsieur? It's plain they have murdered the poor young gentleman."

Chapter Twenty-Three

Marsanne looked from the barmaid framed in the doorway to a thin, intense-looking man peering in over her head, and then with despair she glanced at Philip, knowing he was still poised on one knee over the body of Nicoletti— the pistol still in his hand.

He took his time about rising and answering the barmaid's hysterical charge. His gaze was upon the much more important gentleman behind her. This gaunt man, the local prefect of police, appeared even more forbidding when he stepped forward. In elegant "Sir Philip" clothing Philip might have bluffed his way out, but to be caught looking like a smuggler with a gun in his hand and a man on the floor dead of a gunshot wound. . .

"The gun, if you please, monsieur," the prefect ordered, holding out his hand.

Philip's eyebrows arched in what Marsanne had always considered his "arrogant English way." His deeply blue eyes had never looked more frigid. "You are mistaken, *Monsieur le Préfet*. I did not shoot this man. Your own eyes will tell you he has been dead long enough for the blood to dry on the carpet here—"

"The gun!"

"Do you know what a Bow Street Runner is, monsieur?" The prefect shrugged, and Philip went on, "A man named Hogue, a recognized police officer of England, will return before evening. He will testify to my identity."

"An *Anglais*? I am to take the word of a stranger, an *English* stranger? You have an odd sense of humor, fellow. Your gun. Now . . ."

Philip made no effort to surrender it. The prefect advanced into the room, moving slowly, never taking his eyes off Philip. "I know there is no ball in that pistol, you've already used it upon that gentleman . . . enough of this—hand me the gun—*now*."

Marsanne nearly called out her thought—that Philip's very innocence meant the pistol aimed at the prefect was deadly, loaded and needing only the squeeze of Philip's finger to make them both precisely what they were accused of.

She felt almost relieved as she saw Philip move toward the prefect as though about to hand over the gun . . . and then she stiffened as at almost the same time she saw the landlord's boy silently pass the doorway behind the barmaid. As Marsanne caught his eye the boy put a finger to his lips and shook his head, and since he was also facing Philip it was clear to her the gesture was a signal to him as well.

In his left hand the prefect carried a black stick about the size of a *maréchal*'s baton, its head metal-tipped. Now he slowly raised it until it was pointing at Philip.

"You are a gambler, monsieur?" Philip asked quietly. "You believe I have murdered this man—a hired assassin —and that my pistol is therefore empty. I assure you, monsieur, that I did not shoot him and that this pistol contains one ball which could certainly find its way to your head. Do I make myself understood?"

The prefect lowered his stick and slapped it against his other palm, the sound making Marsanne flinch and seeming to draw the barmaid further into the room, as though transfixed by the by-play unfolding before her. Philip now began to move toward her and the prefect, toward the door too . . . to give himself up? To fire? The tension mounted, punctuated by the prefect's slapping his hand a second time, followed by, "Come, now, no more of this nonsense—"

His voice was cut off by a resounding crash in the hall, on the trail of which came heavy thumps Marsanne suspected to be a series of wine bottles rolling down the stairs. She had no time to think further as she was shoved out the door by Philip amid screams from the barmaid and grunts from the prefect as the barmaid tumbled directly into him.

Marsanne then saw no more of them—Philip had snatched the big key out of the door, slammed the door itself and locked it, tossing the key in the general direction of the ruined tray of dishes and bottles. These in their turn had been hurled the length of the hall by the landlord's boy, who motioned Philip and Marsanne to a room further along the hall.

Marsanne whirled dizzily into the room and saw the boy's weather-cloak hanging on a wall-peg not far from two trundle cots that apparently served the boy and his father.

Down the hall the prefect was now banging on the door with his stick and shouting, "In the name of the king, I order you . . . !"

. The landlord's boy and Philip exchanged a few words in whispers, then the boy ran hard down the hall, making a terrible clatter with his wooden sabots. With the door ajar, Philip listened while Marsanne, silent and shaken, stood behind him.

"Ay, *Monsieur le Préfet*! The key is somewhere on the floor," the boy yelled. "I will find it, monsieur, wait right there . . ."

"Where else could he wait?" Philip grinned. Then he whispered to Marsanne, "Good! I was afraid he would go out the window—"

"You want him to come through this hall?"

"I want him to trust the boy's directions."

Minutes later the boy called out, "Found it, monsieur!" His shoes again clip-clopped over the floor. He unlocked the door, managed a fine hysteria that outdid the barmaid's and flung himself into the prefect's unwilling arms.

"Monsieur—he knocked me down, he and the lad . . . I was on the stairs, picking up the tray . . . you'll not let master blame me because I broke them things . . . Please, you'll not—"

The prefect thrust him aside and rushed to the servants' stairs, his boots crunching broken glass as he hurried down and out past the kitchen area to the alley beyond.

Marsanne expected the boy to return at once and get his "guests" out of the inn, but Philip waited until he saw the barmaid run down the front stairs to her post in the taproom before he closed and locked the door. He quickly explained to Marsanne that Thaddeus, Nate and himself had once escaped the customs guards by this same tactic. "Of course," he added, "it isn't a full-fledged Prefect of Police who pursues us every day. . . . I imagine he came here merely to visit the taproom, and found that damned suspicious barmaid."

Turning away from the door, he walked with his arm around her to the low trundle bed and urged her to sit down. "My poor darling, you are as cold as ice," he said, and began to rub her hands between his. And as he did she felt herself gradually relax, and feel a warmth that even the worst March chill would be helpless against.

"Now, listen carefully," he went on. "We must, of course, first locate Sister Veronique. But remember, there are a score or more prisons, convents, houses of detention where she might be. To find the right one I must seek out the Ministry of Police in Paris. I'd hoped to be able to find out from friends in one of the Bonapartist clubs, but by this time they are sure to be under lock and key . . . if not worse." He saw her eyes widen and added hastily, "Darling, I am talking of active enemies of the king . . . I certainly hope I needn't deal with the Minister of Police himself, but the Ministry files should hold the answer to your mother's whereabouts . . . I hope you haven't become so taken with this pirate fellow that you will no longer want me as pompous old Sir Philip . . ."

She hugged him and whispered, "I will take you, sir, in any guise, especially if it will lead us to my mother."

After that it was a matter of waiting. Marsanne, mindful of the long journey ahead to Paris, had rested for several hours, half-asleep but coming fully awake to hear low-voiced exchanges between Philip and the landlord's son. The boy had brought them a cold luncheon, which they both ate greedily, knowing how long it might be before they could take time to eat again.

At sunset Mr. Hogue arrived with the landlord Besigny, who carried garments from "Sir Philip's" lodgings and a silk gown and shift, a travel cloak and shoes slightly too big for Marsanne.

While Marsanne stepped behind the door of the old armoire to change into respectable female clothing she heard Mr. Hogue explain the awkwardness of his position to Philip.

"Ye'll understand, sir, I've no authority here. These Frogs—Frenchies, what I mean to say—they don't listen to me. Still, I'm going to stay here and try to prove this

Nicoletti chap was killed by somebody else. Not but what it'll be a chore—but you paid me well and I'm not forgetting it."

"I know you'll do your best," Philip told him, not sounding as though he actually had much faith in Hogue's search. Unfortunately there was no substantial proof against "Reynaud." For that they needed Nicoletti's confession—which was now permanently unavailable.

Marsanne reminded him, "And it's possible Reynaud is not the only suspect . . . it *may* have been that awful Hattie Totter, acting on his instructions as she did when she tried to poison me. Mr. Hogue, she's plain, tall and thin, about thirty years old, I'd say."

"Whichever of the two killed the Corsican," Philip put in, "it seems the reason was the same—to keep him from identifying Reynaud as his paymaster."

"Just so, sir. But meantime, you best be on your way with the lady. This town's not healthy for you."

Philip turned to the landlord and his son. "What do you two say for our appearance?"

The Besignys examined their guests in their transformation, and Besigny Senior declared, "You should do very well, both of you. One would hardly associate such respectable citizens with the colorful cutthroats who were about to be arrested for the murder of our Corsican friend.

"And when I speak of Corsicans," the landlord went on without added inflection, "I must tell you, Monsieur Philippe, there are heavy rumors coming in every hour from Paris and the South. It is said that the Emperor has reached Lyon without firing a shot. They say that people are pouring out of the cities to welcome him. But here in Calais, a Breton wagered me Bonaparte would never reach Paris."

Philip nodded grimly. "Do they say so, indeed! Well, let them continue in their delusion."

Besigny gave him a sharp look. "All known Bonapartists have been arrested. Some of them shot. Do you still say I am safe in laying a few wagers, Monsieur Philippe?"

Philip lifted the dunnage bag to his shoulder. "You have my word on that," he said, feeling slightly less certain than he hoped he sounded.

The local police had returned during the hour to remove René Nicoletti's body, and Besigny's boy came in after they'd departed to inform the fugitives there would be at least half a dozen soldiers as well as a member of the prefect's department returning within minutes to examine all the rooms of the Dover Quai Inn.

"They say, m'sieur, they have not found the murderer. They think maybe he escaped by ship to England, but also maybe this murderer left some signs of himself here on the upper floor."

His father waved him aside. "How long before they arrive?"

"Ten minutes after me, I think. Come, Papa is right, there's no time . . ."

They hurried down the servants' stairs to avoid being glimpsed by the barmaid, and then as luck would have it found the girl in the kitchen securing the ingredients of a hot rum fustian. Marsanne wondered if her nerves would survive the brief—and yet seemingly endless—passage by the open kitchen doors. Besigny now took over, abruptly pushed past her and made his way across the stone floor, barking orders, one of which was sharp enough to cause the girl to drop her hot poker and stoop to pick it up. . .

As she did so Philip, Marsanne and the Besigny boy hastily passed the doors and found themselves in the alley beside a strong young mare hitched to a gig. Philip quickly lifted Marsanne up to the seat, jumped in beside her and took up the reins.

When they were out of the alley and beyond the jam of wagons, carriages and other vehicles, Philip drew her

to him and managed firmly, though not ungently, to in-
sinuate her head against his cheek. "Sleep if you can,
sweetheart. It's a long way to Paris and I want to make
stops only for fresh horses."

"Oh, please, anything if we only make fast time!"

He thought about the road ahead—the dark, swift high
road to Paris—and passed the time telling her about his
personal as well as political involvement with the Emperor
Napoleon—to her at best a shadowy figure she'd seen only
at a distance on horseback and glimpsed briefly in the
magnificent carriage of the Coronation.

"I grew up without a father, as you know," Philip began, "and during the Revolution I looked up to Georges
Jacques Danton and Gilę Marsan, your own father. Later,
as you also know, I came to adore your mother. And then
there was Lucien Bonaparte, who introduced me to his
brother Napoleon. You will smile, but I found in this
young general—not ten years my senior—the person I
could happily serve, admire and follow—the father I'd
never had."

"Strange," Marsanne said, "I'd never think of the Emperor as a fatherly man, though I adore his son . . . the
little King of Rome, I believe they used to call him.
Mother was invited to his christening and she took me
with her. I never forgot. I wonder how she thinks of the
Emperor. Perhaps as a son . . . ?"

"God knows he's the only leader we've got," Philip said
emphatically. "We certainly can't go on under that Bourbon family. What idiots! . . ."

When they finally arrived at the Paris customs barriers
they found the customs agents arguing so vehemently with
each other as well as the peasants bringing in produce,
that it took Philip several minutes to attract their attention.

An eternity later the line of wagons, carts and tumbrels
moved on, and when Philip found himself at the barrier
looking down at the customs guards, he could not restrain

himself from putting the question to them that had never for a moment left him during any of the past thirty-six hours.

"May I ask, monsieur, what are the reports on the landing of the Emperor?"

"All reports confused . . . it's generally thought the Emperor will be stopped before he reaches Auxerre . . ."

Yet now, thought Marsanne as she listened closely, *they are beginning to call him "the Emperor" again.* No more the "ogre," or "usurper" or even "the general."

"On the other hand," said the grinning official, "they say a second army is being sent south. Why that, eh? What happened to the first they sent a week ago?"

Marsanne was about to express her own enthusiasm when Philip put a hand on her arm to silence her, and she realized almost too late that these various comments might have been spoken to bring out the true sympathies of "Sir Philip" and his lady . . . sympathies that might condemn them.

She breathed easier when Philip's papers were finally returned to him and the horse and gig were passed through the barrier into the crowded, narrow streets of Paris.

At once it was obvious that a new and dangerously exciting spirit had come over the capital. There were many more Royalist soldiers than Marsanne remembered seeing a month previously, but there were also an astounding number of working class and old veterans wearing fresh violets on jackets, belts and hats.

She remained anxious as Philip gave over their transportation at the stables behind the Café Vaucluse and led her across the Place Vendôme toward the Tuileries palace. All along the noisy streets they had been pushed and shoved by busy citizens, many of whom frantically dragged odd items of furniture or belongings in bedsheets along the cobblestones.

"What do you think they are so afraid of? They lived here under the Empire, didn't they?" Marsanne asked.

"Most of them look like emigrés to me," Philip said. "I would guess they ran away in '89 at the beginning of the Revolution and came back in the pocket of the Allied troops. Now they are running away again . . . not the most reliable of citizens."

Marsanne now heard an outburst of laughter mixed with snickers from the crowd gathered about the railings of the Vendôme column, which had been raised as a monument to the French victory at Austerlitz. As Philip pushed their way through the mob, they came on a placard fastened against the railing, and a limping veteran alongside asked excitedly, "Is it news of the South, have they tried to murder the Emperor?" . . . A heavy-set baker, sleeves rolled up to his apron, offset the veteran's worries with "They've had to send another army south, the first's already joined Napoleon. Shows how they love our little Corporal . . . what does the placard say?"

Everyone pushed and shoved to read the placard:

"Napoleon to Louis Eighteenth: "My Good Brother, It Is Useless To Send Me Any More Soldiers. I Have Enough."

The roars of laughter spread the message of the placard through the square and beyond. Philip and Marsanne joined that laughter, but Marsanne also thought of the palace of the Tuileries where she and Philip were headed, and wondered whether that fat Bourbon king hidden behind gray stone walls had heard of the placard. . .

"Poor man," she said, mostly to herself, as they left the square and crossed the rue St. Honoré. Philip looked at her quizzically. "I mean, the king, he's really only just warmed his throne and already he may be packing his things to do some more traveling—"

"Let's not call him 'poor man' until we find out what he has done to Sister Veronique," he reminded her, with which she readily agreed.

They walked rapidly up the new arcades of the rue de Rivoli until they were opposite the place du Carrousel, where they made their way through noisy excited crowds to the steps of the Tuileries palace. Marsanne had never seen such panic. She counted a score of men, most of them in military uniform, rushing into or out of the long gray palace.

Suddenly Philip stopped, drew Marsanne away from the mainstream of the crowd. He looked about, studying those nearby and then the huge, forbidding entrance doors of the palace. He dropped the dunnage bag down from his shoulder, then off over his hand.

"Darling, I want you to slip this over your shoulder, under that cloak. If anything should happen, if—by any mischance—I shouldn't . . . come out soon, I want you to take this to a friend of mine. He will use its contents to pay for the food and lodging of the Emperor's army as they move northward . . ."

She tried to borrow some of his calm. "But what is his name, where will I find him?"

"You do understand that if I fail here we have no other way to locate Sister Veronique. Then only the Emperor's or his prefect's arrival in Paris can save her from Royalist hands . . ."

She moistened her dry lips. "I believe I understand, Philip. You wish me to go to meet the Emperor at Lyon if you do not succeed in looking into the files. I go to Lyon, or wherever he is now—"

"Between Auxerre and Fontainebleau, I should think, judging by the plans I heard discussed two months ago. Raoul Joubert should be with the advance guard . . . you remember my speaking to you of him?"

She nodded. "You said he used to be Prefect of the Seine under the Empire."

He took her shoulders, looked down at her with that special, wondrously unexpected softness that always touched her so. "My darling, this is a terrible burden to put on you . . . your own mother and—"

"I can do it if . . . anything happens, but I am sure it will be—"

"You will need to find out," he said, cutting her off with some impatience despite himself, "where they are billeted in Fontainebleau, but don't go alone. Send a boy with a message to Raoul Joubert. When he comes, tell him what has happened . . . about Sister Veronique, and about me . . . you understand?" Again she nodded. "I hope it may not happen, that I may get to the files immediately and have no problems, but you understand, my darling, we must be practical . . ." He raised her chin and kissed her. An officer in full gaudy regimentals elbowed him and hurried on, which diverted Philip not at all as he kissed her once again, and with a kind of intensity she'd never felt in him before.

They were almost torn away from each other by a pair of troopers running to mount their horses. Philip, scarcely noticing, looked at her intently. "You must not worry too much. Even if I should be taken I need but call out in the name of the Emperor in the right districts and there are many who should help me escape . . . Wait here, give me at most a half-hour. If I do not return . . . well, then you know what you must do, and you must start immediately. Darling . . ."

She held out her arms. He lifted her off the pebbled ground with his embrace, set her down again and walked off toward the palace entrance doors. He did not look back.

Marsanne waited scarcely a minute, then made her way through the crowd after him, careful not to be in the line of his vision if he should look around. She could still make out his tall figure as he moved inside.

She hurried and entered in time to see him hesitating between the ground floor and the staircase leading to the first floor and the royal apartments above. There was so much confusion, such a panic-stricken mob milling around that Marsanne feared no one could possibly know where the Minister of Police or even one of the *sous-préfets* might be.

Whatever Philip had been told, he backed down from the stairs, thanking the man who'd given him the information he sought, and then started along the crowded lower floor. Marsanne followed at a distance. She did not intend to let him see her, but at the same time she wanted to know as soon as possible where her mother was being held. . . If, God forbid, they should detain Philip she meant to report every circumstance to Joubert and, if necessary, the Emperor himself. . .

Philip was ushered into a large ornate audience chamber by a bowing lackey. Marsanne moved past the tall narrow doors, which remained ajar. Philip approached a stout man dressed in the style of an exquisite dandy, his white cravat so high he could scarcely turn his head. He did seem amiable, though, greeting Philip with a friendly wave of the hand and repeating Sylvie Lesgate's name.

"Indeed, monsieur," he said in a high-pitched, penetrating voice, "I am acting in the minister's place. Naturally with the danger so close at hand the minister must be gotten to a safe place. We are, indeed, familiar with Lady Lesgate. She proved a good and loyal friend during His Majesty's lamentable exile in England . . . But, monsieur, what problem do you bring me at such a time when the Usurper Bonaparte is marching north . . . ?"

"Your Excellency's permission," Philip replied, "to discover where Lady Lesgate's cousin is imprisoned . . . I am persuaded there has been a great mistake, but I should at least like to know where the unfortunate woman may be held—"

"Imprisoned? A lady? . . . Capitaine de Saulx, what are you standing here for? Be off and see to the arrest of those Bonapartist radicals in the Latin Quarter . . . Well,

then, Sir Philip . . . Lady Lesgate's cousin, you say. It's
hard to refuse a request from a friend of Her Ladyship.
One of my men will take you to the city prefect and you
may discuss the prison files with him. I say of the prisoner's release, that is a matter for His Majesty's clemency.
And at such a time . . ."

Among the many men pushing past Marsanne was one
civilian who bowed to the *sous-préfet* from the doorway
and went forward who seemed terrifyingly familiar to
Marsanne . . . his head, the thin neck and graying hair,
the narrow shoulders . . . and just as she was certain it
was "Reynaud," the man pointed a long finger at Philip,
declaring to the prefect, "Monsieur, that man is an assassin, murdered one of His Majesty's agents in Calais! . . ."

Marsanne looked frantically about, wondering how she
could possibly help Philip, though from the contemptuous
glance he turned on his accuser you would have thought
her, or anybody else's, help was the least of his concerns.
"I suggest you ask His Majesty's ministers if I am not Sir
Philip Justin. They know me—"

"He's a damned Bonapartist, Jean-Philippe Justin!"
Reynaud shouted. "The Prefect of Calais is with me, he is
my witness and he is waiting in the antechamber . . ."

Marsanne backed away quickly and was swallowed in
the mass of humanity pouring through the palace toward
the outer doors. But even though pushed rudely back and
forth she somehow managed to keep the prefect's doors at
least in sight.

It was several tense minutes before the doors were
opened again. She saw a guard clearing a path to the
Carrousel entrance. Just a step behind him came Philip
Justin, looking determinedly at ease, scarcely a hair out of
place, closely followed by two guards and a triumphant
Reynaud.

Marsanne prayed that Philip would look her way just
once, then realized that of course he would never call
Reynaud's attention to her. She tried to run after the

guards and their prisoner, but was thrust against the wall by the king's fleeing civil servants.

Stunned and bruised, she pulled herself together, pushed her way toward the doors and found herself out in the place du Carrousel, wondering which way to go . . . to try to discover where they had taken Philip, or to carry out his orders.

Finally, resolving to do what she knew all along she must do, she fought her way against the tide of humanity and headed toward the Marais district and the Hôtel de Sens, where the coaches to the south made up their way-bills.

Her mother and Philip were both in awful danger because of Napoleon Bonaparte. Well, then, *that* particular Corsican was going to save them if Marsanne had to force her way through the entire Old Guard!

Chapter Twenty-Four

The Auxerre coach passed through the barriers at dawn and rumbled off into the countryside. It was obvious by the crowds on the road that something of great interest and moment was happening. After all, it was Palm Sunday, and in normal times a Frenchman would spend his holy day at home.

Marsanne carefully eavesdropped on the conversations of groups near her to gather information on the progress of Napoleon and his entourage, and where she could expect to meet them. She needed to find out exactly which towns he had passed through and especially where his advance guard had spent the night. After that she was determined to follow Philip's instructions to the letter . . . and to put out of her mind as much as possible the terrible realization that she might be losing all at once both him and her mother—the two people who were her whole world. . .

After the coach had passed the Paris barriers the travelers began to speak of the reason for the extraordinary crowd on the dawn coach—it being, of course, elation over Napoleon's return—and each passenger vied to top the others in expressing a real passion to be a part of the Emperor's growing strength. All the while Marsanne busied herself with her plans, including the wording of a note to be carried by the stableboy or some other to Raoul Joubert in Napoleon's advance guard. She could not sleep, though she ached with exhaustion. Instead she nervously chewed on the ends of her gloves every few moments.

Her fellow passengers, in a different mood, excitedly retold anecdotes as they passed through the villages. . .

"The Little Corporal's bound to have moved beyond Auxerre. He never did waste time. He was there last night," one old lady insisted. . .

"Ay," a stout baker agreed. "Did you hear what happened last week, how Marshal Ney marched south promising to bring back his old friend in a cage, and instead—"

"—instead threw himself into the Emperor's arms," finished a young woman. . .

"They say near every regiment sent against him has stove in its drum and joined him . . ."

They went on matching rumors and tales of the return of Napoleon Bonaparte, while Marsanne thought privately, "If you help Mama and Philip, I'll more than join you . . . I'll give thanks to you every day left in my life . . ."

Meanwhile at a village stop to change teams she heard the postilion speaking with the hostler of the inn: "St. Amand-Eglise . . . he's sure to be there tonight . . . they say he wants to reach Fontainebleau tomorrow in honor of his son's birthday . . ."

Marsanne carefully took note of the town's name and got back into the coach—St. Amand-Eglise would be her destination. She would gamble that the gossiping postilion had been right. She had no choice.

When the coach reached St. Amand only the old woman disembarked with Marsanne, who looked anxiously about, feeling unnerved to see so many Royalist troops, all wearing the white Bourbon rosette on their hats and milling about the town square in little groups, now and then looking over their shoulders as if awaiting instructions.

Marsanne quickly crossed toward an inn facing on the square. She knew that when the Bonapartist advance guard arrived they were certain to enter the square; that the impact of this march would lie especially in its spontaneity, in the fact that each new addition to the Emperor's forces was made voluntarily. To do this they would have to be seen in the most spectacular way. And now, doubtless awaiting the Bonapartists, was a Royalist army which had no intention of permitting a further bloodless march. Before nightfall it seemed likely that the first shots of civil war would be fired . . . here in this little market town.

On her way around the square, pointedly ignoring the flirtatious remarks of the soldiers she passed, Marsanne noted that two streets out of the square were sealed off by more troops. A large woman carrying a basket of vegetables came along, and as Marsanne made way for her she asked on a sudden impulse, "Pardon, madame, why is the street sealed off? Do they think the . . . General Bonaparte will take this route?"

"Bonaparte, madame? Bah! Who knows what soldiers are ever up to? They usually seal off the street because the police are taking prisoners to the carts."

"The carts? But why?"

The big woman looked her up and down. "Where have you come from, madame? You do not know that criminals are chained and taken to the coast? And from there to

Cayenne and those other hellish islands in the West Indies?"

"No, I'd no idea." Marsanne felt such revulsion that she could barely allow herself to absorb the full meaning of what the woman had told her. Instead she hurriedly thanked the woman and went on, though she could not resist a quick look in the direction of the sealed-off streets. She was relieved that she saw nothing more than some dogs chasing each other, and in front of them the line of Royalist troops. She could not, though, dismiss entirely from her mind the picture of Philip being sent to one of "those hellish islands" . . .

The landlord of the corner inn was in the taproom, crowded now with noisy drinkers wagering on the results of the conflict sure to come the next day. The landlord was not enthused to see Marsanne but agreed to rent her one of his rooms abovestairs for a night. Though the taproom did a thriving business, no one was willing to spend the night in a room that might be sprayed with gunfire before morning, and the landlord disliked the thought of his customers being endangered.

"It's extraordinary," she remarked, seeing that though the room was bare and simple the view of any activity in the square would be superb. "A view as good as sitting at the Théâtre Feydau."

"That may be, madame, but the prisoners' cart will pass this way earlier and no one likes to see that."

" 'Prisoners'? What are they supposed to be guilty of?"

He was surprised. "Some are from Paris. Some from Champagne and the Loire and other places. Their crimes are sacrilegious murder, crimes against the state or Bonapartist conspiracy." He inclined his shaggy head in what might be considered a bow and left her.

She called out, "When you have time, please send me a boy to carry a message." She looked out into the obscurity of the hall after him. "And also please send a standish of ink, a pen and some paper."

He waved an arm to indicate that he'd heard and went on. She returned to the little room and removed her cloak —wondering where to hang it, and the bag with its precious contents. The floor was thick with dust and the stains of many a drunken guest; there was no armoire or clothespress—only a peg in the wall. Unable to decide what to do with the jewels, she left them on the stained and threadbare coverlet beneath her cloak.

Wondering how long she might have to wait here for the arrival of the Bonapartists and whether a street battle would be fought under her very eyes, she studied the square below the window. If there were a battle fought here, she might well be unable to get a message through to Raoul Joubert. And then . . . there was also, she supposed, a dreadful possibility that the Bonapartists could lose the battle. What then?

The base of a statue in the square was surrounded by a grassy little common. Two officers stood there now, deep in discussion. Where the four roads emptied into the square, the troops were concentrated. Marsanne opened the window and looked out, wondering if the Emperor's advance guard would enter by the south road. She could see nothing there but an occasional woman returning from the fish market, or a tileworker, or several children running after each other in a game of tag.

Suddenly, as she watched, mothers began to call their children with voices raised in panic. Small wonder that the streets were empty. The entire population seemed to know that the confrontation between two armies would take place soon in this peaceful little town. And sensed, rather than knew, that two different ways of life, of *their lives*, might also be at stake.

Marsanne stood there for some time looking out the window, thinking about Philip, wondering where he was at this minute. Was it possible that he had been taken to one of the several places of detention and had seen her mother?

Palm Sunday, she thought with some self-reproach. The first such holy day of my life that I did not go to Mass. . .

Suddenly a knock at the door made her start nervously. Was it the boy bringing the paper and ink? "Who is it?"

An expressionless female voice called, "From the landlord, madame."

Yes. It must be the paper and ink. She glanced at the bag with the box of jewels still under the edge of her cloak and, looking about, saw the dusty floor unswept for months. Obviously, if she put the bag under the shabby bed for the moment, no one would have occasion to look for it there. Having done so, she went to the door and unbolted it.

After that, everything happened at once. It seemed to her stunned senses that a hurricane swirled around her. Her first stunned realization was that this woman standing in the doorway was . . . Hattie Totter, and she found herself backing quickly away from the pointed knife glistening in the woman's steady hand. Crowding the doorway beside her was "Louis Reynaud," whose thin lips spread now in a sour smile. His knife was too familiar. . .

"What a pity you didn't drown!" Marsanne managed to taunt him before the woman's knife blade lodged closer to the bone just under her chin.

"Drown, dear lady? My wife and I were born in Martinique, where one learns to swim before walking. And then, too, I am lucky. Like your lover, who managed to land in a prison warden's office under the care of a Bonapartist. Though he escaped, dear lady, you will not. And you, after all, are our real concern . . ."

Philip had escaped. She'd heard that, concentrated on it, rejoiced in it even in the midst of her panic. The fact that this creature with Reynaud was evidently his wife was a revelation that did not interest her, except as a further explanation of her interest. *Philip had escaped* . . . somehow he would find her . . . he knew she was headed toward the place where the Emperor's advance guard would be gathering. He would follow . . . But of course she hadn't gotten that far. He would not know that she had gotten off the coach at St. Amand-Eglise.

There were soldiers in the square. They might not be Bonapartist, but they were men. She determined to make as much disturbance as possible to attract their attention. She began by pulling back and uttering a shriek that deafened her own ears, hoping it would carry to the square and the troops below her window. Before she could make more than strangled breathless noises, "Reynaud's" surprisingly powerful fingers closed around her neck. She clawed at him, not even feeling the sharp edge of the dagger's blade across her knuckles. She heard him warn his wife: "She is too much trouble. It will be simpler to strangle her and bury her somewhere nearby."

"You fool!" came Hattie Totter's low-pitched ruthless voice. "Her body must be found if we are to claim the estate. And it mustn't be found near us. Far better for that idiot prison guard to clap her over the side of the head. One good blow to end her, and drop her off the tumbrel at the edge of town . . . that tumbrel is the only thing the king's troops will let through today. . . . That way they cannot connect us to her death."

He nodded and started to drag Marsanne, who was grasping frantically at every obstacle—the door-jamb, the wall of the corridor, a stair-rail. . . . He slapped her hand away from these obstacles and muttered to his wife, "I suppose you're right. They certainly won't want the Bonapartist soldiers to get hold of the prisoners. Half of the damned prisoners are Bonapartists."

He had Marsanne under his right arm and was dragging her through an alley whose broken cobbles cut and marred her morocco slippers. She made another attempt at a scream and was cuffed across the head. Her world vanished into darkness.

Later, she came to vague consciousness aware of the afternoon sunlight cutting across her eyes. Hands were

holding her head up. She was lifted high and dropped into
a tumbrel of some sort. She opened her eyes with an effort,
hearing groans, mutters, sing-song moaning and found
herself in the center of perhaps a dozen foul-smelling
prisoners, men and women, all but herself chained to a
big muscular fellow sitting on a plank behind the driver
and facing the prisoners. She had no doubt their neglect
to chain her was based on the arrangement to kill her and
then toss her out when they had passed beyond the barri-
cade of Royalist soldiers.

The tumbrel moved forward and the prisoners' guard
called to the driver, "Avoid the square. The damned
troops!"

Marsanne saw the prisoners begin to twist and turn; a
ferocious woman with straggling gray hair, a firm-jawed,
fiery-eyed man, several creatures so beaten their features
were barely recognizable. They all turned as Marsanne
finally became aware of the peculiar sounds that had distracted them from their own misery:

The distant roll of thunder moving up from the south.

Their guard called over his shoulder to the tumbrel's
driver. "Quick, damn it! That'll be the enemy. There may
not be many of 'em but they are making hell's own
noise."

And still no shots had been fired.

One prisoner called triumphantly to his motley companions in the tumbrel, "It's the Emperor's guard, the
citizens are going out to them."

"Shut your mouth!" Their guard struck out with the end
of the chain. He stood up and stared over the tumbrel
driver's shoulder to see better what was happening.
"What? Is that one closed too? Try the north corner of
the square."

Marsanne tried to get near the guard. "Monsieur, I am
not one of your prisoners. They are going to kill me,
please, *listen* to me . . ." But, of course, she realized with

horror as she said the words, this fellow was the man who intended to do the killing. . .

The tumbrel rattled toward the square, toward the soldiers' backs, the driver hoping to cut across the corner of the square and out the north-east road. Marsanne leaned over the tumbrel's high side and shouted at the top of her lungs, "Help me, messieurs! I am not a criminal, I am not—"

The soldier turned to look at her while the guard swung his chain, which she barely managed to duck in time. At the same moment one of the younger soldiers made a menacing gesture toward the guard, obviously in sympathy with Marsanne. She quickly reached out to him.

"Monsieur, I beg you—" This time she was yanked back so hard she fell into the lap of the man and at the same minute the Royalist commander gave a sharp order.

The soldiers came to attention, their long rifles at the ready. All of them in the square heard approaching hoof-beats, perhaps a dozen horses, and Marsanne silently prayed that they brought the exiled emperor's soldiers . . . with Philip! . . . Oh yes, please . . .

"Get across, get across the square!" called out the tumbrel guard to the driver, "or we'll lose our chance . . ." But by this time the troops dared not move and so the tumbrel could not move. They were all staring, as though fixed, toward the south road. Stray citizens and hangers-on came running along the south road toward the square, some waving hats and cheering, others terrified.

Seconds later the horsemen rode into view. For the most part they appeared to be hussars. Marsanne saw the splendid pelisses and the great dark fur colbacks, the shakoes, on their heads. She did not make out Philip, but as the hussars reined in before the line of Royalist soldiers, she noted the one man among the hussars who wore no uniform, and recognized the striking black and white clothing that marked Philip for her. . . . It must be

Philip, even though the only mark that clearly identified him as a part of the imperial hussars was the small red white and blue cockade of the Revolution and the Empire he wore on his coat, and which was mounted in the shako of every hussar.

The horsemen rode up now to the foot soldiers. There was no sound except the snorting and stamping of the mounts. The leading hussar called out in a stentorian voice: "Soldiers, your general asks his loyal troops to permit his passage through this city."

The Royalist commander shouted back: "Let the traitor rebel advance. We are here to accept his sword in surrender."

The horses stirred uneasily under the tightening grip of the reins, but it was the Royalist soldiers who exchanged the most uneasy glances. The civilian horseman, whom Marsanne took to be Philip, guided his mount along the house fronts bordering the square. He seemed to be headed toward the inn. Could he know that she was staying at the inn?

Marsanne called out to him and held tight to the guard's chain as he tried to lash it across her shoulders. The Bonapartist prisoner, believing his chance was at hand, leaned over the tumbrel's side . . . "Long live the Emperor!" The Royalist troops became even more uneasy. At the same time the imperial hussars grinned and several of them echoed the man's cry.

Hearing Marsanne call out to him, Philip reined in abruptly, then began to swing his horse around in a circle, still unable to gauge the direction of Marsanne's voice, but the Bonapartist prisoner's cry caused him to look over at the tumbrel in the far end of the square. Marsanne, holding on to the chain in the guard's hand with all her strength and trying to avoid the guard's angry fist, called out Philip's name again. It was enough.

Seeing this unarmed civilian now suddenly racing his horse directly at them, the troops parted and let Philip through as he headed for the tumbrel. The Royalist commander once more ordered the hussars to surrender and the horsemen laughed, answering in turn with the demand that *he* and *his* troops come over to the Emperor. But the center of attention became the tumbrel, where several prisoners suddenly joined in Marsanne's struggle against the vicious guard and the tumbrel's driver. Philip had gotten his horse up to the cart, and now reached for Marsanne, his eyes alive with anger.

With the prisoners on the offensive in the tumbrel, Marsanne managed to pull free of the guard and hold her arms out to Philip, who lifted her from the tumbrel and onto his horse. She scarcely heard the soldiers out in the square.

"How did you know I was here?" were her first words once she'd caught her breath and forced back the tears of relief.

"Darling, if you ever want to run away from anyone, never give your true name on the waybill of a stage coach." She nodded soberly, realizing that was also how "Reynaud" and his wife had tracked her to this place. Philip added, "The coach driver in Auxerre told me you'd gotten down here. Fortunately for me—and for you—the Emperor had left Auxerre and was on his way here . . ."

"Speaking of fortune," she said quickly, "your treasure is waiting for you under a very dirty bed at the inn."

He looked at her and nodded briefly. "I suspect I've even better news for you. The prison warden who released me knew where Sister Veronique is being held. . . . She is a rather famous lady, your mother. Most important, I have the order for her release from the prison convent of Ste. Genevieve du Mont in this pocket—signed by the Emperor himself."

"Thank God . . ." and then her instant delight gave way to the dark reality of what was all around them . . . the Royalist troops, and the undeniable possibility that *they* might prevail, and that she would never reach her mother, that the Emperor's release order might become a death warrant instead. . .

Philip's individual breaching of the soldiers' line had brought his fellow horsemen forward and the hussars were now inside the square. At a short distance to the south could be heard other horsemen and faint cries that lingered on the air.

Marsanne looked about in alarm.

"The people are cheering," Philip murmured in her ear.

The new contingent of horsemen approached the square but before the crowd of soldiers and civilians in the square could identify them, the Royalist commander, standing in front of the base of the broken statue, raised his sword. "I call upon you to surrender in the king's name—"

The hussars, now surrounded, might have urged their mounts against the north line of soldiers penning them in, but they waited. As the orders snapped out, the Royalist soldiers wheeled about, raised their rifles. Marsanne could scarcely breathe.

"Aim!"

The soldiers snapped to obey. The dozen hussars found themselves under the guns of a hundred soldiers as the sound of hoofbeats once more neared the square.

"Fire!"

A gasp went up from the crowd at every window facing on the square. The soldiers hesitated, glanced furtively at each other. In the strange, pregnant silence, the new contingent of hussars reached the south line of troops.

"Fire!" the Royalist commander ordered again; this time one octave higher than last—in fact his youthful voice cracked to falsetto under the strain.

But few heard him. Every face had turned to the south of the square. The new contingent of Imperial Hussars had reined up.

In their center, leaning slightly forward as if about to talk confidentially to his Royalist enemies, was the Emperor himself.

He spoke quietly now, yet his voice carried throughout the square. "Soldiers, if you shoot, we will not return your fire. Soldiers! Your Emperor calls upon you to join your comrades. Take back the cockade we wore proudly as one army. We welcome you."

Marsanne had forgotten how small he was, especially emphasized alongside these enormous grenadiers and guards. His face looked a little heavier, slightly more puffy than she remembered, but she recognized the inner power and the glow of great personal magnetism she had heard so much of. It apparently had not diminished.

Marsanne noticed that though he was surrounded by the gold braid and white bandoliers, the elaborate fur shakoes and fur-trimmed pelisses—luxurious uniforms of every description—Napoleon Bonaparte wore his old gray campaign coat and his black tricorne hat with its red white and blue cockade. And Marsanne found the sight painfully moving. He did not have to wait long for their reply.

First one, then two, then a dozen and then all of the Royalist soldiers put down their rifles, and the cry passed from man to man: "Long live the Emperor!"

Each of them now pulled off the Bourbon rosette from his uniform or his helmet, until the cobblestones at the hooves of the Emperor's horse became piled high with white cockades.

"Give us back our tricolor!" some of them called out, and members of the Imperial Guard behind the Emperor, the old guard of sentimental Bonapartists, came forward and passed the tricolor cockades to each Royalist soldier.

Marsanne looked on, relieved and suddenly tired . . . so tired. . . It was surely an earth-shaking moment for her country, yet what still most held captive her pent-up emotions was the fate of her mother . . . and how soon she would look on her again.

Chapter Twenty-Five

For once Marsanne was able to match Philip's long stride as they hurried up the slight elevation of Ste. Genevieve Hill above the Latin Quarter in Paris. She told herself that if Veronique had been alive and well yesterday under the king's rule, she would hardly be in worse condition tonight, since the Emperor's triumphant return to the Tuileries.

"When I was very young," she told Philip breathlessly, "Grandmama told me a ghastly tale about nuns sealed into tombs in the Cemetery of the Innocents and kept alive by food pushed through a slot in the wall."

"Those nuns chose a death in life," he reminded her.

"Not all. There was one whose family put her there at eighteen and she died at eighty-seven. She had fallen in love, and the family disapproved. Would the Royalists dare do something like that to Mama?"

Philip laughed quickly. "I think not. Besides, Sister Veronique hasn't fallen in love."

"Please don't joke. And if there is no danger, then why are you hurrying so fast?"

He drew her closer. "Because the Sisters of Ste. Genevieve du Mont are royalist to the core. Most of them never took the oath to the Constitution. They emigrated to Italy in '92. They only returned last year, so they aren't likely to be entirely cordial to Sister Veronique, who after all has remained a loyal Frenchwoman during the past twenty years and placed her country even above the Church . . ."

When Philip looked back now at the city below, Marsanne guessed that he hoped to glimpse the Tuileries, where the Emperor was said to be back at the business of running France, but the great bulk of the Louvre and other buildings interfered. He shrugged and turned his attention to *his* business at hand.

The little street was a cul de sac running into the great gates and walls of the convent, which still showed signs of graffiti done by both children and adults during the Revolution. The cul de sac was deserted, but the boulevard cross-street a block behind them was teeming with activity, and from here a man called Philip's name and began to overtake them rapidly. After Marsanne's recent experiences she trusted no one and asked Philip anxiously, "Who is it? Don't let them stop us, please—"

She was reassured by Philip's quick laughter and the welcome he gave the pudgy, grinning little man who complained as he reached them, "I'm damned if I ever play the rescuer again. My asthma won't stand it."

"My love, this is none other than Raoul Joubert, who persuaded the Emperor to sign Sister Veronique's release even before he signed such minor papers as the proclamation abolishing all feudal privileges reinstated by Louis the Eighteenth. You see, thanks to Joubert here, your mother's well-being was placed before the good of the nation. We trust you approve."

As they reached the convent gate, where Philip rang for the portress, the stout, hard-breathing Joubert added, "I come with other goods news, mademoiselle. The troops in St. Amand caught two old friends of yours last night, trying to escape through the lines. . ."

Philip and Marsanne exchanged quick glances. "Thank God for that!" he said. The relief was overwhelming.

"Ugly business . . . the woman was killed," Joubert went on. "Tried to knife a couple of the troopers. But there's no question the man will be executed . . . that Nicoletti business if nothing else. His own wife accused him . . . her dying words, matter of fact. . ."

A stern, tight-lipped nun peered out at them now through the portress' window in the wall. Philip did not waste words but held up an unimposing, slightly wrinkled paper in front of her eyes. Her nearsighted gaze moved slowly from the first line to the near-unintelligible signature. Nonetheless, she recognized its authority and signalled to an ancient, toothless gardener who opened one of the gates.

The portress then gestured toward a gloomy gray stone house of three stories whose windows were scrupulously sealed. The Mother Superior, a regal old woman who might have been an empress, ushered them into a chilly stone-flagged passage that seemed to enclose the inmates even more surely than the iron entrance door when it clanged shut behind them. Poor Mama, Marsanne thought. She was always so free, so quick to break rules when they interfered with her purposes. She said aloud, "She must have suffered from the very confinement itself."

Philip did not reply, a fact which troubled her. She wondered if he was less sympathetic than she had suspected when she saw his faint smile. Or did he simply know her mother better than she herself did?

The narrow interior hall became freezing cold. There was no light but the taper borne ahead of them by the Mother Superior. Somewhere Marsanne could hear a curiously passionless—almost by rote—chanting. That too was unlike Sister Veronique, who did few things by rote. Marsanne heard Raoul Joubert wheezing along behind her and was surprised once more to find that this friendly, jovial fellow actually had been, and doubtless would be again, Prefect of the Seine. One could never judge by surfaces.

They passed several doors with tiny barred openings, which she understood were the cells of this strict Sisterhood. At last the Mother Superior stopped, pointed with her forefinger and stood aside while Philip pushed open the double doors to a long, cold room with an extremely high-beamed ceiling—the refectory.

Long, empty tables, rough-hewn but sturdy, were placed in double file the length of the room, which was lighted by barred windows set high in the great stone walls. It was a medieval dining hall very little changed except for the removal of ancient banners that must once have hung from its beams.

But none of the three visitors gave more than a glance at the room itself. They were fascinated by the actions of the room's occupants. Two sweet-faced, determined nuns were hard at work, one washing down the bare inner wall, another on a ladder scrubbing one of the high windows. Most astonishing of all, the third nun—her religious habit heavily disguised by a stained pinafore—was high above the heads of the visitors, standing on a single plank supported by two flimsy ladders and dusting the ancient beams overhead with long, curved broomstraws. It was Sister Veronique. It could not possibly be anyone else.

Seeing this impressive vision, Marsanne could only get out a single, horrified, "Mama!"

Joubert was already chuckling. Philip had restrained his own amusement out of deference to Marsanne, but he called up now to Sister Veronique, who looked down at them, briefly waving her broomstraws and a cloud of four-hundred-year-old dust.

"Is that you, Marsanne? Dearest, can you wait until I am finished here? I see Jean-Philippe is caring for you.

I predicted it that day you left Paris. You remember, Jean-Philippe?"

Marsanne looked at Philip, smiled and then raised her voice. "Yes, Mama. But were you well-treated here?"

"Abominably. They would not set me to work until last week. Had me standing about in the most useless way. Day after day with no means of earning my bread. I felt like a charity patient . . . Come, Sister Marie-Mathieu, just a little more elbow work there. . . Marsanne, darling, are you quite safe?"

"Thanks to Philip, very much so, Mama." She backed away, trying to stifle a cough, and joined Joubert, who was wheezing badly from all the dust. "Philip, your lungs seem to be better than mine, please tell Mama I'll be waiting out in the garden."

He laughed, did as she asked and when Veronique waved at them in response and happily resumed her work, he took Marsanne's arm and they were ushered out by the Mother Superior, whose silence was finally broken as they stepped into the sunny garden.

"Mademoiselle, you are a relation of Sister Veronique?"

Marsanne made a small, instinctive curtsy and agreed that she was. Philip, who guessed what was coming, kissed her cheek and whispered, "Think how happy the patients of the Hôtel-Dieu will be to see Sister Veronique."

"Then, mademoiselle," the Mother Superior continued, "in the name of our patron saint, we ask you: remove this *good* sister from our House, so that we may return to the Peace of God!"

HELEN MacINNES

Helen MacInnes's bestselling suspense novels continue to delight her readers and many have been made into major motion pictures. Here is your chance to enjoy all of her exciting novels, by simply filling out the coupon below.

☐	ABOVE SUSPICION	23101-1	1.75
☐	AGENT IN PLACE	23127-5	1.95
☐	ASSIGNMENT IN BRITTANY	22958-0	1.95
☐	DECISION AT DELPHI	C2790	1.95
☐	THE DOUBLE IMAGE	22787-1	1.75
☐	FRIENDS AND LOVERS	X2714	1.75
☐	HORIZON	23123-2	1.50
☐	I AND MY TRUE LOVE	Q2559	1.50
☐	MESSAGE FROM MALAGA	X2820	1.75
☐	NEITHER FIVE NOR THREE	X2912	1.75
☐	NORTH FROM ROME	Q2441	1.50
☐	PRAY FOR A BRAVE HEART	X2907	1.75
☐	REST AND BE THANKFUL	X2860	1.75
☐	THE SALZBURG CONNECTION	X2686	1.75
☐	THE SNARE OF THE HUNTER	X2808	1.75
☐	THE VENETIAN AFFAIR	X2743	1.75
☐	WHILE STILL WE LIVE	23099-6	1.95

Buy them at your local bookstores or use this handy coupon for ordering:

FAWCETT PUBLICATIONS, P.O. Box 1014, Greenwich Conn. 06830

Please send me the books I have checked above. Orders for less than 5 books must include 60c for the first book and 25c for each additional book to cover mailing and handling. Orders of 5 or more books postage is Free. I enclose $_____ in check or money order.

Mr/Mrs/Miss_____

Address_____

City_____ State/Zip_____

Please allow 4 to 5 weeks for delivery. This offer expires 6/78.

A-8

Sylvia Thorpe

Sparkling novels of love and conquest set against the colorful background of historic England. Here are stories you will savor word by word, page by spellbinding page into the wee hours of the night.

☐ BEGGAR ON HORSEBACK	23091-0	1.50
☐ CAPTAIN GALLANT	Q2709	1.50
☐ FAIR SHINE THE DAY	23229-8	1.75
☐ THE GOLDEN PANTHER	23006-6	1.50
☐ THE RELUCTANT ADVENTURESS	P2578	1.25
☐ ROGUE'S COVENANT	23041-4	1.50
☐ ROMANTIC LADY	Q2910	1.50
☐ THE SCANDALOUS LADY ROBIN	Q2934	1.50
☐ THE SCAPEGRACE	P2663	1.25
☐ THE SCARLET DOMINO	23220-4	1.50
☐ THE SILVER NIGHTINGALE	P2626	1.25
☐ THE SWORD AND THE SHADOW	22945-9	1.50
☐ SWORD OF VENGEANCE	23136-4	1.50
☐ TARRINGTON CHASE	Q2843	1.50

Phyllis A. Whitney

Ms. Whitney's novels constantly appear on all the bestseller lists throughout the country and have won many awards including the coveted "Edgar". Here are some of her finest romantic novels of suspense that you may order by mail.

☐ BLACK AMBER	Q2604	1.50
☐ BLUE FIRE	Q2809	1.50
☐ COLUMBELLA	X2919	1.75
☐ EVER AFTER	P2298	1.25
☐ THE GOLDEN UNICORN	23104-6	1.95
☐ HUNTER'S GREEN	Q2603	1.50
☐ LISTEN FOR THE WHISPERER	23156-9	1.75
☐ LOST ISLAND	23078-3	1.75
☐ THE MOONFLOWER	Q2738	1.50
☐ THE QUICKSILVER POOL	22769-3	1.75
☐ SEA JADE	Q2572	1.50
☐ SEVEN TEARS FOR APOLLO	Q2508	1.50
☐ SILVERHILL	Q2810	1.50
☐ SKYE CAMERON	Q2804	1.50
☐ SNOWFIRE	Q2725	1.50
☐ SPINDRIFT	22746-4	1.95
☐ THUNDER HEIGHTS	22737-5	1.50
☐ THE TREMBLING HILLS	X2807	1.75
☐ THE TURQUOISE MASK	X2835	1.75
☐ WINDOW ON THE SQUARE	Q2602	1.50
☐ THE WINTER PEOPLE	22933-5	1.50

Buy them at your local bookstores or use this handy coupon for ordering: